AGAINST the GRAIN

A NOVEL

LÂLE DAVIDSON

Lâle Davidson

Enjoy!

EMPEROR BOOKS

Praise for Lâle Davidson

"*Against the Grain* combines gorgeous poetry and romance with heart-stopping action, as the daughter of a rich CEO joins forces with a logger's son to stop a huge lumber company from destroying an ancient redwood forest. The trees themselves become surprisingly powerful characters in this rich, multilayered novel. After reading *Against the Grain,* you'll never look at a tree in the same way again."
—Matt Witten, bestselling author of *The Necklace*

"I found the story quite enthralling. Lâle Davidson does a remarkable job of capturing the moods and rhythms of a very special time and place."
—Larry Livermore, *Spy Rock Memories,* publisher of *Lookout* magazine, and veteran of Redwood Summer.

"...vividly illustrates the truth of that old North Coast adage: If trees could talk, nothing short of chainsaws could quiet them."
—Hank Sims, editor of *Lost Coast Outpost*

The dramatic confrontations of 1990's Redwood Summer surge to life in Lale Davidson's bracingly imagined eco-novel, which somehow manages, despite its heady pace, to educate the reader on why trees matter, how they grow, and what they do for us -- if we dare to let them. Vivid with charismatic characters, steeped in environmental history and the conflicts that defined a difficult and bitter time, *Against the Grain* sticks with hope and takes the long view, not unlike the thousand-year-old towering giants at the heart of this rich yarn.
—Amy Godine, independent scholar; curator, Dreaming of

Timbuctoo exhibition, John Brown Farm, North Elba, NY; long-time writer for Adirondack Life.

Against the Grain is satisfying as a thriller, as a poem to the environment, and as a love story. The richness of the characters' relationships with the forest and trees is inspiring, and the plant kingdoms' communications — and use of Sanskrit — was magical. In these family dynamics, politics is made personal, and finding purpose is a tool for healing. I couldn't put the book down.

    —Peter Ferko, author of *The Genius of Yoga* and *Incarnation*.

Dedicated to Charley, Tess, and of course, the trees.

I want to sleep
and dream the life of trees, beings
from the muted world who care
nothing for Money, Politics, Power,
Will or Right, who want little from the night
but a few dead stars going dim, a white owl
lifting from their limbs, who want only
to sink their roots into the wet ground
and terrify the worms or shake
their bleary heads like fashion models
or old hippies. If trees could speak,
they wouldn't, only hum some low
green note, roll their pinecones
down the empty streets and blame it,
with a shrug, on the cold wind.
—Dorianne Laux, "The Life of Trees"

One day, as the three young Aesir walked along the seashore,
their eyes fell upon two little trees, an ash and an alder
standing side by side. In these two trees they saw the makings
of [human]kind—straight as gods and tough as wood."
—Ingri and Edgar Parin d'Aulaire

Never doubt that a small group of thoughtful, committed citi-
zens can change the world; indeed, it's the only thing that
ever has.
—Margaret Mead

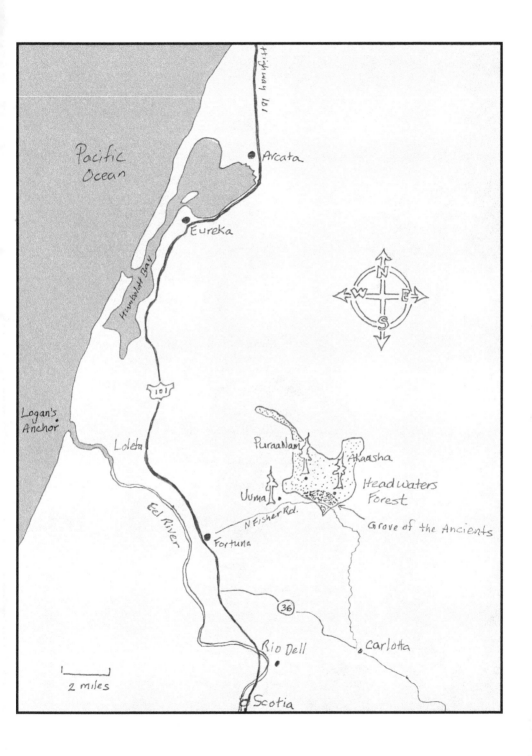

Contents

Acknowledgments

This is a work of fiction. However, it is based, in part, on the research of true events surrounding the Maxxam takeover of Pacific Lumber in 1985 and Redwood Summer in 1990. The time frame of the events for this novel has been simplified and shortened for dramatic purposes, and the main characters, Logan, Diana, Atlas, Zeff, and Jessica, are entirely invented. The Grove of the Ancients is also invented, though the Headwaters Forest Reserve is real. The skirmishes in my novel at the Headwaters are based on several real confrontations, one in 1987, detailed in David Harris's book *The Last Stand* (183-187), and one at Owl Creek in 1990, detailed in Joan Dunning and Doug Thron's book *From the Redwood Forest* (68-70). The two court cases these events are loosely based on, *EPIC v. Maxxam* and *EPIC and Sierra Club v. Board of Forestry*, took years to settle. I have changed the geography of what is now the Headwaters Forest Reserve for dramatic convenience. The bombing of Judi Bari was rendered as accurately as possible from *The Judi Bari Website*, and the accident at the mill is based on her articles in the *International Workers of the World Historical Archives*.

Judi Bari and Darryl Cherney, who are secondary characters in this novel, are real people. Their written accounts of the bombing and the history of these events made it possible for me to plausibly characterize them. Darryl Cherney graciously gave me permission to use his name in the book, though he is not a fan of mixing fact and fiction. Judi Bari passed away in 1997. For his account, please visit https://whobombedjudibari.com/ and http://www.judibari.org/. I am deeply grateful and in awe of them both. Thanks also to the Environmental Protection and Information Center (EPIC) and Earth First!, both real organizations. I've also made reference to several other real people who were hugely instrumental in taking Pacific Lumber to court and forcing them to adhere to environmental law: Greg King, Robert "Woods" Sutherland, and Cecelia Lanman, as well as Paul Watson, an activist famed for sinking whaling ships. These people and so many others risked their lives, their mental health, and their financial stability to hold the timber industry accountable. Many have not been named, such as Macon Cowles, a lawyer who mortgaged his own house to prosecute the case with Mark Harris in *EPIC and Sierra Club v. Board of Forestry*.

There are many others to thank for this novel, chief among them is my husband, Charley Brown. He, along with my brother Loren Davidson plotted the story. Then Charley and I wrote a screenplay version twenty years ago as we jostled our newborn in our arms. My writing group is a source of constant support and wisdom: Jackie Goodwood, Anntonette Alberti, Elaine Handley, Antoinette Martin, and Karen Bjornland. They are an uncommonly intelligent and kind group of people, and we work together in a way that daily restores my faith in humanity. Thanks also to Nancy Seid, Matt Witten, Laura Albert, and Marilyn McCabe for blurbs, edits, and support. Everyone I contacted for help with accuracy responded with uncommon generosity: Doug Leen, Brian Maebius, Larry Livermore, Tom Wheeler of EPIC, Ryan Overbey (Professor of Buddhist Studies at Skidmore), and Hank Simms. Finally, much thanks to my publisher, Stephanie Larkin of Emperor Books, for her generous spirit.

Trees created the conditions that made human life possible and have fed, clothed, and sheltered us since we first evolved. They are our best defenses against climate change. The fight to save them continues today.

To the True Ones

You, our greatest grandparents,
who enfold the globe in air who prepared the earth
for all that creeps and crawls on land,
patiently sunhumming,
translating toxin to oxygen
sweet and slow,
Connect us now
to the allmind
to know and now
our part.

Chapter 1

Trees Don't Talk

1935

"Trees don't talk," the boy scoffed. They stood in the deep woods, on a road of packed earth, between towering redwoods, behind a battered Ford Model T grain truck.

"How do you know?" the old man said. Sun and wind had carved a map of his face. He picked the boy up and set him on the flatbed of the truck, sided only with a wood grate, among neatly tied bundles of scavenged firewood. "Maybe you just don't stick around long enough to hear what they have to say." He pinched the boy's knee affectionately and hobbled toward the driver's seat.

The boy's face lit up as his gaze swept from the base of the trees into the canopy. Columnar trunks soared two hundred feet into the sky, taller than dinosaurs. As the boy's eyes hit the crest of the canopy, sunlight pierced the green with gold, bird calls amplified, and insects clicked. Time slowed to the eternal. The wind picked up, and the giants' whisper was just beginning to form words when the truck rumbled to life.

Uuma

Listen, loved ones, we are all speaking to you. Quiet your bodies. See us. Feel our bark, stippled, shiny, furrowed, white, black, red. We are the True Ones. We speak by being. We have stood for eons before you, alone on Bhūr, the sustainer. Before our time, all was different, nothing crept and crawled. But when we learned to send our seeds abroad, we covered Bhūr end to end, connected by our sister Kulaaya underground, interrupted only by Samudra, the coming together of waters.

We took the sky and bound it to the earth, we injected the sky into the earth and it came out as limestone to Samudra, and that is how we forested the salty waters with corals and shelled ones. That's how the waterbabies could crawl onto land and live. That's where you crawled from, you naked ones, you rootless ones, you cleverest of tongues. You are all our children. Hear us now. So much depends on it.

We have always loved you, ever since you came dancing pretty, waving roots at both ends like seaweed, swirling like water, chattering like rain. While the furred, feathered, and many-legged ones all had their sounds and dances, you clevertongues turned our growth into sounds more complex and beautiful, you spoke in ways that spoke for us as we had never spoken for ourselves, using twigs to make markings that could speak to those yet to come. You entertained and amused us with stories and kindled lightning. Because your roots did not thread the earth, because you had no bark and little fur, because your smooth cambium glowed red as the expanding universe when you leaned close to your kindled lightning, we fed you, we clothed you, cradled you.

When Bhūr turned away from the Bright One, we cradled you in our arms, carried you through the darkside, and brought you back around to the light of all-knowing. For many, many, many circles around the sun, you were the flower of Bhūr's most infinitely wise tongue.

PuraaNam, who has been here four times as long as I, and who lives in the most ancient of groves not far from here, is beyond weary. She says you no longer speak for us, no longer hear us, have forgotten who we are, who you are. PuraaNam's bark is thick. She has withstood many fires, some set by you. She says you will continue to kill us and in killing us send Bhūr so far out of balance that most will die. You will die. You will drag many beloved species with you.

I am young, only five hundred circles around the Bright One. I have loved you clevertongues more than most. That is how I got the name Uuma, friend. Because I am your friend. I tell PuraaNam we should keep reaching for you, that you will hear us and change. Will you?

Chapter 2

Logan Returns

April 15, 1990

A log bumped against the hull of a sailboat anchored for the night below Humboldt Bay. Dawn arrived thick with clouds, a few shades lighter than night. The mountains disappeared in the mist. A few miles off the coast, a squall, like a piece of churning night, darkened the sky and was fast approaching. For now, though, the waves were placid, so the thud of the log wasn't loud enough to wake the boat's lone sleeping inhabitant, but it was loud enough to penetrate his dreams.

Logan Blackburn turned over restlessly in the cabin berth, his brow furrowed, caught in a recurring nightmare of a different storm two years ago.

"It won't hold!" he shouted to his father. "It's too late! Stop!"

The rain came down in sheets, pelting Logan so hard he could barely see. He stood at the edge of a manmade ravine, shouting as loud as he could to be heard above the roar of the D-10 dozer in the storm.

His father sat in the dozer cab, side window down, gesturing with one arm, index finger out, mouthing the words, "One more pass." His face was a smear of light and dark paint in a rectangle.

"It's not worth it!" he shouted.

A few small whitecaps tossed Logan's sailboat a bit harder as the squall neared, but still, he slept, the sounds of the rain, wind, and knocking blending into an avalanche of mud that toppled the dozer, and with it, Logan. Mud and needles packed his esophagus as he tried to inhale.

A few yards away in the water, among the harmless debris, a chunk of redwood was positioned like a battering ram, perpendicular to the boat. When the squall swept in, the log rammed the boat. Logan shot to his feet and shook his head, momentarily stuck between two worlds. The fiberglass hull reminded him where he was. He raced onto the deck. Rain peppered the deck like beach pebbles, roaring just as loud. The boat bucked against the anchor and the squall whipped the waves into a froth. Seeing the dark hump in the water, he glanced from anchor to mast, and back again, then ran aft, slipping and regaining his balance. He laid hold of the anchor line and pulled—but gently—using the line to pull the boat out of the way of the oncoming log, but, *crack*, it hit again.

He pulled a little faster, keeping the line low, hoping not to uproot the anchor. Finally, the boat moved just as the log hit one more time, but this time it was just a glancing blow off the stern before it slid away. He lifted the line and pulled upward, uprooting the anchor and drawing it in with quick, practiced moves. He swiveled, unwrapped the mainsail, released the boom, and yanked the sheet through the cleat. The sail unfolded awkwardly, twisted by the wind, and the boat skittered sideways across the waves until Logan grabbed the tiller and steered the prow into the wind. With the mainsail sheet in one hand and tiller in the other, he aligned himself with the elements and brought the boat under control. He steered it out past the damaging debris. Shortly, the squall passed, the sky cleared, and the water calmed.

In contrast, his head ached with the hangover of his dream.

He'd been gone for two years, on the water and in Hawaii for much of that time. Six months earlier, a longing for the big trees, for Uuma, had stirred his blood. That was how he knew his blood was moving again. He pushed it away again and again, but it wouldn't leave him alone. Finally, he obeyed the summons.

Now, here he was. But as the mists rose from the forested banks of what used to be his home, he surveyed Pacific Lumber's shipping dock in Humboldt Bay. Defeat settled on his shoulders like a millstone.

"I can't do this again," he muttered and turned the boat back out to sea, his movements fast and sharp as knives. As the sail filled with wind and the boat picked up speed, slicing through the waves, his head cleared, and his lungs ballooned with the first easy breath he'd had since he awoke.

Yet, even out at sea, floating through the briny air, the cedar-earth scent of redwoods tugged him back. His father's words stole in, "Whatever the cost."

His hands relaxed, the mainsheet slipped away, and the full-bellied sail collapsed like the wrinkles on a worried face.

Chapter 3

The Setup

October 1985

A massive office complex stood in uptown Houston on South Post Road at the corner of Four Oaks Boulevard. There were no oaks on the boulevard anymore. The office complex housed big businesses like Wells Fargo, JP Morgan, Exxon Mobil, and Titan, the holding company of venture capitalist Atlas Jamison. Holding companies don't make, buy, or sell anything. They're just a place to park assets so that if your business goes bankrupt, you get to keep whatever you parked there. Like nothing else in nature, it can't lose anything and doesn't bear any consequences. All blue-tinted glass and clean contemporary lines, the complex was surrounded by a landscaped park of scored granite walkways decorated by small trees trimmed to perfect globes, surrounded by concentric circles of begonias. The towers were connected above by bridges with potted trees in a row.

From his floor-to-ceiling windows in his corner office at the top, Atlas Jamison could see much of Houston. Gray swaths of asphalt and massive buildings stood behind him, out of sight. To the north, he enjoyed his view of the Spanish-style housing development typical of the area, with terracotta tile roofs. Each house was surrounded by walls that billowed with blooming bougainvillea. He liked the neatness of their lawns, the regularity of the construction. The people in those houses were totally unaware of what happened in these towers, the power he wielded, the roller-coaster twists and turns of the stock market he rode, the maze of laws he spun with the dexterity of a swordsman. What they didn't know didn't hurt them, and what he knew he used to amass his fortune. Skimmed it right off the top, no harm, no foul. Indeed, men like him were the engine of the economy. Not that he did it for these reasons, but his industry made their nice little lives possible.

It was Wednesday, October 25, 1985, and Atlas was on the phone with high financier Matthew Molten working out how to take over the unsuspecting Pacific Lumber company in California. His broad nose and mouth were bracketed by deep creases that made him look permanently stern. His eyes were wide-set, and his gaze was hard and too direct. When he smiled for the camera, it looked like a grimace, his teeth too small, the smile not spreading to his eyes.

"Another 275...million, yeah. Is that a problem?" he said.

"No problem at all. When do you need it by?" Molten said.

"Monday, if the PL report I expect today confirms my projection."

His office was all metal, glass, and minimalist chairs and settees, with a few art objects in lighted alcoves. A Jackson Pollock that predated the drip period called *The She-Wolf* struck a stark contrast, with its thick, energetic lines of red and white.

"We'll just have to rework the repayment schedule, of course," Molten said.

A pigeon flew into a window, ricocheted off the steel trim, hit the other side of the window frame, flopped onto the sill.

Absent-mindedly, Atlas tapped on the glass next to the bird with his knuckle. It didn't move, its neck broken. "Of course. I've already acquired two percent of PL stock, and so far, the price hasn't risen significantly, so we're in good shape. With the one percent your people are holding, and this additional amount, my subsidiary can acquire the final three percent, and then we make our tender offer on Monday."

"You're the man, A.J. I have complete faith in you," Molten said.

The lines around Jamison's eyes deepened slightly. No one had ever called him A.J., and Molten's casual familiarity offended him, but he dealt with those he had to.

"I'll keep you posted."

At the ground level, Detective Scott Barnes, a man in his forties, wearing a cowboy hat, a pinstripe suit, and cowboy boots, passed the gardeners who were trimming the hedges. He pulled the glass doors open with a flourish that caused them to bounce back at him too fast, called out a cheery hello to the security guard at the front desk, flashed his ID, and after the required go-ahead, strode to the elevators, where a younger man stood, wearing a meticulously tailored navy-blue suit and carrying a folded *Wall Street Journal* in his left hand. Barnes noticed the headline, "Another Broker Testifies to Insider Trading," and quickly took stock of the man, waiting for the usual nod before greeting him. But Eddie Cox, one of three junior VPs of Pacific Lumber, stared hard at the elevators, with his chin and eyebrows raised as if readying himself for a fight, to which Barnes took offense. They entered the elevator and endured the ride in awkward silence, surprised when it turned out they were going to the same floor.

In Titan's reception area, Barnes took the power stance at the windows, legs splayed, chin lifted as he surveyed Memorial Park and the housing development, West Oak Village.

"Mr. Barnes, Mr. Jamison will see you now," said Betty Rogers, the receptionist. Betty had worked with Jamison for fifteen years and was devoted to him. People called him a corporate raider as if he was a pirate who boarded ships by force, but he was just a man who did his homework, found undervalued companies that needed to be maximized, acquired a big enough share of the stock to swing the vote, and then made a tender offer the shareholders couldn't refuse. Later, he maximized profits for everyone. Sure, his Savings and Loan had failed and had been bailed out to the tune of 1.8 billion in taxpayer money, but if you wanted to be successful, you had to take risks, and that meant a certain percentage of failure. She'd defend him to the end of her days.

Scott Barnes glanced at Eddie Cox, who cranked his left elbow with a stiff jerk to look at his watch.

"Mr. Cox, Mr. Jamison will be with you shortly," she added.

Barnes grinned and doffed his hat to Betty as he passed her desk.

When he entered the room, he stopped to survey it and whistled under his breath.

"Nice digs," he said, his roving gaze stopping on the Pollock. "That what they're calling art, these days?"

Atlas, standing behind his desk, looked up briefly at the painting, and smiled faintly.

"Your report, Mr. Barnes?"

Barnes handed him the manila envelope.

"Just as you suspected. Pacific Lumber has eight billion board feet. They think they only have five."

Atlas pulled the bound report out of the envelope and turned the first few pages, his eyes gleaming as if from reflected light. "Go on."

"On top of that, they've got an overfunded pension plan—at least fifty million in surplus just sitting there."

"Thought so."

"And they've been practicing this thing called 'sustainable yield harvest' since the 1920s."

"And that means?"

"They only cut as much as they think will grow in other parts of the forest in that same year. The practice has left them with the largest holdings of privately owned 'old growth' in the country. And that stuff is like gold compared to regular wood."

"What about that office building in San Francisco?"

"It could fetch you as much as a hundred mill. Then there's the welding company and some farmlands, another hundred to two hundred mill at least. It's all in the report."

"Very good," Jamison said calmly. "And of course," he said, looking at the tip of Barnes's boots, "I can count on your discretion, as always." With the last few words, he made eye contact with Barnes.

"Of course, sir," Barnes touched the front brim of his hat in salute.

"Thank you for your service," Atlas said as he pulled an envelope out of his top desk drawer and threw it on the table.

Barnes stepped forward to retrieve it. "My pleasure."

Barnes left the office with more than his usual bounce.

Alone in the office, Atlas tapped on the window again where the dead bird still lay. It was a fixed window, so there was nothing Atlas could do about it. He thumped the window adjacent to the bird with the heel of his palm, trying to jolt it off the ledge. It didn't budge. Turning back to his desk, he glanced sidelong at the two pictures, one of his current wife, Linda, and the other of his daughter, Diana, when she was two or three, with Christine, his first wife. Her death from brain cancer had been a terrible mess. All the king's horses and all the king's men....The shadows around his eyes grew darker. But he had soldiered on. Long ago, he had mastered the art of not feeling things that might incapacitate him. Diana was grown and in business school, and things were good with Linda. He sighed and hit the intercom.

"Betty, will you send Mr. Cox in, please?"

"Of course."

Eddie Cox strode in, brows still raised, bright blue eyes wide, jaw jutting. Atlas, still standing behind his desk, didn't raise his eyes. He waited until Cox had stopped awkwardly before him.

"I told you not to come here," he said, eyes still on his desk, right hand moving a file to the side.

"I'm sorry. I didn't want to, but a lot is happening, and," he paused, searching for the right words, "and I was hoping we could discuss my compensation."

"We already have. You will be promoted to vice president after the takeover, and I have stock reserved for you that will more than triple in value once I'm done with PL."

"But I heard you were closing the San Francisco office."

"Who did you hear that from?"

"I—I don't know," Cox fingered his lapel nervously. "It's just a rumor."

"There are rumors?" Atlas's volume rose slightly.

"Well, no. No, it's just," he paused, selecting his next words carefully, "a buddy of mine works for Molten."

"I see."

"I need more."

Atlas's brows went up, but he still didn't look up.

"If word gets out," Cox pushed forward, his voice getting a bit crafty, "that I was the one who gave you the inside track to PL's holdings—I could be in danger. I need protection."

"Security?"

"That, and," he hesitated, then threw his jaw forward and spoke more firmly, "an account."

"An account?"

"You know. An offshore account."

"I see."

"After all, if others find out about your move, the stock prices might go too high, and the whole deal will be ruined."

Atlas leaned on his desk like a gorilla and speared Cox with his eyes.

"I don't take well to being threatened. You want to be a part of this, you do as I say, or the whole deal is off. I don't care. I'll walk away. I've got more money than I could ever spend, and I've got other irons in the fire. You understand?"

Cox paled slightly. "I understand."

"And another thing," he paused, "someone has been buying stock on the q.t. and it's stirring the soup."

"It's a free country, isn't it?"

"Not if you work for me."

"Well, do I? Still work for you?"

Atlas turned his back on Cox briefly, glancing out at the Memorial Park. When he turned back to Cox, his smile looked genuine.

"Of course. In fact, I'll give you a raise and promotion to VP as soon as I own PL."

Cox was taken aback, but thinking quickly, asked, "How much?"

"Double whatever you're getting now. How does that sound?"

"Great."

"Of course."

"Can I—see that in writing?"

Atlas came around from the desk and clapped Cox on the shoulder, turning him gently toward the door.

"Can't do that, Eddie. Gotta keep it all on the q.t. But I'll give you something better. My word."

"I appreciate that." Cox put his hand out to shake on it as Atlas all but pushed him out of his office.

"I'm nothing if not a man of my word," Atlas said as he gripped his hand.

When the door was shut, Atlas muttered, "Worthless."

He looked at the tangled lines of *The She Wolf*. Though he liked neatness in his life, the energy of this tangle aroused him. Most of the people in his circle knew nothing about art. They simply acquired it for status or to launder money. He, on the other hand, felt genuine affection and admiration for his collection. Art history had been one of his favorite courses in college, and he was particularly proud of this acquisition. A wolf had suckled the twins, Romulus and Remus, who founded Rome. A certain ruthlessness was necessary to foster civilization, he thought. It really didn't look like a wolf. More like a steer. And the face, in particular, was beyond consciousness, a coiled spring, a spider eye, two eyes out of sync. It spoke to him in ways he couldn't articulate. And the red arrow shooting from head directly to the gut, that spoke to him, too. Most of all, he admired Pollack's bold brushstrokes, his irreverence, his machismo, his energy. Atlas stroked his chin, sighed, and strolled back to his desk to hit the intercom. He'd taken over a lot of companies, but this would be his best scoop yet if all went according to plan, but it depended on secrecy, surprise, and luck.

"Betty?"

"Yes, sir."

"Is he gone?"

"Yes, sir.

"Get my lawyer on the phone. I've still got a few loose ends to tie up."

"Right away, sir."

"Thanks, dear."

"Not at all."

Atlas bent over and scrutinized the dead pigeon as he spoke. Flies were already feeding off its eyes.

"And order yourself some flowers."

"Thank you, sir."

"And Betty?"

"Yes, sir?"

"When was the last time the windows were cleaned?"

"Monday, sir."

"Will you call to get them back here tomorrow? There's a dead bird I want removed."

"Of course, sir."

After he tied up those loose ends over the weekend, he'd call the president of Pacific Lumber at the crack of dawn, Monday morning, maybe before, to tell him he was making a tender offer. That would wake him up, he chuckled. PL had lousy legal counsel, and they would file a few fruitless lawsuits, then he'd file a few counter lawsuits, and in the end, he'd win. He'd replace all the top brass, sell off PL's extra assets, and commandeer the pension fund to pay off his bridge loans. Then he'd liquidate Pacific Lumber's assets by tripling the tree-felling rate. If all went according to plan, he'd collect his profit in three years, five max, and move on to his next conquest.

Over the next few months, with a few extra dips and curves, all did go according to plan. Until the activists. Goddamned nobodies. He hadn't anticipated how much power they could wield.

Chapter 4

Diana Arrives

April 15, 1990

Diana bumped up the logging road in her new Jeep Cherokee to the Pacific Lumber public relations field station at the edge of a disputed lot 2-86, called Grove of the Ancients by the activists. She was listening to *Local Talk*, a Humboldt State University radio station.

"And once again, for those of you who are just tuning in, this is Sam Seabreeze from *Local Talk*, and I'm sitting here with Jessica Wild, who heads up the legal team for EPIC, the Environmental Protection and Information Center. Jessica Wild is a bit of a local hero. She grew up in Fortuna and left for law school. Then, instead of staying in the big city, she brought her talents home where they are much needed. She's David to Atlas Jamison's Goliath and successfully blocked Pacific Lumber's latest timber harvest plan at Owl Creek. We have time for one more caller. Hello? Daniel?" Sam paused. "Daniel, you have to turn down your radio."

"Okay. That better?" a male voice said.

"Much better, thank you. My notes say you've been logging most of your life. Is that right, Daniel?"

"Yeah, that's right. And no offense, I have a problem with a bunch of outsiders who are more concerned about some little bird than about the people who live here coming in and taking away our jobs. My family has been here for over a hundred years. Scotia wouldn't even be here without the logging industry. And we've got bills to pay. What right do you have to just come in here and shut us down?"

"Do you have a response to that, Jessica?"

Diana took her eyes off the bumpy road for a second to turn up the volume.

"I'd like to respond to all your charges, Daniel. Many of us are from here. My people, for instance, have been here for 11,000 years."

"Oh, is that right? You're Native American?" said Sam.

"Sinkyone, one of many tribes massacred by the Europeans when they came here. But this isn't a turf war. We care about the trees and the thousands of species that depend on them," she paused, "which includes you and your family, Daniel."

"Spiking trees is a funny way to show it. My friend nearly lost his right eye thanks to you!"

"You're mixing us up with Earth First! But Judi Bari, their new leader, has disavowed all violent tactics. EPIC, the organization I work for, pursues mainly legal means to preserve not only the redwoods but your jobs, as well. The problem is that Jamison's holding company, Titan, which now owns Pacific Lumber, has more than doubled its cutting rate. And for the listeners who don't know, Pacific Lumber was one of the oldest and most respected lumber companies in the region, taking care of their own, practicing sustainable yield. They didn't have a union because they didn't need one. They paid better than the other companies, and their workers have a great pension. Well, had. Until Titan took over. At this rate, you'll be out of a job in no time, and the whole town of Scotia will shut down."

"Total exaggeration," Diane muttered.

"See, that's where you're wrong," Daniel said. "Ever since Titan took over, we've been getting overtime and I was able to sell my stock for a tidy profit. We finally had the money to build a room for my five-year-old daughter, thanks to Atlas Jamison."

"That's right," Diana muttered. Anyway, she'd learned from her research that the story of PL as a paternalistic company that took care of its own and never cut more than it could replace was romanticized b.s. Maybe that was how it was back when it was a family-owned company, but since it went public they'd had three different CEOs, and they'd done their own share of clearcutting.

"Daniel," Jessica replied, "ninety-six percent of the old-growth is already gone. There's only four percent left. And PL is damaging the ground so badly with machinery and herbicides, that they won't grow back. These 400-foot-tall, 30-foot-wide giants require 500 gallons of water a day. The Northern California mists have allowed them to grow to this unheard-of size, but it's dwindling with climate change, which means they might never grow to these heights ever again. These trees are one of the seven wonders of the world."

"But isn't it true that PL is planting trees to replace them?"

"Monoculture is no replacement," Jessica said. "And the point is that since Titan took over, they've been filing timber harvest plans without doing the required environmental reviews. Atlas Jamison doesn't care about loggers or trees. He even said so himself when he made that lousy joke about the golden rule."

"Oh, what was that?" asked Sam Seabreeze.

"In his first speech with the company after the takeover, he said his version of the golden rule was, 'Those with the gold, rule.' The man has no shame."

Diana slapped the dashboard. It was a stupid joke. Humor was never his strong suit. It was unfair how they singled him out. This wasn't the only logging outfit in the area. What about Louisiana Pacific? And Pacific Lumber had been a global conglomerate before he took over. They just liked to characterize him as a corporate raider and a pirate because it sold stories. If it bleeds, it leads. The news media were capitalists, too. And the activists were exploiting the opportunity to get more publicity.

Now he was having to spend way too much time establishing public relations to clean up his image. That's where Diana could help.

Chapter 5

Mudslide

February 1987

When Logan's father, Robert Blackburn, caught wind of Titan's plan to clearcut the plot above their land, he'd sued and lost. He knew mudslides were inevitable, and his property and all the trees he'd worked to save would be destroyed. But the judge didn't know anything about forestry and the lawyers said they couldn't prove mudslides were caused by clearcuts, with experts testifying that mudslides were a naturally occurring phenomenon. It wouldn't have been an immediate threat because the roots of the trees would hold the soil together for at least another decade. However, the Jamison clearcut was right below a clearcut from fifteen years ago, where the roots had lost their grip on the soil. The best Robert had been able to do is get permission to dig a ravine that took advantage of the natural topography to divert the inevitable damage.

It had been a painful decision, requiring the destruction of many trees and a few creeks, tearing up topsoil thousands of years in the making, destroying the homes of the spotted owl and millions of other creatures, but it had been the only option left.

Robert owned four hundred acres of redwoods that had been in the family since the 1860s, many of them ancient giants and some of them second-growth. His father was a lumberjack, and his father before that. All of them were avid woodsmen who loved the land that gave them their keep, but Robert had seen early on that there was no kind way to cut down a redwood and that the lumber companies were moving too fast. What was more, most of the old-growth had ended up on private property.

So, he had turned his acres into a demonstration of how to log sustainably, providing workshops and raising awareness. He and Logan were well known by the local activist groups, EPIC and even EarthFirst!, which had been working hard to stop Pacific Lumber ever since Atlas Jamison had taken over. So far, activists had managed to slow things down and draw national news to their plight, but Titan's progress had been inexorable.

Before 1850, two million acres of ancient redwoods shaped the northern Pacific coast. Many of them were seedlings when Emperor Augustus ruled Rome. Most were already 1,000 years old when the first Europeans came to the Americas and began to exterminate the indigenous people. By the 1850s, most of the forests in the United States had been cut down. Robert Blackburn was doing his best to make up for that in whatever way he could. He had always told Logan a man couldn't live his life only for himself. To have purpose, he had to be a part of something bigger. This land, these trees, this mountainside, were worth saving whatever the cost, and they had cost him a lot. Their family lived hand-to-mouth, with limited electricity and gravity-fed water. It had even cost his marriage.

Logan's mother, who had dropped her life-long dream of going to college to give birth to Logan, had returned to college when Logan reached kindergarten. She'd earned her PhD by the time Logan reached fifth grade. She had always wanted to get out of the small town of Fortuna, and when she was offered a teaching position at San Francisco State, she'd leapt at it. She'd asked Logan to move with her, but he'd stayed with his father out of loyalty both to him and the land.

That was twelve years ago. Since she'd left, Robert had gotten more single-minded, teaching Logan everything he knew, often harshly. But the trees were a part of Logan as much as they were a part of his father.

His friends thought they were crazy for digging the ravine, like Don Quixote tilting at windmills, but Logan had worked by his father's side every step of the way, dozing the soil to make beds for the trees they felled, dragging the logs to the water to float them down the coast to the mill. During the occasional light rains in October, topsoil had been sifting down from Pacific Lumber's clearcut right above their property, but in December that year, rainfall had reached a new record. Robert and Logan had sped up efforts to divert the inevitable mudslide, working eighteen-hour shifts, and catching four hours of sleep between. Maybe that's why his father didn't see how crazy it was for him to be on the dozer the day of the storm.

"It's not worth it!" Logan shouted.

Through the blur of pelting rain, he could make out his father nodding his head and moving his lips. Though he couldn't hear him, he knew he was saying, "It is. Whatever the cost." It was what he always said.

Right before he mounted the Cat that fateful morning, he had told Logan "in no uncertain terms" to get to safety. He would finish up and catch up to him. Their house was not safe. It would be in the path of the mudslide because of its lower elevation, but the tree platform they had built when Logan was a child was out of harm's way. He'd be able to keep watch from there. Logan had argued with him, pointing out that anything he could do in the next few hours would make little difference, but his father was a stubborn son-of-a-bitch, and didn't seem to care about his own life. He was fixated on finishing one last detail that he was convinced would make all the difference.

"Go!" his father shouted with an impatient wave of his arm. Logan did as he was told. He'd jumped in his truck, and rattled and jostled his way to higher ground, heading for the back acres of their land that ran up past the Pacific Lumber clearcut and adjoined other uncut forests. He swerved to a halt, jumped from the truck, and slogged up the slope to the great redwood they'd named Uuma. They'd built the platform in the tree when he was five, and it had been a place of solace all his life. He had always felt like the tree hummed to him as it rocked him to sleep at night, saying uuma,

uuma, uuma. Now, with shaking hands, water trickling down his neck inside his jacket, he donned his spurs and clipped himself into the harness. He usually didn't use spurs, because he didn't want to hurt Uuma, but in this rain and emergency, he hoped Uuma would forebear.

He climbed so fast he was panting hoarsely halfway up, but he didn't slow an inch. In the rain, his hands slipped and scraped against the ropes and furrowed bark, but he pushed himself. By the time he reached the platform, his hands were bleeding and his lungs felt like they'd been scrubbed with steel wool. The platform had a tarp roof, but in this torrential rain, it did little to keep him dry. He opened the storage chest at the edge of the platform, dug through the gear, and pulled out binoculars. The Cat was only observable at the top of the ravine between the clearcut and their wooded acres. His father had finished that part and disappeared into the trees below, but the storm roared louder than the machine. Logan swept the binoculars to the clearcut above their land looking for any signs of landslide. Even in the rain, the mustard scars of scorched earth between gray stumps were visible.

The first indication of the slide was a log moving near the top of the clearcut. Then a few branches on the ground moved simultaneously in three or four different places, more or less in a row.

"Shit. Shit," Logan said, his scalp tingling with adrenaline. It was only when he spoke that he realized his jaw ached from clenching it so hard. He swept the binoculars over the trees where his father had disappeared. He couldn't see anything but trees and rain. He swept the binoculars to the bottom of the ravine to where his father should be emerging. "Come on. What's taking you so long?"

He was soaked to the skin, and his body began to shake with cold, his teeth chattering. He swept the binoculars above their land, a dizzying sweep of trees through the lenses, and focused on the first log he'd seen move. It was tilted in the other direction, wedged between a few stumps. A few more branches lurched here and there across the slope, but he couldn't see what was moving them. They stuck again.

He thought he heard a rumble of his dad's Cat through the pounding rain, but he couldn't see him through the trees. He whipped the binoculars back to the clearcut. The stumps appeared to be rising in a way that didn't make sense. A flash of heat shot across his skull and through his stomach nauseatingly, as the earth buckled, rose, and tumbled, folding huge stumps into a wave of red mud that began to slide downhill. Even through the roar of the rain, he heard unearthly screeches, moans, pops, and cracks, as the wave headed for his father's ravine. "Jesus. Fuck!" Logan said. It wasn't as fast as a snow or rock avalanche, but the more it rolled, the bigger it got, at least a hundred yards wide and ten feet tall.

He refocused the binoculars on the road where his father should emerge, "Come on, come on, you stubborn motherfucker!"

A crack, pop, and screech drew his attention upward. The wave hit the ravine at the top, just as they had anticipated. It splashed in slow motion against the opposite bank. Smaller trees along the edge of the ravine caved inward, but it appeared to be working as they intended, diverting the wave away from the rest of the property. He'd read that these waves could travel ten miles an hour, and he knew a D-10 could only get up to about nine miles an hour, but his father had a good lead, so he should be okay. He scanned the road at the bottom of their property, where the ravine emptied into a culvert. No sign of his father.

Mud and stumps formed a dam at the top of the ravine, and now the dam was catching the whole hillside.

"Oh my god," Logan muttered to himself, realizing that though the dam was holding and giving his father time, it might divert the slide right into the rest of their property and bury the trees.

"Come on, come on!" Logan yelled, looking at the road at the bottom where his father should emerge. How long could it take? What the fuck was he doing? A second roar from above drew his attention. The dam filled to the brim and broke with a terrible scream. The wave, now double in size, roared down the ravine after his father, disappearing faster than ever under the canopy his father had disappeared into. Logan held his breath.

When waves emerged from the tree cover and washed over the road below, Logan's body went cold. His mind split in two, one side saying, "Shit! Shit! Shit!", the other side clinically telling him that a wall of mud that size was big enough to roll the entire D-10 into it and keep going. The first side of his brain told him his father could have jumped off in time and made it to higher ground, maybe grabbed onto a tree that had fallen across the ravine, and swung to safety like they always did in the movies.

The other side told him his father's body was little more than a branch cut from a tree, engulfed, battered, and suffocated by all that he loved.

———

His best friend, Zeff, had been with him when they found his father's D-10 after the mudslide, a tread sticking up out of the mud. They never found his father's body. For a long time, Logan fantasized that his father had been struck on the head and was living somewhere with amnesia. A few friends of the family offered to help him plan a funeral, but he'd refused. The house had been spared and much of their land. But none of it meant very much to Logan at the time.

His mother stepped in and organized a funeral even though there was no body. He was furious. She had left *them,* so who was she to step in and take over after the disaster? Logan had to sit next to her at the funeral, but he stared straight ahead. He almost relished the pain in his mother's face when she looked at him across the crowd at the funeral. Almost. It had been a big crowd. His father was well known and respected.

After a year, Logan erected a wooden grave marker where the tread of his father's Cat stuck up out of the mud. They hadn't bothered to pull it out. He took some small comfort from the fact that his father was buried where the county would never have allowed it.

Jessica Wild, an old high school friend he'd had a bit of a crush on, had encouraged him to attend EPIC's calls to action to stop Atlas Jamison. But mud seemed to run in his veins. He was angry at his father, angry at his mother, but most of all, he was afraid that if he ever came face to face with Atlas Jamison, he would kill him. And that was wrong. He knew that if you fought your enemy too hard, you sometimes became just like them.

He'd given up the fight to save the trees. He couldn't bear to sleep in their house, and the one time he climbed Uuma, he couldn't hear her thrum anymore.

Instead, Logan equipped his twenty-seven-foot sailboat with food and water and set out west, not sure where he'd land. He ended up in Hawaii.

Uuma

There used to be a clevertongue child who climbed me and slept in my branches on and off for many circles around the sun. He came at first with his forbearer. After much chatter, they both would lie quietly in my branches, and as Bhūr turned away from the Bright One, I would carry them through the Darkside until we came brightside again.

His forebearer's mindroot was like a tree who has reached the twilight stage, with only a few fresh channels to receive nutrients, but the child's phloem and xylem were flexible, mutable, nimble. His mindroot grew like a field of grass with many tendrils sensitive to the merest vibrations. I hummed to him, and in only a few trips to the Darkside, he learned to hum back. When I Uuma'd him, he said my name. I called him Laghu, for that was close to what his forebear called him. Nimble. Truly, he was nimble of hand, foot, and wit. I knew he would protect me as I protect him.

One day, the cutting came to the grove next to mine. Jagged-edged waves flooded Kulaaya. I have felt the death-judder of True Ones far from me before, but this was quake after quake. Then holes appeared in the net up the slope from us like stars gone out in the sky, entire banks of net gone dark, young ones and ancient ones down.

Silence.

We breathed.

The web reformed in different directions. We sent signals, sugar, nutrients, to each other as always, our messages back-and-forthing. But we were fewer. A wide hole above us never filled in.

Laghu grew to a sapling, and he was working for us. I rejoiced whenever I felt his particular vibrations. His vibrations are like a windbear with a hint of raptor. He hummed with all of us far and wide. The animals weren't afraid of him.

But one day during an unusually rainy season, he and his forebear began to scour Bhūr with their machines. I cried out to him, our feathered and furred relations scolded him, but he didn't respond.

The rains came often and harder than they had ever come in my journeys around the Bright One. One day, it was as if Samudra fell from the sky. Mrid filled up, and because the net was broken, there was no place for the waters to go, so Mrid became liquid, rose up and traveled on legs down the slope near mine, taking many more of us with her.

Laghu climbed me then, vibrating discordantly. I almost didn't recognize him.

Then the storm passed, and Laghu came no more. His forebearer's vibrations were gone.

For a time, I could feel Laghu's vibrations through Kulaaya ever so faintly, but after a circle around the Bright One, even that was gone.

Chapter 6

Pacific Lumber Plots

April 15, 1990

Morning mist rolled through the redwoods, stippling needles, melding with other droplets, and dripping down in a fine rain. This had been going on for millions of years.

It was Saturday, 9 a.m., and Harry Stanton, a short muscular field manager for Pacific Lumber, waited for Vice President Eddie Cox at the demo logging site at the edge of lot 2-86. It was a trailer deposited in a stand of second-growth. Unlike the other field trailers, this office had been sided in redwood slabs, the part of the log that was sheared off when it was squared at the lumber mill. It formed a wavy, rustic "clapboard" on which hung a sign, "Pacific Lumber, a division of Titan. We're on Your Side."

Eddie, or Mr. Cox, as they were now required to address him, had said he wanted to meet Stanton there to get a first-hand account of the recent sabotage by the goddamned tree huggers. Both the time and place were unusual requests, and Stanton was worried.

Age fifty, he had worked his way up to the management position from the bottom, as was the tradition at PL before the takeover. Cox, fifteen years his junior, had skipped a lot of steps and was promoted to executive VP by the new boss, the Texan. Stanton had been next in line for the VP of operations. But Cox, having an appetite for all the new corporate bullshit that most old-timers disdained, had sent one of his toadies to the mill floor with a stopwatch, the motherfucker.

"A fuckin' stopwatch?" Stanton muttered, recalling it.

Cox had no idea of the kind of danger they were dealing with. Cox was unhappy with their haul, so he didn't promote Stanton, and had hired some other outsider for the position, another corporate monkey, probably some relation to the Texan. Stanton sighed. This was the new way of the world, and he would have to adapt.

He surveyed the damage. Spray-painted slogans defaced the redwood-sided trailer, "Earth First!" and "Greed = Death." A wire cutter had been used to cut a human-sized hole through the chain-link fencing that guarded dozers, skidders, and loaders. Each logging station was equipped with a trailer office, storage sheds, and fenced lots. This particular site was the display area— where press and others were brought for inquiries. It was situated in a second-growth grove to emphasize how quickly the redwoods recovered. Right next to it was a prime example. A circle of hundred-foot tall trees stood around a stump twenty-five feet wide that was cut in the 1920s. In seventy years, the trees had shot up and reached diameters of six or seven feet.

He popped a stick of gum in his mouth and tucked the wrapper in his shirt pocket. Bleeding heart liberals getting in the way of logging wasn't news in Northern California. In the early days, it was rich people who bought property and donated it to the government. That's where the Redwood National Park and Humboldt Redwoods State Park came from. They had their parks, but that didn't stop them.

Starting in the 1960s, hippies began to invade the region, and they weren't just protesting logging on federal and state land, they had the nerve to protest logging on private land. And they played dirty, spiking trees, sabotaging equipment, and tree sitting.

Eddie Cox pulled into the clearing in a brand new short-bed Chevy Silverado that was so clean and you could eat off it. Like he was ever going to need to haul equipment again. Eddie jumped down from the cab. He was dressed for the weekend, in baggy cargo shorts, brand new hiking boots, and a Hawaiian shirt. He strode toward Stanton holding his hand out.

"Mr. Stanton, glad you could meet with me."

"Sure," Stanton said, irritated by the use of his last name. "What did you want to see me about?"

"Like I said on the phone, I've been hearing about the eco-terrorists, and I want to take a more active role—sorta close the gap—the disconnect—between operations and the front office. And I've been crunching numbers...and I wanted to see the damage for myself."

Stanton stiffened. "What's the matter, don't trust me?"

"No, no, nothing like that. It's just time for the company to tighten up its act. We've been underperforming. I want to see if there's anything I can do to help, maybe shuffle some money around and make some...assets available to you."

"Assets. You mean, like, equipment."

"Yeah, or security."

"Okay," Stanton chewed his gum a beat. "That's good news," he said neutrally.

"So, what's the damage?" Eddie said with too much energy, smacking his fist into his palm.

"Well," Stanton scratched his head, "we've got two dozers down just last week. Motherfuckers poured sugar in the tanks. And a couple of men caught a spike in the tree. Destroyed a saw. One of my guys was hurt pretty bad, so I expect there will be some disability claims. Then one of the skidders...I just don't know. And that's on top of some equipment that broke down last week due to lack of maintenance. It's definitely gonna knock us off our mark."

"Yeah. What are you doing to fix it?"

"You can see, we've erected ten-foot fencing around the lot, and we've got cameras stationed so we can catch the buggers, but they climb like monkeys and knock 'em down. We hired armed guards on three of the sites, and when we catch them, we make sure to do some damage, if you know what I mean, before we turn 'em over to the cops."

"Sure do. So, it sounds like you could use more security?"

"Well, sure. And we're gonna need that equipment replaced ASAP.

"Done."

"Now that's what I'm talking about." Stanton finally relaxed and slapped Eddie on the back.

"Sure thing. Now listen. There's something you gotta do for me."

"Oh, yeah?"

"This is why I wanted to meet in private."

Stanton looked at him uncertainly.

"I tracked down a rumor from the truckers that the independent outfit we hired to timber lots 78 and 79 have been overcharging us."

"That right? The gyppos?"

"The men were saying that they have been charging yarder rates for logs they actually got by Cat and that this has been going on for years. You hear anything about that?"

"No, can't say I have," Stanton spat and rubbed his brow with his forearm. gyppos, outside outfits hired to increase their cutting rate, charged the company by the foot. Yarder was the term used for trees harvested from steep slopes, where cables and hoists were used. It was slower, more dangerous work. Cat rates referred to trees that were harvested by dozers and cranes on level ground. The gyppos marked the logs according to their harvest method, which determined the payout.

"Thing is, I was just looking at 78 and 79 before I got here, and they are pretty flat. I don't see why anyone would be using cables and hoists on those lots. Am I right? Aren't 78 and 79 your responsibility?

"Sure are, yeah. And you're right. Cats are all you need to do the work there—'cept maybe the northern edge of 79."

"So, how come more than half the haul is billed at yarder rates?"

"God damn. That right?"

"Thing is, Harry, you've been overseeing these guys for the last five years. From where I sit, there's no way you could have missed this."

"Now, wait a minute. I'm not sure I like what you're implying."

"Don't get your panties in a twist. I'm not here to come down on you. And I'm not gonna tell Jamison about it either. I understand that the old way of doing things was less—formal, shall we say."

"Well, yeah. Okay. We more or less guesstimate the yardage. But I'll get right on that and put a stop to it, immediately."

"No, you don't have to do that on my account. I just want to be a part of it, if you know what I mean."

Stanton paused, digesting this. "Like..."

"Yeah, exactly like. You report to me, and I'll make the final call and see that everyone gets their fair share."

"Okay," Stanton said slowly, not quite sure what he was agreeing to.

"You've got nothing to worry about," Eddie said. "But I want those truckers to stop talking about it. Can you do that for me?"

"I think something can be arranged."

"Good man. See, I'm a man with a plan, and I need a partner on the ground to pull off a few of these ideas. Would you be willing to be that man?"

Stanton looked Eddie over. He didn't like him. There was something about his face. His head was too large, his lips too thin, his skin too pale. Stanton saw himself as a basically honest man, who maybe didn't report all his income on his taxes, but who did? Eddie, on the other hand, had something of the lizard about him. But he didn't have much choice. "Yeah," he said slowly, "I think so."

"Well, see, this group, EPIC, has filed a stay for the cutting of lot 2-86. That's all old-growth. We've got millions of dollars in that grove alone."

"Tell me something I don't know," Stanton said.

"If they succeed, the whole northern half of our holdings will be tied up in court for years...so we've got to head them off."

"I'm listening."

"I say we take the whole grove down before the stay order is issued. Today."

Stanton snorted. "Not possible. It would mean moving equipment and taking men off other logging shows. They're already working double shifts and with all the sabotage—"

A red Jeep Cherokee pulled up and parked near Eddie's truck. They both stopped talking. Neither of them recognized it. The paint was still glossy, a condition that didn't last in these parts. A blonde woman opened the door, stepped out, and paused. The trees drew her eyes inexorably upward, immobilizing her for a nugget of eternity.

"Can I help you?" Stanton said with an edge as he moved toward her.

Eddie stepped forward with a big smile on his face, offering his hand to shake.

"Well, *this* is a pleasant surprise."

Diana didn't recognize him, but clearly, he recognized her. "Hello?" she asked, shaking his hand.

"I'm the new executive vice president of PL, Eddie Cox. You're the boss's daughter, right?"

"I hope I wasn't interrupting anything."

"No, no. Harry, have you met the big man's little girl?"

Diana smiled like the edge of a carving knife.

"This is Harry Stanton," Eddie continued, oblivious, "one of our field managers."

"Will you be introducing me that way when I own this company?" Diana said as Stanton stepped forward.

Cox reddened.

She extended her hand to Stanton and he shook it. "Mr. Stanton," she said more neutrally. "I have a lot to learn before that ever happens," she added with a more sincere smile. "I'm organizing my own internship this summer."

"Nice to meet you, Miss Jamison. Uh. Sorry to cut out on you, but I've gotta check some equipment. Let me know if you need anything." As he turned, he and Eddie's eyes met.

"You'll talk to the gyppos?" Eddie said.

"Will do. See you around."

Eddie turned back to Diana. "I'd be glad to show you around."

"Maybe later, when I get to the front office. Today I literally just want to get the lay of the land."

"Be my guest."

"I'm a stockholder and daughter of the owner, not a guest."

"Of course," Eddie said, blushing again, much to his own dismay.

PuraaNam

Many circles of the sun ago, the naked ones cut down Tunia at the edge of our grove. Tunia had lived three thousand circles around the sun. Her earth-net used to span the world once upon a time, interrupted only by Samudra, the gathering of the waters. We were able to send food to her through our sister Kulaaya, whose fine white filaments spread faster and farther than our roots, feeding us as we fed her and sending messages back and forth between us. Thanks to Kulaaya, Tunia sent out a circle of new shoots that are now almost as tall as she once was. Together we hum as we always have, and so, the circle never ends.

Bibi has not returned from the twilight for at least a circle around the Bright One. She used to return every half-circle or so. She is no longer accepting our offerings. We have all said goodbye. Sap flows only in a few narrow paths up and down her trunk. But Bibi will stay upright for many more circles. Already our furred and feathered relations have moved in, and Bibi is alive with the life of others, and so, the circle never ends.

Hairs of mind from new seedlings probe the uppermost kernels of soil all around. We send them sugar, water, and other nutrients, and so the circle never ends.

But now the uprooted ones grow out of balance. They have been extracting death from Bhūr's belly and spraying it into the air. They have fashioned tools out of Bhūr that amplify their power far beyond their natural reach. Wherever they grow, they cut, grind, and burn us. When they began to burn us en masse south of Bhūr's belly, the death of millions sent shudders through us all. The Bright One itself grew dim, and Kulaaya was interrupted so that we couldn't speak to those far from us. Our sap slowed, and the steady beat of our rhythms faltered.

Bhūr has been changing. She grows hotter and colder, dryer and wetter. If we do not remove the Uprooted ones, they will destroy us with them. Even if we do remove them, Bhūr has changed in such a way that we will never be as we now are again along these shores. The net will be too broken.

The Uprooted plant rows of trees that are all one kind, but these seedlings break soil for the first time in isolation, so Kulaaya does not thread their roots, and they cannot speak. They are thrust into ground that has been churned and poisoned so that nothing else grows between. If they are alive, they are asleep. Bhūr cannot find balance within them, and so our furred and many-legged relations cannot grow amongst them.

Now the Uprooted ones are cutting up the earth between me and one of my oldest friends, Candra, and where they cut, the energy sizzles like sap on fire. My mind shoots have always curled inside of Candra's, I feel her sap rising or falling. When the wind blows, our trunks sway together. When ground clouds roll in off the ocean, the water droplets that seeded her needles also seed mine. We have formed a branch cage up top, where our children grow. We are as good as one, but I can barely feel her anymore. The ground between us is so dense that Kulaaya cannot get through, and I do not know if the seedlings will ever be able to penetrate that ground again. I am darker, different.

Uuma thinks we can still reach the Uprooted, but they are traveling in something heavy that shakes the ground and crushes Kulaaya's net in a line straight toward our grove.

Chapter 7

Old Friends

April 15, 1990

The temperature dropped fifteen degrees as Logan stepped into the redwoods onto springy ground formed by thousands of years of decomposed branchlets. His whole body relaxed as the scent of soil and greenery enveloped and cooled him. Tiny muscles around his eyes and scalp he hadn't realized were clenched let go. He could almost hear Uuma call him, the bass hum he'd picked up so early in life when he was alone in the platform he and his father had built. It formed the texture of his childhood. He'd learned to relax into that sound like lying in a hammock. He could twist and turn inside the strings of sound wherever he was, pluck them with his body or swim among them. The giants were like relatives, great aunts, great uncles, and great-great-grandparents.

His mother had been furious when his father insisted that Logan take part in building the platform when he was only five years old. His father reasoned that a child was safer in a tree than any adult because they "bounce" when they fall. He was only half kidding. He'd tied Logan into a harness the entire time.

For a moment, now, as he picked his way across the forest floor, he almost relaxed into the hum, but the memory of the mudslide slashed across his mind, and his body tensed and shut it off.

For the last four hours, he'd been hiking along the Eel River, which used to be blue-green. Now it was most often brown due to the silt from logging. Wide sandy banks showed how much it had dropped over the years. It still had a few holes popular with fly fishers looking for steelhead, coho, and trout. He had left the river after Fernbridge, and angled northeast toward his home, traversing back roads, and patches of recovered and devastated forest. With a mixture of memory and compass, he navigated straight to the Grove of the Ancients located in the heart of the Headwaters Forest, where some of the oldest and largest old-growth trees still towered.

The forest, which held six old-growth redwood groves, was owned by Pacific Lumber but had been named by Greg King, investigative reporter, and environmental activist. King, like Logan, came from a long line of lumbermen. Unlike Logan's family, his family had owned the largest redwood mill in Sonoma County, and the King Mountain Range was named after them.

The deeper Logan hiked into the oldest growth, the darker and quieter it grew. By now, he estimated he was trespassing on Pacific Lumber Company land. If he was caught, he'd be arrested. But since he was bushwhacking and had learned to walk without sound, there wasn't much chance of that. Not much grew between the redwoods but ferns, sorrel, and moss, which covered everything. Still, navigating was tricky, as it was easy to punch a hole through the humus made by a hundred-thousand years of fallen redwoods. Often it was best to walk along the moss-covered, sorrel-covered trunks of fallen redwoods. He forded a stream, one of the tributaries of Salmon Creek, and was careful not to step on frogs and banana slugs. A giant salamander, still in its aquatic stage, hid in a pool, with a brown ruffled mane sprouting from the gills behind its ears. Logan was slightly out of breath as he bushwhacked ever upward.

He'd been hiking for nearly six hours when a rustle behind him made him freeze and duck behind a six-foot fern.

Zeff Tolliver, a surfer-turned-activist, formerly known as Joseph, crept through the woods with his two friends Jim and Brian, unaware of Logan as he passed. Logan smiled to himself, and right after they passed, stepped out soundlessly and tapped Zeff on the shoulder.

Like a cat, Zeff crouched and whirled in one move. His two

friends dove headlong into the underbrush. If he'd had a tail, it would have been bristling like a bottle brush. When Zeff recognized Logan, he scream-whispered, "Holy shit!"

Crackling with frenetic energy, he threw himself onto Logan before Logan could open his mouth, "Bro!!! Dude!" and crushed him in a hug so tight Logan's laughter turned into a cough. "You're back!!!" Though inches shorter, Zeff lifted Logan nearly off his feet as he jump-hugged him a few more times.

"Whoa. Glad—chill!" Logan couldn't even free his arms from Zeff's embrace.

Zeff let go, backed up, and clapped both hands on Logan's shoulders. "Let me get a good look at you." Logan clapped his own hands over Zeff's tattooed shoulders, their arms wrapping around each other like trees grown close together. "I've *missed* you so much, Dude! Not even a *postcard* for *TWO years*?" Zeff talked in perpetual italics, even when he whispered, which he was doing now.

"Sorry, man. I just needed some time to get my head together."

"No, I get that, totally. I'm sorry about your old man. He was solid."

Logan's eyes flickered as he tried to shunt off the reference, and Zeff, seeing his mistake immediately, said, "Where've you *been?*"

"Sailing."

"Right. I knew that. But for *two* years?"

"Well, I ended up in Hawaii."

"Dude! Hawaii? That is *so cool."*

Logan smiled and looked down. "Yeah, it was, man. The mountains there are really," he paused, looking for the word. "I don't know. They *grip* you."

"I totally dig that," Zeff continued to whisper. "When did you get back?"

"Last night. Anchored too near a doghole left by Pacific Lumber companies. Slash from the most recent cuts woke me up."

"Oh man, that's PL for you, our good ole PAL. Cutting continues apace. But this is so *kismet*, man. I can hardly believe it. We—," he turned around as if just realizing that his friends Brian and Jim weren't standing behind him. "Yo, guys. Come on out. It's safe!"

Brian, a lanky tattooed twenty-something-year-old with a full beard, and Jim, a dread-locked ginger, slowly emerged from the ferns blushing, eyes darting from the ground to Logan's face and back.

"These are my mates, Jim and Brian. We're all part of the Earth First! Redwood Action Team!" Brian stiffened a bit and looked at Zeff with alarm. "Brian, Jim, this is Logan Blackburn, a righteous dude. Me and him grew up together in Fortuna, more or less. Logan was a country kid, and I was a townie, but that didn't stop us from being best buds."

"I thought everyone out here was country kids," Jim said.

"Spoken like a true city boy," Zeff said, giving Jim's butt a squeeze.

"Oh, is that how it is?" Logan said, noting the gestures.

"That's how it is," Zeff said, and both Jim and Zeff blushed.

"Logan's dad used to run sustainable logging workshops on a sweet gem of land not far from here. He's practically an Earth First!-er himself."

Logan grinned and proffered his hand to shake theirs. Brian grabbed his hand in both of his, and Jim gave him a half hug, hairy armpit grazing his shoulder and dreadlocks grazing his ear. By high school, Logan and Zeff had started to party with the Earth First!-ers, but Logan was wary of them after some tree spiking incidents that had injured loggers.

"Brian grew up in Eureka, and Jim here was a city kid from the Big Apple before he went feral."

"Cool, cool," Logan said. "So, you've thrown in with Earth First!"

"*Totally*. I know we always had that argument—legal-illegal—but, thing is, one hand washes the other, dude. And you gotta do what you're built to do. And *you*, my friend, are built to climb—" Zeff turned to Brian and Jim. "Logan taught *me* to climb."

Brian pressed his palms together and bowed and Jim added a salaam.

"So, what, may I ask, are you doing here?" Logan said.

"Staging our next attack. Our good PAL has been threatening to cut the Grove of the Ancients since you left. Did you hear about Greg King's highway 101 stunt?"

"I've been avoiding the news."

"Well, he hung a banner saying 'Save the Redwoods.' Got us a lot of press. A logger nearly pulled him out of the tree and he was arrested. But we've been doing political theater and everything. We're prepping for Redwood Summer, man! People are coming from all over. It's gonna be *massive*."

"Oh? And what part are you playing?"

"A picture's worth a thousand words, bub. I'll show you."

A wall shot up inside Logan. He didn't want to go, he just wanted the silence of the trees, but he also didn't see how he could refuse without seriously offending Zeff.

As they hiked further into the woods, Zeff narrated the ups and downs of the movement over the last two years, seemingly oblivious to Logan's silence. Zeff told Logan how Darryl Cherney had fallen in love with Judi Bari, and how she—a former labor organizer, had become the de facto leader of the north coast chapter of Earth First!, not that they had any official leadership. There was another organizer who was advocating real violence in the name of self-defense. Much to everyone's dismay, Judi had recently disavowed violent protest and was trying to bring the loggers into the movement. Dave Foreman, who founded Earth First!, was not happy, saying the Marxists and anarchists weren't helping things, and that Earth First! is about—well Earth—not people. Other people thought he was just sexist and resented Judi.

"She a *force,* man," said Brian

"There's no denying it. But we're *Earth* First!, not *loggers* first. Much as I care about the loggers, that's not the point." said Zeff. "Fat-Ass Jamison and PL don't care about their workers. It's all about prof-it," Zeff continued as they picked their way between six-foot ferns and over streams. It was easy to imagine the dinosaurs walking among them. They bore the same ratio as the redwoods, and the species dated back to their time.

"And then the FBI—the *fuckin'* FBI," Zeff said, still in a stage whisper. "The fuckin' FBI *infiltrated* our meetings." Logan, who was ahead of Zeff and had jumped off the log, turned and looked back, and Zeff stayed where he was as if born on the stage. He was a good-looking guy, Logan thought. Small, and fine-featured, but with outsized energy that made you think he was bigger than he was, with long curly hair, large eyes, heavy brows, and a goatee. From his stage on the log, he towered. "This guy—I fuckin' *knew* there was something off about him, *Nick* something, called himself 'The Terminator.' I mean, *the terminator?!* Wrong fuckin' milieu!"

Logan laughed at his choice of words.

"He pitched this whole plot to sabotage one of the powerlines feeding the mills in Scotia...and Dave—he didn't—like *go* for it, but he gave this guy a copy of *Ecodefense*, and they fuckin' arrested him on criminal conspiracy. Can you fuckin' *believe* it?"

"It shows you're more powerful than you think," Logan said.

"No shit! Anyway, they have been building this Death Road to the Headwaters Forest, and they've been filing dozens of THPs to clearcut the whole thing. All six *groves.* We've been doing everything we can to stop them, tree-sitting, disabling their equipment, you name it. Even came to blows a few times!"

Rage pressed against the wall in Logan's head, a dam threatening to break. Sometimes, before and especially after the mudslide, he had seriously contemplated bombing Pacific Lumber headquarters. He was always quick to suppress the thought. but that was why he had to stay out of the fight.

The Grove of the Ancients was up a steep slope, and the increased incline and thick root and moss growth required their mental focus to navigate. Talking was no longer possible, but with each step upward, as the width and height of the trees increased, the silence around them deepened, as if the voice of the trees was a decibel beyond hearing, perceived only as a cottony silence of blocked eardrums. They were stepping back into the timelessness of millennial beings, dwarfed to the size of ants.

They finally arrived at what appeared to be their destination, a tree that had a dead core but was very much alive at the circumference. Brian and Jim dropped their packs, pulled out ropes and climbing gear, and began attaching harnesses with lanyards, carabiners, and ropes. Brian pulled out a rope with a beanbag weight at the end of it, swung it like a pendulum, and expertly let it fly eighty feet into the air to the first branch. When it dropped back to his feet, he attached a climbing rope and began rigging the tree.

Zeff looked Logan up and down mockingly, and whispered, "Think those sea legs still know how to climb?"

"Does a bear shit in the woods?" Logan mocked back.

"I can lend you my gear," Zeff said as he unloaded his.

"Brought my own," Logan said, letting his backpack slide to the ground.

"Such a Boy Scout!" Zeff said as he readied his throw line.

Jim and Brian agreed to spot them, and when they finished rigging the harnesses and knots, they both dipped their hands into the chalk bag.

"Race you to the top," Zeff said. "But try to keep to this side."

"Why's that?" Logan asked, clipping himself in.

"You'll see."

They leaned back into their harness and set their feet to the tree, then hoisted their ropes. They worked in silence, settling into a steady rhythm, step, step, hoist, step, step hoist. Logan began to take the lead.

"Oh man," Zeff said. "Such a showoff." But Zeff was small-boned and wiry, and with a few focused hoists, he was ahead of Logan

Logan smiled.

"So, did the ocean treat you good?" Zeff said.

"Pretty good," Logan said, thinking. "It empties the mind. How about you? Been on that board lately?" Logan caught up to Zeff and passed him.

"Nope. Last time I was in the water was the day you left."

"Why's that?"

"Turns out I have a calling, man." Zeff caught up.

They were both breathing hard now and were about sixty feet off the ground, so they paused to catch their breath.

"I picked up where you left off, man," Zeff said, "but I've been going the illegal route."

"Takes all kinds," Logan said, looking up at the tree.

"Oh yeah? You've changed your stance on that?"

"I don't have a stance anymore," Logan said. He yanked on his rope and restarted his ascent.

"I dig that. You know EPIC and us have stopped them from doing any more cuts in the Grove of the Ancients."

"That's something," Logan said, but he sounded disinterested as he pulled ahead.

"Sure is."

"How about All Species?"

Zeff hesitated, catching up. "Greg King is occupying one of the last trees standing."

Logan fumbled a step and hit the truck and swung around. Zeff reached out a hand to steady him. "Whoa," Zeff said.

"It's pointless," Logan said, as he caught his footing. "See what I mean? Pointless." He took off with rage-filled vigor.

It wasn't long before they were too out of breath to talk. An hour's climb and two hundred feet later, they pulled themselves up onto a platform built into a natural hollow caused by the confluence of the dead and the living. It had been topped a long time ago by a lightning strike and had sent up a new lead branch that continued to the side up another thirty feet, sparsely needled in tufts. The tree formed a cradle, like a giant eagle's nest about ten feet wide where its own soil had collected over decades. Zeff had built a balcony of sorts to one side that extended the space another few feet. Smaller trees had taken root in the soil and created a natural screen all around. A camouflage net stretched overhead to help them escape detection from helicopters, which were sometimes used to dislodge tree-sitters.

When Logan planted his feet on the platform floor, they vibrated slightly. Nights swaying in Uuma's branches under the stars flooded his mind, but he locked his knees and squeezed his calves to stop the vibration.

Zeff pointed to a metal chest locked by a chain around the base of the lead branch and bolted to the wood platform that was also lashed to the tree with ropes, so as not to injure it in any way. "We keep our equipment locked in here. So far, the loggers haven't found this hideout. It's totally invisible from all angles, ground, and sky."

"Cool," Logan said, hoping Zeff wouldn't detect the underlying deadness that had been steadily taking over.

"And the thing that is so great is that we can sleep in this soft area in our bags. We've got one set of buckets to send the shit down, and another to pull food up. All kinds of volunteers keep us fed. We use this for surveillance, right now, mostly." He turned back to Logan and unlocked the chest.

Zeff handed Logan a pair of high-power binoculars and directed his gaze.

Through the lenses, the forest careened and Logan caught a flash of white on the ground about two hundred feet from the edge of the grove. He adjusted the focus and zeroed in on a trailer, fenced dozers, and the sign, "Pacific Lumber, a Division of Titan, Inc."

His heart sped up when he recognized the grizzled figure of Stanton. His father had worked with him a few times, and Logan had stood across from him at public hearings. Next to him was a man he didn't recognize, with pale skin and a bulging brow, who just looked like a prick, even from that distance.

"Doesn't that make you wanna puke? They filed another THP to cut this grove *next week*," Zeff said, looking through his own binoculars. "Now, check this out!" Zeff moved his binoculars and gestured for Logan to take a look.

Logan saw an odd-looking burl about fifty feet off the ground.

"That's a parabolic mic and it's recording everything they say. Brian retrieves the recordings whenever possible and transmits them via walkie-talkie. We've got scouts everywhere, that's how we know where they're going next and where to set up."

"In case you missed the logging road," Logan said, mock-serious.

Zeff punched him in the shoulder. "Anyway, they don't know we're here, yet, but we have a demonstration planned for the day after tomorrow, and Brian and Jim and I are gonna do some damage to their equipment tonight. Also, we're gonna start our tree-sit." He held up a banner that read "Respect your Elders." That's why running into you is so *kismet*. You gotta join us."

"I don't know."

"How can you say that?! You of all people?"

"I sorta washed my hands of all this, when..."

Zeff's scorn softened instantly. "I get that. But you're here. And that's no accident. We need you, man."

"Looks like you've got plenty of help."

"Come on. You know there's never enough. Every man counts."

"I'll think about it."

"Man, you've changed! The Logan I know wouldn't need to think."

Logan looked at Zeff, and the logs that hit the hull of his boat that morning seemed to hit the hull of his stomach, beating through the hull of his heart with the nauseating persistence of ocean waves.

Uuma

What's this I feel? A hint of summer field in the arms of Akaasha, a familiar vibration. Laghu! My friend. A thin whiff of him came to me off Samudra's breeze a few Darkside's ago. Now he is inland. Akaasha takes root not far from PuraNaam. I hum to Laghu through Kulaaya. But the rootless ones are always so restless. He may not stay long enough for my message to reach him. It does! But it flattened and went dead as soon as it entered his branches. Like a dormant tree, his mind-root has grown rigid. I try again, but something dark and heavy pushes my vibrations back at me.

Chapter 8

Atlas Surveys the Damage

April 15, 1990

A tlas Jamison arrived at the demo logging site in a chauffeured Range Rover. He wasn't a man to waste money on pointless luxuries, but this luxury left him free to work, so it was a necessity. Also, the car was practically a work of art. It was only twenty-four miles from the PL office in Scotia to this spot, but it had taken more than an hour to traverse, and Atlas was annoyed by how much of the trip was in the wilderness. The logging roads were so bumpy they drew his eyes repeatedly to the outdoors where the sun flashed black and white through the trees, making reading nearly impossible. He was more at home in the sunny, urban Houston landscape, humid though it was. Stepping into the woods was like stepping into a freezer, only it was dark and endless, and put a bad taste in his mouth. He could have drawn the shades, but part of his purpose here was to take stock of the cause of the unrest. The activists had been holding up quite a bit of business over the past five years, and the Molten loans were coming due in eight months.

The car slid to a halt, and as he stepped out, the trees seemed to force his gaze upward. His shiny, plain-tipped Oxfords slipped on the rubbery needles. He glanced down at them and shook the needles off his shoe like a hawk shaking out its feathers. The trees were taller than his office building, their trunks like the Ionic columns at the original Museum of Fine Arts in Houston, but three times taller. Grudgingly, he admired them. Cox was waiting in front of the trailer.

"How do you like the great outdoors, A.J?"

"Excuse me?" he spoke quietly, scowling.

"Mr. Jamison, sir."

"I prefer the office, frankly." He looked up at the trees again and adjusted his blazer, his gaze taking in the random placement of trees, ferns, and branches. The ferns were taller than he was. The colossal proportions of everything here diminished his size to a child. Less than a child. Swift's Lilliputians. He'd read that book, what was it, five or six years ago? He shook off the feeling. He preferred the symmetrical plantings around Titan headquarters in Houston, with trees that were neatly shaped and trimmed to his size. "I don't know what all the fuss is about. Seems like there are plenty of trees, and they're all bigger than anything that grows in Texas."

"Exactly. The protesters are mostly communist potheads on welfare. I mean, this—here—is seventy to eighty years of growth," Eddie said, gesturing to the brown and red ridged columns. "One acre is anywhere from a hundred to two hundred board feet."

"So, what's the current damage?"

Cox gestured toward the fenced-in lot, and they strolled in that direction. "We've got several machines down, but Stanton tells me the men are eager to pick up extra shifts."

"Has anyone claimed responsibility?"

"There's a group that calls themselves Earth First! Of course, they deny any sabotage, but they organize the rallies, and one of their leaders, Dave Forman, has his name on a monkey-wrenching manual."

"What do the local authorities say?"

"They've made some arrests. The FBI had infiltrated the group and got Foreman on conspiracy. They're keeping their eye on Darryl Cherney, a clown with a guitar, who writes really annoying songs. Seems to be the rally leader—and his heartthrob, Judi Bari who has ties to the Wobblies."

"Wobblies?"

"The fuckin' Industrial Workers of the World. They're totally socialists and have been out here organizing for most of the century. Bari writes for their rag."

Jamison bowed his head, wrapped his hand over his brow, and rubbed his temples.

"Stanton is setting up more security. We've got cameras here, here, and here," Cox said, pointing to various trees.

"Good," Atlas said. "What about this environmental protection group that has been filing all the court documents?"

"They're a serious threat on the legal side of things. Up until now, the Department of Forestry has been rubber-stamping all our timber harvest plans, but EPIC has been challenging them in court."

"Over some damn bird."

"The marbled murrelet, yeah, but more importantly—it's about habitat. That's why we've got to get this next lot down as soon as possible. Lot 2-86, which they have named the Grove of the Ancients to foment public outcry. It's about a hike that-a-way," he said, gesturing.

"Oh?"

"First off, it's old-growth—which is like gold—as you know. And second—it's situated in the middle of five other groves which they've named Headwaters Forest, again, just for publicity."

"If that doesn't take the cake. Trespassing on *my* land and then naming it, for God's sake."

"We take down that grove, all those other ones are no longer considered habitat."

"I like your plan. Maybe it will take the wind out of their sails and they'll walk away."

"One can only hope," Cox said, shaking his head. "But I think we might need to take more direct action."

"Such as?"

"A little, shall we say, roughing up before we turn them over to the police."

"I don't want to know anything about that."

"Understood."

"Anyway, who says money doesn't grow on trees," Cox said, grinning.

Jamison scowled at Cox's crassness.

Just then, Diana stepped into the clearing from behind a six-foot fern. She looked surprised to see Atlas, but she quickly composed her face.

"Hi, Dad," she said with a big grin, coming up to him and kissing him on his cheek.

Jamison accepted the kiss with a flicker of a glance at Cox.

"What are you doing here?" Atlas said, momentarily flustered, then covering.

"I'm doing internships this semester. Thought I'd spend the rest of it here. The summer, too."

"No one told me about this." He turned his back to Cox and tried to herd her back toward what he now realized was her car, but she held her ground.

"I did, at Christmas. Clearly, you weren't listening. We are required to do internships for my program. Anyway. You always said if you own stock in a company, you should do your own research."

"Give us a minute," Atlas said to Cox, who nodded and disappeared into the trailer office. Atlas took her by the arm and walked her toward his car.

"*Dad*," Diana pulled her arm out of his grasp. "What's got into you?"

"Young lady, you don't know what's going on out here. It's dangerous. All these anarchists and communists. You don't know what they'll do. There are way more powerful actors in this thing than I realized. And, a bunch of them are crazed and strung out."

"Oh, come on. They're hippies with bad b.o."

"They've been spiking trees, injuring loggers, and damaging equipment. You'll be a target. They'll use you to get to me."

"God, when did you get so paranoid?" Diana said, smiling.

"When I started getting death threats."

Diana stopped smiling. "You've been getting death threats?"

"I didn't want to worry you. Mostly, it's nonsense. They can't get to me. But you're a different matter."

Diana looked at the ground. She felt like she was sinking into a web. She put her hands in her back pocket, elbows akimbo to stop it. "Look, Dad, you need my help. I could do some PR, take some pictures of you holding a seedling, improve your image. They've got you all wrong."

"For once in your life, just do as I ask."

Diana examined his face for a half-second. "I wouldn't be a Jamison if I did."

"I can't bodily remove you, but if you insist on staying out here, I'll assign you a bodyguard."

"*Dad.* No. I don't want some creep stalking me. My best defense is to blend in. Cozy up."

"You don't have a choice in the matter. I'll make sure he's discreet."

Just then, a worn Volvo wagon pulled into the clearing, and a woman in her late twenties with light-brown skin and jet-black hair hopped out. "Atlas Jamison?" she said, striding toward them, porcupine quill and seed earrings swinging as she strode.

"Who's asking?" Atlas said, coolly.

"I'm Jessica Wild, legal counsel for EPIC. This is a stay order for the Grove of the Ancients, known to you as lot 2-86. Humboldt County Superior Court has ruled in our favor. Until you have completed a full study of the environmental impact of your timber harvest plan in compliance with CEQA, you can't cut so much as a blade of grass."

Atlas took the paper from her and looked it over. "We will do the study. And we will win."

"We'll see about that," Jessica said, turning on her heel and striding back to the car, her straight black hair flashing as it whipped behind her.

Chapter 9

From the Nest

Up in the nest, Logan and Zeff watched the whole thing through the high-powered binoculars.

"So, Jess is still at it," Logan said.

"Of course," Zeff said. "And she's making a lot of progress. She's now the head of EPIC's litigation arm. And Woods—you remember, the dude—"

"Yeah, I *know* who Robert Sutherland is, a.k.a., The Man Who Walks in the Woods. I've been gone, not lobotomized," Logan cut in.

"Sheesh. *Okay.* Anyway, Woods thinks EPIC is getting too professional—or something—and he and Cecilia Lanman have been working on this Forests Forever thing—like a ballot vote that comes up in September. I don't know."

"Oh? Sounds promising. What's it do?"

"Like, limits the amount of clearcutting and adds more rules and regs that make it harder for the timber companies to do what they want. Me, I want to be part of the direct action. Without us, they'd get nowhere."

"Jess wanted me to file charges against PL after the mudslide," Logan said, still looking through the binoculars.

"Did you?" Zeff lowered his binoculars and looked at Logan.

"No. Just couldn't deal with it."

"That's her. All legal mumbo-jumbo and 'work within the system.' Oh sorry. You still have a thing for her?"

"What?"

"In high school. You—never mind. Anyway, money won't bring your dad back."

"Yeah," Logan said, keeping his eyes glued to the binoculars. His feet vibrated again. "What did you say this tree's name was?"

"I didn't," Zeff said. "But it's Arcadia. Just came to me one morning, after I'd spent the night here."

"Home of Pan," Logan said.

"You got it. The goat god of the wild, man. Trickster extraordinaire. That's my man."

Logan smiled wanly.

"Speaking of home. Must have been tough seeing the house again."

"Haven't been back, yet." Unthinkingly, Logan squeezed his calf muscles to stop the vibration.

"No?"

"Came here first."

"Ha! Home is where the heart is. I *knew* you couldn't stay out of it, no matter what you say!" Zeff thumped him vigorously on the back, and for just a second, messages from the tree gently wafted up Logan's legs.

Chapter 10

Diana

He was a stern father who seldom smiled, but he wasn't who the press made him out to be. Truth is, I was a little afraid of him until I was about eight. But he was more present to me than my mother. He was never one to talk much—at least at the dinner table. When he was on the phone, it was a different matter. He talked in a steady stream. I was amazed at the different personalities he evinced. Like a Shakespearian actor, sometimes he was winsome and charming, and when he talked that way, he talked with his whole body, smiling and making jokes to whatever CEO or banker or stock trader was on the other end of the line. Other times he was aggressive, commanding, invincible. Other times frighteningly brutal, whatever it took to get the job done.

The first time I realized he loved me—the real me, and not the perfect daughter he expected me to be—was when I was about eight. He scolded me for leaving my bike out in the driveway. As I headed to the door to get it, I rolled my eyes because we both knew I had gardeners and house cleaners who would do it for me. When I guiltily shot my eyes back at him to see if he had seen me, I caught him regarding me contemplatively, with this tiny curve in the corner of his mouth, like he was sitting back a hundred yards from the whole scene. From way back there, he liked what he saw, but he wasn't sure if he should encourage it. The lines around his eyes relaxed, which let more light in, and he suddenly looked so much younger, like a person who could smile naturally.

I began to test it, and it turned out it happened quite a lot. He was always correcting my posture, scolding me about a bad grade, telling me to clean up after myself, but every so often, in those accidental moments, he showed that he was proud of me when I stood up for myself. It was a secret. He didn't want me to know because he thought it would spoil me, and the most important thing he thought he should teach me was discipline. But I knew that cold look in his eyes was for other people, not me. I stopped being afraid of him. So, we had an oddly formal relationship, but it was a certain vintage of love that got me through childhood and the death of my mother. I clung to that brand of love, idealized it, milked it for all it was worth.

I attended several "Bring your child to work days" before I graduated from high school, and that ignited my ambition, which became a kind of light in my life. In college, I pleased him with my 4.0 average, but I began to wonder if I was anything more to him than a very special pet or a projection of himself. I wanted to be his equal. He is so much smarter than most people.

He's a good man, deep down, capable of real love. The press paints him as the poster child bad guy, a man whose sole purpose is to get rich. But that's not what it's about for him. It's like a chess game, a vast puzzle that he knows he alone can figure out. Once he's on the chase, he's a man obsessed. He'll study and research for weeks, late into the night. The money is just proof that he was right, that he won, that he figured out the riddle or discovered something everyone else had missed.

He's not like some of these Wall Street stockbrokers who drink all day and snort coke and give wild sex parties staffed by underage prostitutes. He isn't a drinker and never wasted time on TV. He is bookish and learned. When he's all done with business, he reads the classics. Tolstoy and Shakespeare, things like that.

I wish other people could see him when he talks about his art collection. I grew up with it, so I took it for granted. I remember once he pointed out this Calder mobile that hung high in our lofty living room. I had always been peripherally aware of it but had never truly seen it.

"Calder grew up rootless," he told me, "so he understood intimately that everything in life is always in motion. See how this sculpture never fully stops moving?" As he spoke, the disks and fine rods moved with impalpable air currents. "He found a way to balance all the complex parts of life, to harness the impermanent essence of mass, time, space, and turn it into something lasting." It made me wonder about his childhood. He never talked about it, and I didn't know how to ask.

You have to be capable of real love to understand art like that. I'm convinced that is how he sees his work.

Chapter 11

Accident at the Mill

March 15, 1990

Paul Anderson called himself a nobody, but he was proud of that. He was twenty-three, just married, his wife Sarah was three months pregnant with their first child, he had a good job at Pacific Lumber, and he was really, really good at that job. Oh, and they'd just bought their first house, a little bungalow built in the 1950s. That was enough for him. He'd grown up in Mendocino County and was the son of an "old-time lumberjack." Everyone congratulated him when he'd gotten a job at PL five years ago, citing PL's great track record with workers. But it quickly became clear that things had changed—or that the myth was overblown.

He pulled on his flannel shirt this morning, smiling slightly at the loud smell of Bounce fabric softener that Sarah used when she laundered his clothes. It was nice having this scented reminder of her care for him. Married life was good. But the cheer vanished quickly as he looked ahead to his workday at the mill.

He was an off-bearer, one of the most dangerous jobs at the mill. He made the first cuts on the big logs. The saw towered over him, designed for cutting trees up to fifteen feet in diameter, with a flexible band of tensile steel easily thirty-six feet in circumference and a foot wide. It was so powerful that "You could cut through three trees after you turned it off," he said. A hard knot or a fencing nail could chip a sawtooth and send it flying, but his ear was finely tuned to all the sounds the blade made, and he wore protective gear. He could tell when it was approaching a knot, and he knew to scan the logs before-hand for the telltale stains that nails and spikes left. When the saw hit a nail, it made a high-pitched sound that gave him time to shut it off and step away. But lately, the saw had been rattling ominously even before it hit the log. He'd examined the blade and found some hairline cracks.

Shuffling to the kitchen, he found his wife, Sarah, in her green nursing scrubs, with the coffee already made. He kissed her on the neck as he reached into the cabinet for his coffee mug but couldn't help slamming the melamine doors and cursing under his breath.

"What's wrong?"

"We still haven't got that new blade. Dick keeps telling me he ordered a new one, but nothing happens. No way it takes that long. We're not even people to management."

The back of Sarah's neck prickled. She set down her coffee and focused on Paul. He was normally such a happy-go-lucky guy.

"I don't want to go this morning," Paul said, feeling a twinge of embarrassment. "Lately, it's been like pulling teeth to get myself to go."

"Don't go," she said quickly, with certainty. "Call in sick."

"Honestly, every day, it gets a little harder, but it will put us seriously behind."

They both let it go and finished their breakfast in silence, and Sarah kissed him goodbye like she did every morning and left for the hospital.

At work, Paul greeted Sam and Cliff. Sam assisted Paul with the saw, and Cliff was one of two shop mechanics who maintained the machinery.

"Any word on that saw blade?" Paul asked.

"I filed another work order yesterday, but The Dick says it's on backorder," Cliff said.

"Fat chance," Paul said. "It's probably still on his desk."

Cliff shook his head. "Drink after work?" he asked both Paul and Sam, as was their custom.

"Sure thing," Paul said. Sam gave the thumbs up.

It was a beautiful spring day. Paul pushed past his dread, donned his headgear and protective apron, and inspected all the logs that were lined up. He knew they'd already been inspected, but double-checking was always a good idea. He turned the machine on. It clanked a bit discordantly right after he flipped the switch, but it quickly warmed up and whirred into its familiar smooth whine, muffled by his headgear.

He was halfway through a foot-wide log when a loud crack followed by an unearthly screech struck terror into everyone within hearing distance. Paul was on the ground before he fully registered the sound. Sam and Cliff came running.

He clapped his hand reflexively to his neck, but he couldn't get his hand around the steel blade that he realized only dimly was wrapped around his body. The look of horror on Sam and Cliff's faces as they leaned over him made him realize the seriousness of the situation.

"Don't move," Cliff yelled, "I'm getting my torch. I'll be right back!" He darted out of sight.

"Hey, buddy," Sam said quietly. "You're alright. Take it easy. We got you." As he spoke he carefully reached around the blade to press his hand to Paul's neck to staunch the flow of blood.

Everything sounded like it was underwater for Paul. Blood choked his airways. He struggled to sit up, but Sam pushed him back down.

Others crowded around. His blood was all over Sam. How did that happen? It was a lot of blood. His brain told him matter-of-factly that he was dying. That pissed him off. He searched the crowd of faces for The Dick.

Cliff was back. As the blowtorch roared to life, Paul spotted Dick at the edge of the crowd talking into his walkie-talkie. Paul tried to speak, but his jaw didn't work, so he gestured to Dick. If he could just get him close enough, he would squeeze the life out of his neck. It was the one thing he needed to do before he died. Then he blacked out.

It took an hour for the ambulance to come, and Paul survived thanks to Sam holding his veins together as Cliff and other co-workers cut the blade off him. His jaw was broken in five places, and he lost a dozen teeth.

Weeks later, when Judi Bari interviewed him, he told her, "The blade hit me flat. If it had hit me teeth first, I would've been decapitated."

Pacific Lumber wasted no time in exploiting the event. Headlines ran "Tree Spiking Terrorism," and "Earth First! Blamed for Worker's Injuries." The county sheriff's office put out a press release that traveled the nation overnight, "This heinous and vicious criminal act is a felony offense, punishable by imprisonment in State Prison for up to three years. Still undetermined in the investigation is the motive of the suspect or suspects, to deter logging operations or to inflict great bodily injury and death upon lumber processing personnel."

"This is probably the first time we've made international news," one Earth First-er told a San Francisco newspaper, "and we weren't even involved in it."

Dave Foreman, co-chair of Earth First! who had endorsed tree spiking and even published a how-to manual, told papers, "It's unfortunate that somebody got hurt, but, quite honestly, I am more concerned about old-growth forests, spotted owls, and salmon—and nobody is forcing people to cut those trees."

That pissed Judi Bari off. She wanted Earth First! to disavow the tactic, not only for obvious ethical reasons but to bring loggers over to their side. Shortly after Foreman's quote was aired, she wrote an article for *Industrial Workers of the World*, calling Foreman arrogant and contending that his statement made them sound like cut-throat terrorists.

Later, it was determined that the log had come from private land that bordered PL. The owner of the land had been furious about how many times Pacific Lumber had logged across the boundary onto his land. He'd called and argued with them numerous times, but when they kept doing it, he spiked his own trees along the border of his property.

That didn't stop Atlas Jamison from instructing his public relations office to go on the offensive against the activists. This was an opportunity not to be lost.

Someone from the PL public relations department visited Paul at the hospital to ask him to go on tour to denounce the whole ecological movement. He refused.

"I'm against tree spiking," Paul told the press from his hospital bed. "But I don't like clearcutting either."

Sarah told the press about the condition of the saw blade and her husband's complaints. "I hate Pacific Lumber," she said. "I like trees."

But the press never printed that. Later, when Paul recovered and went back to work, he was put on the night shift, and though Pacific Lumber had been willing to put out a $20,000 reward for information on who spiked the tree, Paul only got $9,000 in worker's compensation.

Chapter 12

EPIC Meeting

April 16, 1990

Arcata, referred to fondly by some and not so fondly by others as "Hippie Haven," was a college town twenty miles north of the Headwaters Forest. Unlike many Western towns, it had a central square with a statue of President William McKinley in the center, standing rigidly with one hand out as if offering instead of taking. This statue was the source of some controversy, with most of the liberals demanding its removal because of McKinley's racist and imperialist policies. The rest of the town was a hodgepodge of gabled houses, one and two-story flat-roofed retail and business offices, and a few official buildings. The office of the Environmental Protection Information Center (EPIC) was located in a former corner grocery store downtown, not far from Beanheads, the coffee shop that was the central hangout of most of the activists. The town had opinions on both sides of the logging dilemma. Some places had stickers in the window, "Earth First! Not Welcome Here." Trucks with bumper stickers, "Save a logger, eat an owl," parked alongside those with bumper stickers of Chief Seattle's quote, "The Earth Does Not Belong to Us; We Belong to the Earth." The EPIC office was sparsely furnished with plastic folding tables covered in stacks of literature, metal folding chairs, a ratty couch, and two discarded metal office desks with hulking putty-colored desktop computers.

The day after meeting her father in the woods, Diana strode into the office and lasered in on a volunteer stuffing envelopes.

"Can you direct me to Jessica Wild?"

"She's talking to someone from the *North Country Journal*, but she's almost done. Have a seat. Wanna help stuff envelopes?"

"Oh, no, thank you." Diana's eyes skimmed over the olive green couch with distaste and scanned the folding chairs for one that wasn't piled with boxes, bagged lunches, and sweaters. Finding none, she moved a stack of flyers on a metal chair to the floor, taking one to review as she sat and listened to the interview.

"Can you clarify? What is lot 2-86?" asked the reporter, a thin white man clad in jeans and a black T-shirt with the Rolling Stones' hot-lips logo.

"That's what Pacific Lumber calls it," Jessica replied. "We call it the Grove of the Ancients. See, the Headwaters Forest has six groves in it, but the Grove of the Ancients is in the center of it all. It's the key to the kingdom, if you will." She flashed a quick toothy smile that shone brightly against her skin. "It's the heart of a much larger ecosystem."

"How do you plan to stop them?"

"Last week, the marbled murrelet, a sea-going bird which nests in the spiked tops of redwoods," she pointed to a picture of one on the wall of what looked like a downy, short-beaked duck, "was put on the endangered species list. If we can prove that the Headwaters is a habitat for them, we can stop the cutting because of the Endangered Species Act, which was passed in 1973. The CDF has agreed to review PL's THPs, and we have a hearing with the CDF on Friday."

"I see. And just to confirm, by CDF you mean the California Department of Forestry, and the THPs are the timber harvest plans that all lumber companies are required to get CDF approval of?"

"Correct."

"Is it the California Board of Forestry or Department of Forestry?"

Diana pulled a small glittery notebook out of her purse and began taking notes.

"It's both: The *Department* of Forestry oversees the current timber laws and is controlled by the *Board* of Forestry, which has mostly rubber-stamped everything the logging industry asked for until recently. It was created in the 1880s when they were worried about running out of lumber (even then!). They believed industry professionals knew what was best for the economy, so it was stacked with lumber industry professionals."

Just then, Logan Blackburn came in off the street. Diana and Logan spotted each other at the same time, and for an instant, their eyes locked. They both looked away quickly. She didn't like long-haired, un-groomed men, but she couldn't help noting how neatly his waist tapered beneath the yoke of his Icelandic sweater, how softly he stepped despite wearing boots, and how his boots looked like they were a part of him. For his part, he noticed the quick intelligence of her glance and her overall physical vitality, but her tweezed eyebrows, blow-dried blonde hair, professional-quality makeup, and nail polish were a turnoff, especially as it suggested she was conventional, if not conservative.

As if sensing his disapproval, Diana blushed and looked at her feet, then caught herself, and looked back at him defiantly, noticing that he had ridiculously long and dark lashes for a guy, and they framed his blue eyes in a way that was hard to stop staring at. The blue lifted up out of his sun-weathered skin in a slightly unearthly way. A tiny smile curled at the corner of his lips, as he noted the flash of anger in her eyes. He was intrigued. Something about the assiduousness with which the blow dried blonde took notes amused him and softened him toward her, makeup and all. He sat on a metal desk that gave him an easy vantage point from which to watch both Diana and Jessica.

Jessica was looking good. Her lack of makeup and well-worn clothes suited him better. When he was a freshman in high school, Jess was a senior, and he had been in awe of her. At the time, he thought she was out of his league, because she was a whip-smart senior and because she was Native American, not to mention good-looking. She organized and led a high school chapter of the Save the

Redwood League, which did a lot more than the usual high school bake sales. He didn't think she'd be interested in a white guy, no matter how dedicated to the cause he was. She'd come back to the area right about the time Titan took over PL, this time armed with a law degree, and she'd taken up the fight again. She and Logan crossed paths all the time in their common pursuit. All the usual suspects knew each other.

"Do you condone the recent spate of Earth First! vandalism of logging equipment? People are calling it eco-terrorism," the reporter asked. He towered over her like a question mark.

"We do not engage in that kind of direct action, and neither does Earth First! to my knowledge. These are the acts of a few individuals. However, Earth First!'s direct non-violent actions of tree-sitting and blockades have bought us important time for court filings to stop PL's illegal logging, while the police, the FBI, and the California Board of Forest have turned a blind eye."

"What about that millworker who was nearly decapitated last month?"

"As I'm sure you well know, that log was traced to the property of a neighbor of PL who was disgruntled by their tendency to log beyond their property line. You may not know there is a serious question about the condition of the saw blade itself."

Diana crossed her legs and folded her arms, gritting her teeth. Logan noted this, smiling slightly. Her political stance was obvious.

"But *do* you condone these kinds of actions?"

"We do not condone anything that may result in injury or destruction of property. We *do* recognize the right to protest even on what is considered private property when the proposed cuts have an impact on the health of the ecosystem and the planet and by association all people. Protesters have been arrested, pepper-sprayed, and on occasion beaten badly."

"Are you saying these injuries were unprovoked? Because we all heard about Judi Bari exchanging blows with Mrs. Lancaster at the Whitethorn riot."

"People on all sides are emotional. We care about the forest and the loggers. If PL has their way, all the logging towns in the area like Scotia, Rio Dell, and Fortuna, will be out of work in a matter of years."

"They're saying the same of you."

Jessica grinned at the ridiculousness of the implication and brushed past it with practiced ease.

"Look, this is perhaps where we differ from Earth First! We believe that people can work respectfully with nature in a mutually beneficial way, just as my ancestors, the Sinkyone, did before white people came to this area."

"Oh, thank you for mentioning that. I heard you are a descendant of Sally Bell?"

"Yes, she was one of the few survivors of the Sinkyone Massacres, and she is, in part, what fuels me on this quest. We are still riding high on our success in preserving the grove that was named after her. We think we will be victorious again in saving the Headwaters Forest."

"By we, who do you mean?"

"Robert Sullivan, also known as The Man Who Walks in the Woods, and homesteaders Gil Gregori, Cecilia Lanman, Greg King, and many more."

"Got it," said the reporter, noting these names and closing his notebook. "Thank you for your time, Miss Wild. I'm sure we'll be meeting again."

"Thank *you*."

The reporter headed for the door.

Diana jumped up and launched a rapid verbal barrage. "Ms. Wild, my name is Diana Jamison, the daughter of Atlas Jamison, and I just want to tell you that you are completely mistaken. Pacific Lumber is *not* clearcutting on a large scale, certainly no more than Georgia Pacific or Louisiana Pacific, and we're replanting where we *do* cut. As I'm sure you're aware, the clearing of some of the dead-wood is actually good for the forest. It allows light to come in and new trees to grow taller and prevents forest fires. We always file our timber harvest plans according to specifications and adhere to environmental law. You saw yesterday at the demo site how careful our operations are in preserving the...."

As soon as Logan heard Diana's name his heart started to pound, and a part of him detached from his body.

Jessica, who had folded her arms as Diana pelted her, stayed in that position with one eyebrow raised, otherwise impassive.

Diana stopped speaking abruptly, seeing the expression. *"What?"*

"Well," Jessica said, "I'm trying to decide if you are knowingly lying through your teeth or if you are just incredibly naive."

Diana was taken aback. "Exactly what do you mean?" A blush crept up her pale neck.

Logan stood up from the desk where he had been obscured by Diana and came into Jessica's line of vision ready to jump into the fray.

"Excuse me a second," Jessica said. "Logan!" She hugged him tightly. "I'm so glad you're back! Where have you been!?"

Glancing from Diana to Jessica, Logan tried to keep it short, mildly surprised but flattered by her exuberant greeting.

"Here and there. I ended up in Hawaii."

"Did it help?"

"It helped. But it didn't fix things."

"No. There's no cure for a grief like that. I'm sorry," she looked down at her feet and then grinned up at him. "But I've got a couple of ideas about how you might transform it."

"I'm sure you do. Zeff has been working on me, too."

"We need all the help we can get, and you've got such good experience. Ms. Jamison, this is Logan Blackburn. A mudslide two years ago caused by a Pacific Lumber clearcut above his land killed his father and nearly destroyed his house."

Diana looked at him, speechless. "Well—I'm sorry for your loss. B-but mudslides are common to the area. We follow established timber practices, and—"

Logan looked at her in an unfocused way, just getting the outline of her, debating whether or not to unleash the full load of his anger on her.

"And you must know," Jessica cut into the momentary silence, "that the field headquarters is a public relations front. The selective cutting they're doing in that area is something most of us support. Before your father took over, Pacific Lumber filed maybe thirteen timber harvest plans a year. This year alone, they've filed fifty-three."

"I don't know about that. But what I do know is that this is our land, and the last time I checked, this was the United States of America, and you have no right to tell us how to run our business."

"Your land?" Jessica grinned. "Your people invaded this land and slaughtered my people, and you want to call this *your* land?" She shifted her weight to one hip, still smiling.

"My people had nothing to do with that." Diana was red-faced now, and shaking, "And I'm—I'm very sorry about that—I really am. But I don't see what we can do about that now—" She was confused by the contrast between Jessica's message and her delivery.

Meanwhile, Jessica was enjoying watching her squirm.

"What you can do," Logan said, "is remember that nature—trees, animals, insects—have an equal right to exist. And that without them, we don't exist at all. What you can do is take care of the land for not only its own benefit but for the benefit of us all. Pacific Lumber—not just you—the whole consumerist corporatist cancerous growth that it represents is throwing everything out of balance and—"

"Oh, for God's sake, you just want to shut it all down? Go back to living in caves?"

"Actually," Jessica cut in calmly, "the Forest Practices Act of 1973 gave the public oversight of the eight million acres of privately owned forest in California because we have a public interest in it that trumps private property rights. So, you *don't* have the right to do whatever you want with your property." She made hand quotes around the last two words. "My question is, have you spent any time in these forests?"

"A bit. And I love nature just as much as the next person, but—"

"I don't mean the demo site. I mean have you spent any time in one of the old-growth forests? Have you slept there? Have you ever seen a clearcut?"

Logan stabbed her with his eyes, his brows startlingly dark in contrast to his sun-bleached brown hair, "I'd gladly give you a tour."

Diana assumed he was mocking her and was trying to come up with an answer when Jessica said, her wide face opening and brightening, "Now *that* is an excellent idea, Logan."

Logan's brows shot up, and he glanced back and forth between Jessica and Diana.

"I wasn't—"

"No, but I think if Ms. Jamison truly understood—felt these trees in her body—she'd have a better understanding of what we are talking about. She seems like a decent sort, underneath it all. So, what do you say?" She looked back and forth between Logan and Diana.

"Well. I suppose I could," Logan said slowly.

"You think I'm stupid enough to go off to some remote area with a complete stranger? You could be a rapist for all I know."

"Don't worry, I'm not attracted to you," Logan shot back, surprising himself. Where was this energy coming from?

"*Attracted to me?* You think rape is about *attraction?*" Diana looked like she wanted to kill him.

"Whoa there," Logan gestured palms outward.

"Logan, shame on you." Jessica whacked his arm with the back of her hand. "That was uncool. Apologize."

"I wasn't making an equation between rape and attraction. I was just saying I'm not attracted to you."

"That was not an apology," Jessica said, grinning.

Diana blushed again fiercely. "Who said anything about attraction?"

"I am sorry to have offended you." Logan made a bow with a sweeping gesture.

Diana was not amused.

"For real, Logan," Jessica chided.

The mockery vanished as Logan straightened and said more quietly. "I apologize. And to make it up to you, I will make good on my offer. All you need is a pair of hiking boots, some water....and a security guard."

Jessica hit him again.

"I don't need you to show me around my own property," Diana said coldly. She spun on her heel and strode out of the building.

Jessica and Logan watched her go in silence.

"That was... interesting," said Jess.

"Interesting isn't the word I'd use."

"Did I detect a little sexual tension there?"

"Are you crazy? She's not my type at all."

"I don't know. The French say the best way to learn a language is on a pillow. Maybe it's the same for environmental awareness—substituting a bed of moss, of course," she grinned again.

"Shut up," Logan said.

"Anyway, I see you haven't lost your fire."

"Nor you. That was a whopper you laid on her, about your ancestors and all."

"You white people, man. Sometimes you gotta hit you over the head—with words, of course."

"I don't know how you keep going, especially given the history."

Jessica paused and her eyes relaxed to the soft focus on something inward. "I have faith. And we've been winning in the courts. We're also prepping for a summer of activism. It's going to be exciting. You know Judi Bari and Darryl Cherney?"

"Of course. Their names have come up a few times today, in fact."

"We're calling it Redwood Summer—you know, like the Freedom Summer in 1964, in Mississippi?"

"Oh, cool," Logan said, without enthusiasm.

"We've been publicizing far and wide. It's getting national attention. It's gonna be three months of action."

"I just don't have the energy for it anymore."

"It's okay to pass the baton once in a while, but I think it might *give* you energy."

"No offense, but I don't see this strategy working long term."

"Both are working—the direct action brings us press, and we litigate. Hand in hand—sometimes out of hand—," she smiled. "There are a lot of arguments, not just between the bad guys and the good guys, but between us as well. It's often hard to tell, but we *are* getting somewhere."

"They just keep coming back, though."

"And so will we."

"I don't know," Logan sighed and then smiled tiredly. "Poisoning them would be so much easier."

"Well, think about getting back into the fight."

"I will," he said, but his mind was already canceling the promise.

"In the meantime, you could do a little soft activism with you-know-who." She gestured with her head toward the absent Diana and wiggled her eyebrows. "It might be a way to the head-honcho's heart. Save a few trees with a roll in the hay." Jessica whipped her back on Logan playfully and headed back to her desk and work.

White people, she thought. So touchy. Thank the all-spirit Logan wasn't a wannabe Indian, like so many of the activists she depended on in this fight. She smiled ruefully, thinking about the ever-present Chief Seattle bumper sticker. His actual words were never recorded. Few people knew those words came from a movie poster. It didn't matter. It made an important point, and she'd take whatever help she could get to save the trees.

Chapter 13

Doubts at the Ingomar

April 18, 1990

A few nights later, Diana and Atlas were having dinner at the Ingomar Club, owned by Pacific Lumber and housed in the Carter Mansion, a Queen Anne Victorian built by one of the richest lumber barons of 1885. Personally, Atlas found the grand staircase irritating, with its redwood pilasters, excessive rosettes, and balustrades. The stained-glass windows at the first landing depicting men in Renaissance clothes were garish and pretentious, while the floral brocade wallpaper was oppressive. It was a hodgepodge of turrets, gables, and corbeled porches in a confusing array of Italian, French Gothic, and Stick-Eastlake styles, not that Atlas paid much attention to those things. He was a modernist, himself. But it was the only decent place on the northern coast where he could maintain privacy and security. And the food was not bad.

Diana had been questioning him about the unrest in the area, and he had been answering her curtly, looking at his food most of the time. They were the only ones in the dining room.

"Look, any time you make a change, people are going to be upset about it," he said.

"I just don't trust that guy Eddie Cox. He's so sleazy."

"He's not my favorite. But he serves a purpose. Keep your friends close and your enemies closer."

"Does he have something on you?

"Of course not. What are you implying?"

"Nothing. I'm just trying to understand what people are saying about PL not being responsible—"

"Responsible to whom?" Atlas interrupted. "Titan, Inc., took on a huge risk to acquire Pacific Lumber. We are making the company more efficient, and that's good for everyone. We have to look out for the shareholders."

"But what about the people who live here?"

"Workers who owned stock saw it double in value when we bought Pacific Lumber. They made a pretty penny selling it to us, and now everyone is working overtime. Have you noticed all the new construction in the area? That's because of us. I wish you'd trust me on this," he said, wiping his mouth with a cloth napkin and pausing to take an almost dainty sip of his eighteen-year-old single-malt scotch.

"Of course, I trust you, Dad. You're the genius. I just want to learn all I can," she said, trying to catch his eye with a smile to soften him up. "I think that's why Mom left her stock in Titan to me."

"To make sure you were financially secure, whatever happens to me."

"No, I think she wanted me to be involved in a way that she never was. I think she thought I'd have a good influence on you."

He flicked a scowl at her. "I told you I don't want you out here," he said, holding his scotch up against the light. "It's dangerous."

The "I don't want you" hit her like a blast from a freezer, but she shunted it aside, her enjoyment of the parry as powerful as the hurt.

"With a little PR, people could be convinced that you're on their side. A couple of photographs of you holding a seedling. That kind of thing. I mean, I went to this office, EPIC—"

"My god. You're not wasting time with a bunch of potheads on welfare, are you?" He threw his napkin down beside his plate.

"I was just—"

"You can't get through to those people. They're ne'er-do-wells. They hate us because we're successful. They just want to control everything. Besides, my publicity department is on it. We've successfully driven a wedge between the workers and the activists. You're not needed here."

A wave of anger washed through Diana. "Seems like they're pretty successful in court. Didn't they just hand you an injunction?"

"That's nothing. It will be overturned. Trust me."

"Dad, it's not about trust. I just want to learn."

"Learn somewhere else."

It was the third blow, and it knocked her outside of time for a second. She examined his face. The bracketed mouth, the dead-on-flat stare. Not a speck of emotion. She understood, suddenly, why he was so easy to demonize. She threw down her napkin and stood up. Atlas reached over and grabbed her wrist so fast she didn't see him move before she felt it. Even though his face was soft, the violence of the move set her heart thudding.

"Look, it's not that I don't want to see you. I just don't want to mix business and family. I have a lot to think about, and I don't want to have to worry about you."

There was a moment where she could choose to soften and hug him, play cutesy Daddy's girl, and shrug it off. But the next moment, the choice was already made. She yanked her wrist away. "You don't have to worry about me. I'll take care of myself." She spun around and stalked out, the carpet muting what would have been satisfying heel strikes. She pulled the dining room door too hard, and the host leapt in alarm to catch it before it slammed against the wall.

She flounced past him and out the front door of the club. It felt good, but even as she did so, a part of her hurt for him.

Chapter 14

Diana

I thrive off conflict and competition, so fighting with Dad at the Ingomar Club was fun on some level, like driving a hundred miles an hour on a Texas freeway in a red Mustang convertible. Nothing could stop me, and fuel was fast and easy. But something worried me. I didn't believe he was banishing me for my protection. There was more to it. It felt like a crack in the foundation of our relationship. Even in the best of times, our relationship was never warm and cozy, but he always took some care. I'd seen his cutthroat side, before, I guess, but it had always been on the phone, directed at someone else. Was this a change? He had Linda, but I only had him.

My mother, Christine, died when I was eleven. It was a big deal, but I barely remember her. I feel guilty about that, even now. I have a few sweet memories of the little things we did together when I was maybe three or four. Once she threw Cheerios on the floor in the kitchen and let me stomp on them just for the sheer joy of the sound. It was wantonly naughty, and such a novelty to be allowed to break the rules so openly. But those instances were remarkable because they were rare. My mother was always busy. She didn't have a job, but she sat on a lot of boards, worked for a lot of charities, and planned a lot of required parties. Entertaining was part of maintaining my dad's status. She was gone a lot or in "the morning room," as she called her study, a place of filtered sun with a vista of the pool and trimmed gardens.

I had a series of nannies, some of whom I loved. There was Francie, who was English—I loved her accent. She was thin and pale with dark glossy hair. She did a little light housework for us, as well. When she did the laundry, she had to cross from the back door of the kitchen to the utility room where the washer and dryer were. I used to love to hide behind shrubs and jump out at her. She'd scream in such a delightful way. There was this other nanny, I can't remember her name. Heidi, maybe? She was overweight and played guitar. She took me to Memorial Park and played "Puff the Magic Dragon," and that song about a giant puppy. She didn't last long.

Even though we had a chef who cooked for us five days a week, and gardeners and repairmen visited the grounds often, as well as two different cleaning ladies, I was alone a lot in our huge house. It's a lovely house, designed with my father's help. Clean lines, high ceilings, six bedrooms, and ten bathrooms, fireplaces bracketed by floor-to-ceiling windows on either side, all furnished with low-profile couches and long-lined tables. Great swaths of space were punctuated by the figurative sculptures by Coderch & Malavia, and the more abstract work of Henry Moore, Calder, and Kaminski, not to mention sketches by de Kooning and Kline tucked into the corners.

I had friends over, of course, but we were always watched. Even though I had a bedroom and adjoining study and sitting room, we had to play in the dining room or living room with the nanny present. My father explained that we had to be extra careful. When you have money as we do, people want to hurt you. So, it was a lonely childhood.

I went to a prestigious private school—where all the kids of the movers and shakers went. We knew everyone who was anyone. I thrived in that environment. I was zealous about completing my homework and winning competitions. I loved making huge, color-coded charts and organizing everything.

Things changed, at some point, without me quite being aware. My mother started staying home more and sleeping a lot. Whispered conversations among the adults in the kitchen and bathroom stopped when I entered, and now, besides a nanny, there was a private live-in nurse. You'd think I'd remember the moment when they told me my mother had brain cancer and that she was going to die. But I don't. I came into that knowledge without words or fanfare. It was a wide-open, empty thing, this knowledge. Like a living room with a twenty-foot cathedral ceiling.

I have a few memories of trying to keep her company when she got sick, but she acted strange, with odd facial expressions. Her teeth turned gray, her hair fell out, and her face got puffy. She didn't look like herself at all. I had never seen her without her makeup, and her eyes were a completely different shape. Before my mother got sick, she had never been effusive with praise. She treated my award announcements like slightly annoying but obligatory interruptions, and she would pat me on the back or head and say something like, "Hard work pays off." When she got sick, she would squint at my lips, ask the same questions over and over, and the nurse would cut short my explanations of my current projects. I was only telling her about them to cheer her up. But they didn't. After a while, I didn't know what to say to her, so I avoided that wing of the house. I was more afraid of having nothing to say to her than I was afraid of her dying. She became just that woman attended by a private nurse, in the other room, who was always sedated, who I was supposed to have feelings for, but for whom I didn't. I knew I shouldn't share that lack of feeling with others, and I didn't. Not even with my father.

And then she was gone.

I regretted not doing more. The house was colder without her. I hadn't realized how much she warmed it. And then, slowly, I began to miss her more than I ever had. She became the perfect mother.

Dad was stoic about her death. He has never been much of a drinker, and this was no exception. He enjoys a good scotch for sipping. But he never finishes it. It's his signature, that last untouched swallow in the glass showing that nothing controls him. It's possible her death caused him to work harder. But I was a child and wasn't thinking about him. These are thoughts that occur to me now: Every-thing in our house spoke of infinite space, infinite wealth, infinite beauty, as defined by Dad. Nothing was supposed to die. But also, nothing was supposed to live in any way that he hadn't prescribed. My mother's death struck a blow to my father's core, like an axe to ice. And the crack wasn't that he had lost his soul mate. It was that he had lost control. Death was a thing that all the money in the world couldn't fix. He hated that.

I was a sophomore in high school before he married again. It's hard to imagine a woman being attracted to him—because he has that grim expression and those wincing smiles. Even his jokes are slow and deliberate like a bad actor rehearsing for the part of class clown. He's anything but. His thoughts are always way in front of his words, running a completely different set of calculations while talking to the person in front of him as if they were a slightly dense child.

You had to respect him for finding a woman close to his age. So many of my friends' fathers divorced their families and took up with a sexy trophy wife twenty years their junior. Linda is all right. She'd inherited her wealth, so we knew she wasn't marrying my dad for his money, and she managed her own retail stores and brands, so she had her own business sense and ambition. I just didn't have time for her in my life. I ran my life with a tight economy to stay at the top of my class. To blot out the loneliness. It was easier to ignore her. She didn't seem to mind. She more-or-less ignored me, too. And it worked out fine.

It all happened on a silent level, like a movie with the sound turned off. It's hard to tell which are memories and which are me putting the pieces of the puzzle together now. Perhaps I am making it up. Memory is like that.

I guess what worried me about that conversation at the Ingomar Club was that I hadn't seen that tiny little smile in the corner of his mouth, signaling his approval of my rebellion. That was the thing that truly connected us. It was how I knew he loved me. It was gone. Really gone, like my mother.

Chapter 15

EPIC Victory

April 21, 1990

A crowd of people filled the sidewalk in front of the Humboldt
County Courthouse in Eureka. It was a gray slab built in the
1950s adjoining the five-story county jail with a mural of a giant
lumberjack in the foreground, his axe dwarfing the redwoods behind
him. Three non-native palm trees were planted out front.

Jessica Wild, surrounded by reporters, exited the building into a
crowd of demonstrators, followed by Atlas Jamison and his lawyers.
The crowd was a mix of EPIC activists and supporters, mostly
dressed in jeans and sneakers, Earth First! activists, in dreadlocks and
Birkenstocks, and loggers, in plaid, jeans, and boots. The crowd
immediately formed circles around Atlas and Jessica waving signs
like "Stop Sacrificing Virgins" and "Save a Logger, Kill a Tree."
Mixed into the crowd were Zeff, Jim, Brian, and Logan, and farther
back was Diana. Amid the shouting and cheering, several reporters
shot questions simultaneously at both Jessica and Atlas in their separate circles.

"Ms. Wild! Are you pleased with the outcome?"

"We've had a victory, yes," Jessica answered, chin high, broad
cheekbones emanating their own sunlight. "The Court upheld our
Writ of Mandate, and ruled that the California Board of Forestry
improperly approved the timber harvest plan for the Grove of the
Ancients, and that Pacific Lumber must conduct a survey to establish
the impact on the population for the marbled murrelet, which was

finally added to the endangered species list." Cameras flashed. "Since we already know that the Headwaters Forest *is* a habitat, we are very pleased. These small creatures are helping us save these giants, and thereby the world."

Activists cheered while loggers booed. Brian and Jim, who had climbed a juniper tree that was trimmed from its natural bush shape into a lollipop shape, shouted in unison at Jamison, "Pig! Murderer!"

Reporters around Atlas called, "Will you comply with the court order?"

"Absolutely," Atlas said, utterly composed. "We've made it our practice to obey not only the letter, but the spirit of the law, environmental and otherwise. We are confident that once the survey is conducted, cutting will continue apace." More camera clicks and shouts and jeers from the crowd. "Our primary commitment is to our employees and shareholders, but we also do our due diligence with regard to the environment. After all, we want our profits to be as sustainable as the trees."

Some loggers cheered at this, though others spit and shook their heads.

Zeff jumped in front of Atlas and shouted into the Channel 9 camera, "Here's a grand welcome from the Commie-Eco-Freaks," wiggling his ten fingers and ending with two middle fingers. The camera veered back to Atlas, whose face remained impassive. The creases around his mouth deepened slightly, but his eyes remained expressionless.

"That will be all," Atlas said. "Thank you."

The crowd began to disperse here and there, while elsewhere shouting matches emerged between activists and loggers.

Logan watched Zeff from a few people away, shook his head, and smiled. He spotted Diana at the back of the crowd in a beret and hip-hugging jeans. He wove in and out of the thinning crowd to get to her.

"So...what do you think of the ruling?" he said.

Diana turned around, surprised. She recognized him instantly and flushed.

"It seems fair enough until we conduct a survey. I'm not the capitalist pig you think I am," Diana said.

"And I'm not the unemployed communist, you think *I* am," he rejoined. "Though, I am—currently—unemployed," he added with a hint of irony.

Enjoying the sparring match in the offing, her eyes gleamed and she looked straight into his eyes, "You and your friends *are* trying to regulate what my father does on his *own* property."

"Hey, I'm a property owner myself," said Logan

"So, how do *you* feel when people tell you what to do with your own land?"

"Ownership means stewardship. We are only tenants, dependent upon the health of the Earth. As the saying goes, 'the earth doesn't belong to us; we belong to the earth."

"Well, PALCO is all about sustainable yield," said Diana.

"Since the takeover, your father has tripled the clearcuts and aimed primarily at the old growth. Some of those trees are 2,000 years old."

"Doubled. And it was all part of the plan before he stepped in."

"Look—it doesn't matter who started it. Even if you don't care about the trees, it's not good long-term planning."

"I do care about the trees. But people need jobs. Look at this place. It would be a ghost town without the logging industry."

Only a few stragglers were left at this point, and the news vans were also gone.

"That's what they said about Love Canal, the Exxon Valdez, Three Mile Island, Tar Creek, and the hole in the ozone layer," Logan said, suddenly losing any hint of flirtation and going straight to barely contained rage. "Jobs, economy. It's a false dichotomy cynically calculated to divide us so they can continue to destroy the planet for profit alone."

Adrenaline burned along Diana's forearms and the back of her neck, and she was just about to answer when her father stepped between them, facing Logan. "Step back," he said with deadly quiet.

Logan, caught off guard, obeyed unthinkingly. Atlas had a few inches on him as well as the girth of middle age.

"Dad," Diana said, annoyed, stepping to his side. "What're you doing?"

"I thought I told you to stay away from here," he said over his shoulder, keeping his eyes on Logan.

"And I told *you* I was staying."

"You," Atlas said, pointing his finger at Logan. "What's your name?"

Logan paused long enough to irritate Altas, and then said in neutral tones, "Logan Blackburn."

"Well, Logan Blackburn, you stay away from my daughter, or I'll have you arrested for harassment."

Logan, unperturbed, said, "That's up to her, isn't it?"

"It certainly is," Diana said as she skirted her father. "And far from harassing me, he was showing me around. When are we meeting for that hike tomorrow?"

Logan, surprised, recovered quickly. "Beanheads, Arcata. Seven a.m. sharp. Bring boots and a backpack with water. And lunch."

Atlas and Logan locked eyes, and all of Logan's anger welled up, making his eyes burn bright blue. Atlas looked away first. Logan was too angry to feel victory.

"Seven it is. Beanheads," Diana said, her words nudging him out of the danger zone.

Logan turned around and crossed the street to where Zeff, Jim, and Brian were waiting for him.

Atlas's Range Rover slid up beside him, and he tried to steer Diana toward it, his hand lightly on her back.

She pulled away. "I will *not* be treated like that."

Atlas's brows went up, and for a second he almost went to that faraway place of amused admiration. Instead, he collected himself and opened his mouth to issue another command. Before he could get a word out, she added, "Don't forget that I own stock in Titan, Inc. From this point forward, you will treat me with the same respect you give all your stockholders." She whipped around and walked away.

Atlas stepped into the Rover, picked up the car phone, and dialed. When the detective answered, he said, "Mr. Barnes, I've got a job for you."

"Yes, sir," Barnes answered.

"Logan Blackburn. Find out who he is. See if he has any criminal records. I want to know where he lives, who his friends are, and what color his underwear is...if he has any."

"No problem."

"And tomorrow, 7 a.m. at the Beanheads Coffee Shop, Arcata, my daughter is meeting him. Follow them. Make sure she's safe. Call me immediately if you have even the slightest concern."

"Will do."

Chapter 16

Pacific Lumber Board

April 21, 1990

Later that day at the Pacific Lumber main office in Scotia, various lawyers and unit leaders were assembled in the redwood paneled conference room. Atlas sat at the head of the glossily finished redwood table. "What the hell is a marbled murrelet, anyway? Is it like an eagle or something?" he asked.

"They don't really care about the bird," Eddie answered. "They're just using the Endangered Species Act to stop us from cutting."

"Wasn't the timber harvest plan already approved?"

"The California Board of Forestry has always seen our point of view," said Stanton. He stood out among the suited board members in his Carhartt jacket and jeans. "But EPIC, Sierra Club, Save the Redwoods—every day there's a new organization—even school projects—they have been challenging our THPs in court, and now the Department of Forestry is breathing down our necks, and the Board of Forestry has been getting more cautious."

"We've also been getting a lot of bad press. It makes a good story —you know—outsider corporate raider from Texas takes over the paternalistic old-times logging company, blah, blah, blah," said Eddie.

"Jesus. You'd think we were drug dealers," Atlas said. "Do they have recourse after we submit our findings?"

"We've already had an initial survey done, and the entire forest, of which 2-86 is one of six groves, is likely to be murrelet habitat. If our finding contradicts that, there will be appeals," said one of the lawyers.

"However, Judge O'Connell is getting pretty sick of these cases, so he may find in our favor," added the first lawyer. "The problem is, this is all going to take time."

"And time is money," Eddie chimed in.

Altas flicked him a look of disgust, more for the cliché than the concept. The rest of the table ignored Eddie. "How much time?"

"Months, years...," a lawyer answered.

"What's the importance of this lot? Why don't we turn our attention elsewhere?"

"2-86 is in the center of five other groves," explained Stanton, pointing to a map of the area. "To be a habitat for this damn bird, it has to be at least five hundred acres. They can't just declare any pocket park a habitat. If we clear this grove, no more habitat."

"Er, that's not exactly—," said one of the lawyers, but he was shushed by another lawyer.

"Why don't we just focus on the second growth?"

"That's what I was saying," said Eddie.

"The old-growth is where the money is," said Stanton. "See, the older trees grew slower, and there's no comparison to the grain and quality of the wood to second growth. It's harder, more durable, tighter grained, free of knots. That's why everyone wants it for decking and furniture. It's water-resistant and fire retardant."

"We've had our THP approved for lot 4-72, what they call the Allen Creek Grove as well as fifty others. We can file a hundred more like those. They won't be able to keep up. Any THP that isn't challenged in thirty days automatically becomes legal."

"Do it," Atlas said. "And finish that study by this time next week."

"But—," said one of the lawyers

"Meeting adjourned," Atlas said.

Eddie hung around after everyone left.

"Yes?" asked Atlas irritably.

"I have an idea," Cox said.

"I'm listening."

"We pop that study in the mail ASAP and then cut as many trees as we can before it even hits the court."

"Go on."

"We can take down a tree in thirty minutes. If we concentrate our teams and fan out across the grove, we could cut a million dollars' worth in a matter of hours before they can challenge the study, and that will disrupt the habitat if there is such a thing."

Atlas thought it over. "Not bad." He thought more. "What are the legal consequences?"

"A fine. Jail time supposedly, but that's never happened. Courts around here don't take those laws seriously. And once those trees are down, you can't put them back up."

"Talk to Stanton about it and the lawyers. But, don't do anything yet. Meanwhile, cut whatever you can around it."

"Will do!" Cox said, with renewed energy.

When Atlas left the room, Eddie checked his reflection on the glossy tabletop, adjusting a tie that needed no adjustment. He thought about the half a percent of stock Atlas had allowed him to retain. He knew Stanton held another half a percent. Now that he had Stanton by the nose hairs, he could rope him into his other plans. He had a mind to do the same thing to Jamison that Jamison had done to the Pacific Lumber board, but he had to get all his ducks in a row.

Chapter 17

Triple Threat

April 22, 1990

Atlas sat up in bed, breathing hard. The red numbers on his digital clock glowed 6:30 a.m. He'd overslept. For an instant, he thought he was back in Houston, but as the busy Victorian trim and floral curtains crowded into his vision with grating insistence, he remembered he was still in Eureka, and the phone was ringing, not the alarm. He picked up.

"Yes?"

"Mr. Jamison, sir. I hope it's not too early. I have news."

"Go ahead."

"The young man, Blackburn. It seems his father owned property west of yours. You tried to buy him out, but he refused to sell. Do you remember?"

"No. But go on."

"Well, there was a mudslide."

Barnes kept talking but faded into the background as Atlas vaguely remembered news reports about this, and images of the littered slope. Thoughts of his daughter's safety spiked as Barnes's voice faded back in.

"...anyway, I'm outside the coffee shop now, what do you want me to do?"

"What? Oh. Stay with them. Does this guy have a criminal record?"

"None that I could find."

"Don't let them out of your sight. There's no telling what these people might do. Report back to me every hour on the hour."

Chapter 18

Beanheads

April 22, 1990

It was misty and cool that morning, as it often was in spring in Arcata. Whereas Logan and Zeff's hometown Fortuna was a working-class town, Arcata was in the center of the weed-growing country, and home of Humboldt State University. This morning Beanheads, the most popular coffee shop in town, was buzzing with young and old. Zeff, Brian, and Logan had been up all night celebrating the victory with the leaders of the north country Earth First! chapter, Judi Bari and Darryl Cherney. Judi's fiddle case hung over her shoulder, and Darryl had his guitar. They were on the way to do a concert at Humboldt State to recruit for Redwood Summer. Judi had been a labor organizer on the East Coast and various jobs brought her to California. She'd moved north only about five years ago with her then-husband. This morning she was relating Pacific Lumber's accusation that she and Darryl had blown up a transmission tower in Santa Cruz.

"That's just FBI misinformation. They weren't blown up. They were taken offline with a hand saw and a chisel. Very low tech," Judi said.

"We wouldn't blame you if you did!" shouted Zeff.

"You seem to know an awful lot about what tools they used," someone in the crowd rejoined.

"No, no, guys, we need to tone it down. Pacific Lumber and the FBI have been planting fake press releases with our name on it calling for tree spiking and violence," Judi said. When her face went serious, her strong brows and high cheekbones formed shadows around her eyes.

"Fortunately, they spelled our names wrong," Darryl said, and the circle of friends laughed. He had a six-inch afro and bushy black beard.

"When the cops questioned us about it," Judi said, "I told them, I didn't do it, I was home in bed with five witnesses." Her grin transformed her face, shadows gone from the eyes, light brown hair parted in the middle streaming away from her face like Venus on the half-shell.

Everyone laughed loudly, sipping from the large steaming cups of coffee they cradled to their wool-sweatered chests.

"You should have seen Logan give it to The Man yesterday," Zeff said. "He and Jackass Jamison went head-to-head, and Logan shot him this look—like two blue lasers—that just about sliced him in half. The dude visibly shrank to the size of the most spent roach you've ever seen." He pinched his fingers together and everyone laughed. Logan smiled tolerantly, staying quiet. "It was *so-o-o righteous*, man," said Zeff.

"But seriously," Judi said, "We've been getting death threats."

People nodded their heads knowingly, their faces going somber.

"I heard the FBI gave a bomb-making workshop to police on Louisiana Pacific's property just last month," a person in the crowd said.

"No shit!" Zeff said. "Fascist motherfuckers."

Logan's scalp tightened. Things had gotten way grimmer since he'd left.

Diana entered the coffee shop in brand new hiking clothes that stood out against the well-worn crowd. The place went quiet, as if everyone stopped breathing. She took in their stares and said, nonchalantly, "Don't stop on *my* account."

Out of politeness, people turned away and resumed their conversations.

"You came," Logan said, stepping forward.

"I said I would," she said, looking him eye-to-eye. They were evenly matched in height. They paused awkwardly, not knowing what to say and aware that they were being watched.

"Let me order you a coffee to go," he said, pulling a steel travel mug out of his backpack. Diana noted his use of reusable ware. He turned away from her and handed the mug to the barista behind the counter. "How do you take it?" he asked over his shoulder.

"A latte, if you don't mind. Three shots."

"Logan," Judi said, coming forward with a grin. "Consorting with the enemy?"

Logan was trying to think of what to say when she gently punched his shoulder. "Just kidding. This is exactly the kind of thing we need to do. Humanize each other." She turned to Diana and offered her hand. "Judi Bari."

"I'm Di—"

"Yeah—we know."

"How—"

"Small world. Word gets around."

"I've read about you, too," Diana countered.

"Don't believe what you read *about* me. Read *ME*. Among other things, I'm a journalist. And a good one at that, if I do say so myself. Check it out." She pulled a few papers out of a satchel and handed Diana a copy of the *International Workers of the World*. "You may have heard of us, the Wobblies. We've been active since 1905."

"Thank you."

"I'm giving Ms. Jamison a tour of the Grove of the Ancients," Logan explained to Judi.

"A *private* tour?" she asked lewdly. "No. Seriously. That's great. As Jonathan Muir said, 'No one with a soul can hike that forest and be unchanged.'"

"Except Reagan," said Zeff. "What'd he say, 'You've seen one redwood, you've seen 'em all'?"

104 Against The Grain

Logan handed Diana the steel coffee mug, now full. "We'd better get a move on."

Zeff and Brian whistled, "*Move* on, yeah."

"Shut the fuck up," Logan said, smiling but serious, and steered Diana out the door.

"Not a particularly friendly place," Diana commented.

"Keep in mind, most of these people have been fighting your father for five years. They've been fighting the whole logging industry for most of the century."

"Felt like an ambush. Did you tell them I was coming?"

"No, no. It's just a very small town."

Diana accepted this. "Your car or mine?"

"Since I haven't started my car in two years, I think yours."

Chapter 19

Hike Out of Time

April 22, 1990

Diana was more comfortable driving, anyway, and they headed south in her Jeep with Logan navigating. "That's my Uncle Chester's spread," Logan said as they passed a field with a split rail fence penning two donkeys. "My dad's land begins at that ridgeline."

Twenty minutes from town, they pulled off onto the trailhead. The fog had not lifted.

"So," Diana said, as they hopped out of the car. But her voice was jarringly loud against the silence of the forest, and she dropped to a whisper. "What's the itinerary?"

"We'll hike through a grove of the second-growth," Logan said, his low voice naturally blending with the surroundings, "and then we'll reach a completely undisturbed old-growth stand by lunchtime. We'll have to go off-trail to get there. I'm envisioning a five-hour hike. You up for that?"

"I work out every day."

"Oh yeah? What do you do?"

"Running, Stairmaster, Nautilus."

"This kind of hiking can be harder than you expect because you have to constantly watch your step and negotiate your balance."

"If I faint, you can carry me, right?"

"Not a chance."

As they started the trail, the faint rumble of a pickup truck reached their ears.

"Let's hike quietly for a while to give our ears and eyes time to adjust," Logan said.

The idea surprised Diana. "Where you lead, I follow," she replied in mock subservience.

Over the next half hour, Diana kept having to quell her natural urge to spark witty conversation, a skill at which she excelled. However, navigating the path required concentration, and Logan seemed mired in silence as he walked ahead. She had never done this...walk in silence in complete wilderness. Texas desert was all red rock, sky, and oil rigs. Her parents weren't the kind to go hiking in national parks. The long straight roads in Texas afforded easy eighty-mile-an-hour car travel, and land was a thing you had to get past to get to the next city. The only forests she'd walked through with her nannies were the manicured and fenced greenery in Memorial Park in Houston. The fog was so thick that they couldn't see much but dripping ferns and the trunks of trees. Too much was unseen. It made her uneasy. Logan silently pointed to the six-inch banana slugs across the trail so they could avoid stepping on them. She stepped over them with suppressed shudders.

Walking in silence lulled her into a dream state. The spicy-sweet aroma of earth infused her with calm, and her heart slowed. Billions of fine drops of water hung in the air, and the passage of her body made them swirl like a silk veil. Mesmerized, she stopped and blew out a puff of air to watch the particles eddy, spiral, and divide. However, as the heel of Logan's boot disappeared into the mist ahead of her, she hurried to follow.

They had been hiking at a healthy rhythm for a half-hour or so when Logan stopped, put his finger to his lips, then guided her into a hollow snag.

Seeing the look of apprehension on her face, he tapped his ear and cocked his head back in the direction from which they'd come. Clumsy footfalls approached with the sound of heavy breathing. Scott Barnes came into view as he passed their hiding place. Diana's eyes widened and she clenched her fists. Once the sound of his steps faded, she whispered. "That guy works for my father. I can't believe he's having me followed."

"I've been listening to him for a while now," Logan whispered back. "Once I was sure he was following us, I turned to the west. He's going to wind up in one nasty swamp in about an hour."

They shared a conspiratorial smile.

"This way," he said, as he steered her in the opposite direction. Diana looked at him with enhanced respect.

As they continued, the sounds of bird calls, gurgling water, and creaking trees intensified. The fog thinned to reveal a floating garden sitting atop a fallen redwood, which leaned at an angle against others, forming a bridge seeded with sorrel and purple trilliums.

Further on, a triple ring of thirty trees, all sword straight and clean-limbed, surrounded a giant stump swathed in emerald moss. It reminded Diana of Aslan's stone table from Narnia. She stopped to study it for a long moment, then pushed her way through the three concentric circles. Logan retraced his steps to find her.

"It looks like a family standing around the tombstone of their mother," she said, looking up.

"She never died, though. The other trees continued to feed her, and this is all her, growing again. This area was logged in 1910 or so."

"The forest completely recovered in only eighty years?"

"Not completely. Wait until you see what it used to be."

"But clearly this grove has recovered," she said with a sweeping gesture that took in the rampant and diverse wildlife.

"You need to understand that these were cut by hand and probably pulled out by horses using only one skid row, which left the stumps, the soil, and the roots intact. Logging companies today are doing something very different."

"How so?"

"I'll show you later. Let's keep moving for now. I'd like to reach the old-growth by noon."

They hiked a few more hours in silence. Occasionally, Logan looked back at Diana. He was glad not to have to make conversation.

He had been amused and slightly disgusted, at first, that she had put on makeup to go on a hike. Who does that? But as the hours passed, her face seemed to open and become less conscious of itself, and more outwardly focused, reflecting and receiving rather than digesting and calculating. Every time she stopped and looked at a leaf, or insect, or fungus, it gave him a thread of hope. And the trees calmed him. He could let go of all that was human here, all the anger, grief, buying and selling, lies, and relentless greed. It all faded away to just beauty, simplicity, all-ness. Greg King, one of the activists leading the tree sitting charge, had said this was the true reality, and the way humankind lived made reality seem unreal.

Their progress slowed as they went off-trail. A few hours later, they were almost at the top of a ridge. The fog had cleared completely and shafts of sunlight pierced the shade only intermittently, between trunks fifteen feet wide. The sound of trickling water, buzzing flies, and droplets of mist tinkling off branches elongated, coalescing into a low thrumming that filled Diana's ears and gave her slight vertigo. The infrequent chatter of Steller's jays served only to heighten the silence. The scale of these trees, massive trunks, thick bark, canopy so high it hurt the neck to look up, the abundant and disorganized overflow of plants, the closeness and darkness of it all lifted her into a different time. It could have been 800 A.D. or B.C. for all she knew.

"Welcome to the Grove of the Ancients," Logan whispered. "These are some of the oldest living beings on the planet. There are no roads here. No trails."

Diana needed to sit down. Logan handed her a bottle of water. She looked up at the trees in a daze.

"You okay?"

Her eyes flicked back to his face and she woke up a bit. "Yeah. Fine. I guess I'm just a little tired."

He fished an avocado out of his backpack, sliced it open with a jackknife, and from an outer pocket pulled a small vial of mixed salt and pepper, then speared a green slice and handed it to her.

She reached out for it with her fingers, but then checked them for dirt, and after a micro-pause, leaned forward and took the slice into her mouth. The food had an almost instantaneous effect. Her eyes focused and the usual flutter or expressions quickened her face.

"That was so refreshing! Thank you! What a surprise you are. Some kind of roadside restauranteur or environmental epicurean. You could win at *Let's Make a Deal*. What else do you have in there, a bed?"

A small smile curved the corner of Logan's lips as he fished two spoons out of his knapsack and handed her the rest of the avocado half, keeping the other half for himself.

"From here on out, we have to be careful where we step. Not just for the sake of the plants, but the topsoil is made of thousands of years of fallen and digested trees. A lot of hidden holes. It's safer to walk on the logs."

He stood and offered her a hand. She accepted it and he pulled her to her feet. As they hiked down into the grove toward the creek, time slowed.

The trees here were like buildings twenty stories tall. The biggest she'd seen yet. Most were single pillars that narrowed only slightly as they rose, but there were double and triple trunks that spanned twenty-five feet easily. As they descended, the grove grew darker and cooler and smelled of clay. The sound of the creek grew louder as they approached.

Diana slowed to a stop before one of the double-trunked trees. She put her hand against the bark, and its furrows were so deep it swallowed her hand. She leaned in and rested the length of her whole body against the tree as if to merge with it.

"I don't know why I feel so tired," she said.

"The trees emit aerosols that calm us," Logan said.

"Yeah, but also...I feel so...small...and overwhelmed and—sort of...lost—or maybe—found, like there is no California, no America. Just this...and it's too huge to take in."

Logan folded his arms and smiled in satisfaction. Then a look of concern crossed his face.

"Oh no. Your other hand is in a patch of poison oak."

"Oh, damn it!"

"Not to worry. The antidote always grows close to the poison," he said, eyes searching the undergrowth. "Stay here for a second. Try not to touch your hand to your face."

He disappeared into the ferns. Fifteen minutes later, he emerged, slightly out of breath, with a bouquet of blue flowers.

"You shouldn't have," she said, deadpan.

Logan grinned, a white, toothy grin that nearly split his face open, transforming it from brooding to pixyish as it tilted his eyes up at the outer corners. She liked him much better this way.

"Come with me." He grabbed her other hand and led her down to the creek where the grove was darkest and coldest.

"These are California lilacs. They like sun, so I had a bit of a time finding them. They are the first things to grow back after a clear cut, which is one of the reasons PL sprays herbicide after a cut. They grow faster than the redwood seedlings, and PL thinks they inhibit the trees' regrowth, when in fact, they protect the seedlings from too much sun while they aerate the soil." As he was talking, he used a flat rock to grind the flowers against a larger rock making an improvised mortar and pestle. He splashed the resulting mixture with water until the flowers formed a lather.

"And you are giving me this botany lesson because...?"

The grin again. "They are the antidote to poison oak. Give me your hand."

Dianna offered her hand gladly, and Logan began to lather her hand and arm. At first, he was all business, but despite himself, his hands slowed as they moved over her forearm and down between her fingers. She enjoyed the firm grace of his touch. His hands came almost to a stop and they both could barely look at each other. Finally, he caught himself, and, flicking a look at her from under his dark brows, he finished up.

"You can rinse off now."

"Thank you."

She knelt beside the creek and immersed her arm in the cold water. He stood behind her, watching her bent head, her blonde hair fanning out like a fringe of falling rain, and his emotions surprised him.

"Do you need a rest?" Logan asked.

"No," she said standing up. "I'm okay."

"It will be warmer up on top, so if you can stand another hour, we'll lunch there."

"Lead on."

Logan was impressed by her physical stamina. He had expected this city girl to whine and complain the whole way, and then have a hissy fit about a broken nail.

At the top of the ridge, though the trees were just as dense, it was lighter and warmer. Just behind a row of trees, sunlight shone powerfully, too powerful for the depth of the woods they were in.

They sat to eat lunch, Logan pulling out a glass jar with leftovers, and Diana unwinding a white bread PB and J sandwich from plastic wrap. Logan glanced derisively at it and away.

"What?" Diana said in mock exasperation.

"Nothing."

"I was worried about spoilage. Aren't you worried about breaking that jar?"

"No—just—we take out what we carry in."

"Of *course*. What do you think I am, a barbarian?"

"Barbarians were a lot easier on the environment than we are."

"I mean—"

"I know. I'm sorry. I was making assumptions. I apologize."

Diana looked confused for a minute. "Apology accepted." She was silent for a beat. "So, you grew up here?"

"Yeah. My family has been here since the 1860s. Lumberjacks going way back."

"Really?" Diana was genuinely surprised.

"Why does that surprise you?"

"I just assumed you were against logging."

"I guess I'm not the only one making assumptions."

"I'm sorry," she said.

"My great grandfather started working as a choker at the age of seventeen. That was the standard entry-level position. He ended up part-owner of a small logging operation below the Eel River."

"So, your great grandfather owned his own logging company."

"They were still using handsaws and horses then. By the time my father came along, things had changed quite a bit. They were still using axes and things, but also tractors, railroads, and cranes. It was becoming more mechanized. It used to take two men three days to cut down a tree. Now it takes thirty minutes. The big logging companies were taking over, and my father began to hate what he saw. So, he turned our land into a preserve and started giving workshops on sustainable yield and selective cutting."

"Did you cut down trees, also?"

"I was a topper for my dad. You climb the tree and cut the top off so that it makes a clean fall."

"Did you feel bad when you killed them?"

"Every single one. That's why we only ever did it when we had to. And grief turns to gratitude. When you do your own work, you appreciate your connection to the elements. You see how the energy of the tree is turned into warmth for you, how you become part of it in a way. Also, we never cut the old growth."

Diana lay down and sighed, looking up at the trees above. "I know it sounds stupid, but never realized how alive they are."

Hope and cynicism wrestled within Logan, as he saw his method was working on her. Most loggers love the wood, but they could still kill trees without remorse. They did so by being excessively proud of their job and its history, the culture of masculinity, daring, and physical prowess.

He looked off at the edge of the forest where the light was unnaturally strong, feeling a bit guilty about his next move.

"We'd better get moving. There's one more thing I want to show you."

Diana rose eagerly and happily, making him feel even worse about what was coming next. They climbed to the top of the ridge. "I'm sorry," he said as the reason for the increased sunlight immediately became clear.

Eighty acres of clearcut rolled away from them down to the other side of the mountain. All the ambient sounds of the forest went dead at the edge. Before them lay a chaos of burnt stumps, broken, tangled limbs, and white pampas grass. Bulldozer treads had carved roads between every stump in a crazed pattern like a spider on too much caffeine. What had once been rich topsoil was now tan dust, packed to a polish in places, and eroding in others. It looked like the giant carcass of a plucked chicken on its side.

Diana wordlessly walked out from under the cool of the trees into the hot sun. It was just past its apex and beating down hard on everything it touched: stumps, slash, scarred earth. Flies darted past, and mosquitoes rose from the oily puddles now dwindling in the heat at their crusty edges. Her whole body turned to bagged sand.

"Once they clear, they burn off the brush, which kills all the fungi that keep the soil fertile. They spray herbicide to prevent what they call 'weeds' from growing. Then—if they replant—which this area isn't scheduled for—they plant a mono-crop of firs in rows. It's not a habitat. It's not a forest."

Diana dragged herself over to one of the stumps and sat down hard, bent her head, and burst into tears.

Logan stood behind her and put his hand on her shoulder.

"I had no idea," Diana said. "This is so...wrong."

They were silent for a time.

"We need your help," Logan said.

"I'll talk to my father. For sure."

"Thing is—it doesn't have to be done this way. We can keep the old-growth, and then if you do even a fifty percent selective cut, with planned skid rows, you leave enough shade and soil intact that the forest recovers faster. It's a win-win. Loggers get to log, stockholders earn money, the trees recover, and we get to keep on living in a safe climate. It doesn't have to be this wild, reckless race to extinction."

"I'll talk to my father. I will. I'll make him understand."

"Many have tried."

"I can get through to him."

"I hope so."

"We'd better get going if we want to make it back before sundown," Logan said. "We'll make better time if we go this way," he pointed through the clearcut down the mountain.

"Can't we....go back the way we came? Through the forest? I just don't think I can bear it."

Logan debated internally. "Tell you what, we'll get back to your car, and I'll take you to that tree I was telling you about."

Chapter 20

Logan and Diana Ascend

April 22, 1990

By the time they reached Logan's tree, Diana had lost all sense of time and proportion. The sun hovered eight feet off the ground, a tiger's eye gemstone that shafted tines of light between tree trunks, which pulsed orange wherever they were touched. She was an insect suspended in amber as Logan clipped her into a harness, tied knots, and checked the gear with firm tugs. He was talking all the while, explaining how to climb, but amber suffused her ears, her throat, her mind. She was a wordless creature that existed before time, outside of time, in no time. She watched him from this new and wonderfully wordless place, as he coiled the connecting rope over his shoulder and hopped off the ground into the climbing stance. He pulled the rope, and it hoisted him a short distance, then he pulled and hoisted, sometimes bracing his feet against the trunk, ascending a few feet at a time. She watched how his back muscles triangulated in different configurations, how his hair swung out and away from him, how confident, yet calm his movements were as he inched his way ever upward.

When he was about the size of a coffee mug, slight vertigo set in, and she stepped back quickly to catch her balance. Her neck ached from looking up. Then she remembered to breathe. Cool air filled her lungs, so vibrant, so full of messages, so unlike the sterility of the indoors. She shook her head to clear the amber. What did the trees in Texas look like? Why was she here? What was she feeling for this man, so high up he was now the size of a mouse, scrambling over the lip of a nest and vanishing?

Huffing, Logan pulled himself onto the platform and into a kaleidoscope of times, many pasts and one empty present. His father stood behind and he was five, swinging at a nail with his hammer and missing. The polished horn of his father's calluses rubbed against his knuckles as his father closed his bigger hands over Logan's small ones, repositioned them to the end of the handle, and moved him through the swing twice. At the same time, he was also still Logan, the twenty-five-year-old, who had been stripped of everything he cared about. His different selves unraveled. He could smell his father's pipe-tobacco-coffee scent as he zipped boy-Logan into his sleeping bag, telling him to hush. There was Logan the reluctant activist, doing God-knows-what. Trying to convert a spoiled city girl to call her father off? And there was teen Logan in the hiss of the propane lantern, dangling his feet over the edge of the platform next to his father, feeling the burn of scotch from a silver flask his father had unexpectedly passed to him, sharing their angry freedom from the woman in their life. He didn't want all these feelings that welled up in him now. He was tired of them, and he thrust them down angrily, but they only surged up more powerfully. He was about to get lost in an emotional labyrinth when his feet vibrated. His body warmed.

Uuma. He felt her. He wasn't comfortable telling others how much he used to talk to Uuma. How she always talked to him. Even though there were plenty in his circle of friends who were into crystals, tarot, and native spiritualism and would understand, he never wanted to cheapen the experience with Uuma by putting it into words. His feet vibrated again. With that sensation, his split selves melded back together like a rope fraying in reverse. The past fell away, and he was just here, now, brushing the debris off the platform, rigging his gear above his head to belay himself downward and pull Diana up. He checked the rope and looked down at Diana who was about the size of an acorn.

"Ready?" Logan yelled.

"Ready," she called back, her voice carrying up to him through the air surprisingly clearly. He leaned back into his harness to test the rope, then let himself fall backward off the platform, keeping his feet braced against the edge. After one last check of knots and gear, he let himself fall. As he descended, Diana rose, the brakes on the rope keeping the movement steady. When they passed each other midway up the tree, Logan braked fully.

"Enjoying the ride?"

"Beats the way you got up," she said, now glittering with excitement.

"I take it you're not afraid of heights."

"Oddly, no. But it's a hell of a time to ask."

Logan grinned, fully inhabiting his body now, and noticing this. "See you up there in a bit," he said as he continued his descent.

Diana let out a hoot as she ascended.

When she reached the platform, she grabbed ahold of it and heaved herself onto it, looking back to where Logan was now just hitting the ground. She was awake, fully alive, fully present. And though they were miles from civilization, she didn't feel alone. Instead, she felt like a child among a group of serene, indulgent grownups, so unlike any of the grownups she had ever known. It was much brighter up here. To one side, beyond the tops of trees, the mountains cascaded in descending shades of blue. To the other side, the Pacific ocean glittered. The sun was no longer as close to the horizon as it had seemed from the ground, and it was no longer a tiger's eye, but the ball of flame she had hitherto taken for granted. Now it seemed an amazing thing. She breathed in the rich air. She was starving, but that made her eyesight sharper. She lay down to wait for Logan to join her and sent her mind into the blue sky.

"This is so beautiful," she said later after he climbed aboard. "Which part of this is your property?"

"None of it. But if you mean what we say we own, it's that way," he gestured to the northeast. "My dad built this platform thirty years ago. Rumor has it I was conceived here. He brought me up here from the time I was five. We'd bring a few hammers and nails and add to our little house up here." He pointed to the half-roof and what looked like a dry sink and cabinet.

Diana smiled at the thought. Logan fished around in the cabinet under the dry sink, and while he did, Diana grew pensive.

"I wish you could show this to my father."

"It's hard for me to believe it would make a difference."

"You know, he's not a bad man."

"Good is as good does. If money is his bottom line," Logan added, "and saving these trees is not profitable..."

"It's not his bottom line, and also, as you've explained, it is profitable in the long run. I can make him understand that. Money isn't the only thing he cares about."

Logan, not wanting to argue, pulled out sleeping bags that had been tightly wrapped in plastic bags. From his backpack, he pulled out a one-burner Primus stove. "How about some tea?"

"You brought tea?"

"I collected a few herbs while we were hiking."

"You did not!"

"I did."

"Jesus. I don't think I've ever had tea from anything but a paper sachet. Do you happen to have a juicy steak in that pack, too? I'm starving."

"Would you settle for beef jerky?"

"I'd settle for anything."

The two talked for hours, chewing on the hard bits of meat and a few granola bars, discovering they had more in common than they thought. They had both been raised by obsessed fathers who loved them, but who had little room for anything but their fixations. Both had lost their mothers, Diana to cancer and Logan to divorce.

Diana drew out Logan's family story increment by increment. The sun set in its usual glory of oranges, pinks, and purples, and Logan switched on a small, battery-powered lamp as the mists rose. His parents had been high school sweethearts in the 1960s, he explained. They married right after graduation, but where his father was already running the family business, his mother had dreams of college and travel—leaving Fortuna. College wasn't a common dream for anyone in the 1960s, let alone women, or people in Fortuna, and his father was critical, but "allowed her to do it." However, when they got pregnant during her sophomore year of college, she dropped out to raise him. That was what women were expected to do.

Nevertheless, her itch for education returned in the mid-seventies feminism reawoke in even the most rural areas.

"My dad had always been a 'my-way-or-the-highway' kind of guy, but the more involved he got in the fight to save the redwoods, the more stubborn he got. Maybe he had to."

The fight was constant and frustrating. They'd save one stand of trees, only to lose three others. They'd get a politician on their side only to be traded off for a political favor from a lumber baron. It made his father bitter. His father was called away to more and more meetings, and he couldn't understand how his wife could be more interested in books—in fiction and poetry— when something as important as the trees, the planet, and the climate hung in the balance.

"I had totally followed in my father's footsteps, but my mom read to me every night until I was at least eight."

He had loved their nightly reading sessions, snuggled under a handmade quilt in yellow lamplight, as evil Bill Sykes loomed over Oliver Twist or Mrs. Mike went into culture shock when she moved from the city to the wilds of Alberta, Canada. He'd loved the legend of the Norse God Odin's sacrifice for knowledge by hanging himself from the tree at the center of the universe, Yggdrasil. Legend had it that during his nine-day trance of suffering Odin discovered not only how to write, but he understood its far-reaching power. The twigs of Yggdrasil spelled words, and Odin realized this would make it possible for dead men to speak to those yet unborn. The takeaway for Logan was that the life of trees and the life of the mind were inextricably connected. Loggers and intellectuals in this country were operating under a false dichotomy. Logan shared his mother's cravings and admired her for her return to college.

But one cold November day when he was eleven, his mother took him aside and explained that she had completed her master's and been offered a university job in San Francisco. She said that she was leaving his father, but not him, and that she wanted him to come with her. He couldn't imagine abandoning the family business, the mission, the trees, and his father. She moved, anyway, and he had never forgiven her for it.

"Do you see your mother now?"

"No," Logan said.

"Why not?"

"Because deep down...," he paused, searching for the words, "I blame my mother for my father's death."

"Oh!" Diana gasped. The tree swayed and she couldn't tell if it was the tree moving—or surprise at what he'd said. "But *why?*" Diana struggled to see his face, but the light from the electric lamp barely illuminated his hands.

"Because...," Logan paused. He'd never articulated this to himself before. "Maybe if she hadn't left him he would have been more careful with his life...Maybe he was reckless because he had less to live for."

Diana kept her misgivings to herself. The wind blew and the tree rocked, the lemon-cedar scent of the redwoods drifted with the breezes.

"When did it happen?"

The moon had risen, illuminating a blanket of mist below them, punctured by black treetops here and there. Logan shut off the lamp.

"Two years ago."

"God, so recent."

He pulled her to her feet, clipped her harness into the tree, and, straddling a branch, showed her how to scooch on her butt until they were out on a limb facing northeast. He pointed past the trees to another clearcut with evidence of the mudslide. In the moonlight, the shaved and broken baldness of the clearcut glowed like white in ultraviolet light, a broad scar in the black fur of tree cover.

Literally out on a limb, shame washed over Diana—was the tree swaying again? She couldn't tell.

When they climbed back onto the platform, they stood close together in silence looking out over the ocean of luminescent mist with the tips of the giants poking through like new saplings. In the Acoma creation myth, thought Logan, humans lived in darkness until they climbed a tree up into the light, into a new world. Maybe this view was where that story came from.

"It feels like we're in a different world," Diana said, as if hearing his thoughts, her voice barely above a whisper. She trembled inside, but she couldn't tell if it was the cold air that night was dropping around her or this new reality.

Logan unzipped a sleeping bag, wrapped it around both their shoulders, and pulled their bodies closer together. Their scents mingled in the uprush of warmth.

The fullness of this world, the trueness, the sheer presence of it, filled a vacuum Diana had felt all her life. In all those years with her friends, getting facials, buying buttery leather bags, drinking Veuve Clicquot in Paris—even those high school debate competitions, chasing the ecstasy of victory, there had always lurked this emptiness, this question. What was it all for? What did it all add up to? Tonight this tree, this palm of earth offered to the sky, had told her THIS. THIS is what it was all for. They were meant to live in harmony with all of this and *for* all of this. The stars, which were so much more numerous here than they were over Houston, pierced her like silver spears, connecting her to them with cords of light. People didn't have to be at odds with all this. The realization washed over her like moonlight, cool and shivery. They didn't have to choose between life as they knew it—in their square, man-made houses—and this infinity. They didn't have to choose between human life and the life of the trees. They were the trees. They could have it all, an Eden, a heaven, right here. All they had to do was choose, and the rest would follow. They could figure it out. But the choosing had to come first.

Her eyes returned to earth as she reviewed her father's choices. "I am so deeply sorry," Diana said, "but those words are utterly...inadequate."

Logan looked at her face, amazed that a person could change so entirely, so truly, in a way that was so unlike his father or hers. He believed her, believed in her goodness, her intelligence, her conversion.

"Did you know that the root of the word tree is truth?" Logan asked quietly. "To be truthful is to be as steadfast as a tree."

Diana smiled. "It makes so much sense," she whispered. "I almost feel like this tree is talking to me."

A memory stabbed Logan's heart. "When I slept up here as a kid, I could swear this tree was talking to me, too, in this low, humming voice."

"Yeah. That's exactly it. Do you still hear it?"

"No. I don't know," Logan said. He looked down at his empty hands in silence for a moment, and then out at the ocean of trees. "I mean, there are spectrums of light our eyes don't see and frequencies we don't hear. Our sense of smell is nothing compared to a dog's. We only take in a small amount of what's around us, so...it's possible. I've just...lost touch."

They studied each other's faces in the moonlight. She had creases under her eyes and a bump in her nose that he liked. An owl hooted. She was mesmerized by the triangular plane beneath his cheekbones, by the corner of his mouth. She tried to take her eyes off his lips. The unlikeliness of this match, of all the disparate things that had called them together, the odd intersections and commonalities despite all their differences, the ancient aerosols of the trees, the complexity of the web of life of which they were a part filled them both with wonder. The urge to kiss was overwhelming. They succumbed, and soon the heat of their naked undulating bodies glowed incandescent in the cool of the night.

Uuma

Laghu! He sleeps in my branches. It is good to feel him again, the sky-bear-raptor of him. His dead alleys are open and thrumming tonight. He has brought another clevertongue. Her mindroot feels foreign, shaped at the angles so peculiar to the clervertongues who live far from us in stone forests. As I gentle her corners, a tiny lightpath opens. I thrum through them and we are all one loop spinning darkside to brightside.

Chapter 21

Judi and Darryl Rally

April 23, 1990

Judi Bari addressed the crowd of all ages and dress from a platform in front of Pacific Lumber's sawmill in Scotia, a long yellow building with stacks of logs beside it that would fill a football stadium to the top.

Short and strong-boned, with a long forehead, and pronounced nose and chin, Judi spoke as if the relentless force of the ocean was at her beck and call.

"California used to be covered with two million acres of old-growth. Now, only four percent remain. We have to act, or they will be gone forever. They cannot grow back because the atmosphere they created goes with them, and the climate conditions that allowed them to grow in the first place have already changed, thanks to the arrogance of big oil companies."

"These are the lungs of the planet," she said, pointing to stacks of logs behind her in the mill yard. "We cannot rip out the lungs of the planet to pay for pick-up trucks and corporate executives' multi-million-dollar salaries."

The crowd hooted and clapped. Diana stood with Logan in the crowd about twenty feet from the stage. Among them were people in costumes of spotted owls, elk, and mountain lions. At the edge, loggers and families booed and waved signs saying, "You're Barking Up the Wrong Tree," and "Don't Park My Job," referring to the National Parks.

Darryl Cherney struck a chord on his guitar for the opening of his song "You Can't Clearcut Your Way to Heaven." The crowd clapped and hooted as they recognized the song.

Now my momma used to read the family Bible

Judi joined in with her fiddle.

And it said thou shall not covet, steal or kill
But then I coveted the forests and the mountains
And I stole my mother nature's gems at will

As Darryl sang, many in the crowd joined in, clapping, swaying, and dancing.

Then I killed off many creatures to extinction
But I'm sure God must have made them by mistake
"Cause I had to keep my job
Where I plunder, rape and rob
But I swear to you it's for my children's sake.

"Judi and Darryl are my Gods," a man behind Diana and Logan said. His voice sounded as if it was coming through cloth. Diana glanced behind her. The speaker was a man wearing a two-foot-square paper-mâché elk head. She looked away but continued to eavesdrop.

"Yeah, they're great," a man with reddish dreadlocks and multi-colored tattoos said. He was wearing an Indian print skirt.

"Personally," said a woman, face painted with whiskers and wearing a leotard and cat ears, "I hate how they're dragging all this communist doctrine into the fight."

"What do you mean?" said the dreadlocked man.

"They keep talking about workers' rights. Did you see that article she wrote about the tree spiking incident?" she said.

"No. What happened?" asked the Elk.

"A millworker was practically decapitated."

"That wasn't Earth First!" the dreadlocked man said.

"I know, I know, but she really went after Dave Foreman. Called him arrogant, and all that."

"Who's Dave Foreman?" said Elk-head.

"The founder of Earth First!, dummy!" said Dreadlocks.

"Watch who you call dummy, idiot." Laughter all around.

"It's not about the workers," the lioness continued.

"She's just thinking strategy," said Dreadlocks. "If we can win the loggers over, we have a better chance of winning."

"Anyway, it's a false dichotomy," someone else behind them joined in. "We are the earth, and workers' rights matter, here. These mega-corporations think it's okay to make a profit off the bodies, animals, and trees. It's just wrong."

"Damn straight." All of them nodded their heads, high-fived, and fist-bumped each other.

"The whole concept of private property is a construction," said the tattooed one.

Diana started to tune them out. It was amazing how they used the same exact words Logan had used. It was a bit cultish. "Pigs!" a young woman called.

"Hey, that's an insult to pigs!" a man in a pig mask rejoined. More laughter.

Diana looked at Logan uneasily. She could still smell the scent of his body on hers. He was clapping vigorously as Darryl's and Judi's song came to an end, his strong eyebrows pulled into a black scowl of approval. *She* was the pig they were all talking about. No one in her circle back home or in college had talked like this. She resented their sanctimoniousness, their overly simplistic solutions, their hypocrisy. Their very presence at this rally depended on the institutions and roads built by government and business interests. Simultaneously, she was embarrassed by her resentment. Logan looked back at her, and his scowl broke into that wide grin that tilted his eyes slightly off-balance. The flash of last night's intimacy hit her full-on, almost knocking her over. She grabbed his arm to steady herself. He squeezed her hand.

Darryl's next song cut in:

> Cutting down the forest, hauling it away
> Rumble of your lumber trucks at the break of day
> Last of the baby redwoods hit that forest floor
> Run 'em through your chipper to make your
>   waferboard

"Do you really believe what that guy was saying, about private property? Being a construct?" Diana said.

Logan absorbed her tone of incredulity. "Uh. Basically."

"What do you mean?" She stepped back.

Logan looked at her more closely and considered before answering. "I mean, yeah. None of this land belonged to anyone. The Mattole and the Sinkyone lived here before we came. They don't believe in ownership. Our culture does. But at its core, the idea of property ownership is a belief, not a fact."

"Okaaay. I'll grant you that. But surely you don't believe we should just abolish all private property. I mean my dad has put a lifetime of work into his holdings. These logging companies have made huge investments. Their business pays for the lives of thousands of families and contributes to the whole of society."

Logan stepped back from her slightly. "And I, in turn, will grant you that our entire nation is built on the construct, so it would tear the whole thing apart if we were to suddenly abolish the notion of private property. But yeah, I don't believe any property is truly private. It belongs to all of us; we belong to it."

"Then why don't you give up your land?"

"I did in a sense. The whole thing was a demonstration of sustainable logging that we used to teach workshops. But also, the property you call mine is an isolated postage stamp."

She knew she should let it drop. Instead, she said, "You could donate it to a Native American."

Logan grimaced and shook his head. "So, what are you saying? That I'm a hypocrite?"

"Kinda." She wanted to backpedal, but she was also triggered.

A group of loggers pushed to the edge of the stage, their shouting drowning out Judi and Darryl momentarily. A few organizers shouted back from the platform, and others tried to pull them back.

"Huh," Logan said, noticing the developing fracas. Then he looked back at Diana, really focusing on her. His heart started to hammer. Had he imagined what he'd seen in her? She had drive, ambition, energy, and last night, he thought he'd seen a willingness to change. But people don't really change, and she was born to a level of privilege he couldn't imagine. Anger, never far away, welled up inside him. "So, giving up my dad to the cause. That's not enough?"

"Oh. My God." The sharp look on Diana's face broke apart. "I'm sorry. I—" She stepped toward him, putting her hand on his forearm.

He whipped his arm away from her hand. "You and your dad can keep on destroying the planet because, hey, we're all guilty by association. Right?"

"No, I—"

"You people," he said, his voice dripping with disgust. He turned away from her just in time to see a logger try to jump up on the stage and one of the band members push him back.

"You *people?*" Diana said to his back as he shouldered past the people in front of him.

The logger fell backward and sprang back at the stage. The other loggers now mobbed the stage with him. Soon punches were flying.

Logan made it to the stage just as one of the loggers was pulling back his arm to land a punch in Darryl Cherney's face. Logan grabbed his arm. The logger punched him in the jaw instead.

Logan stood a moment, dazed, as his brain juddered in the soft tissues inside his skull. Then the numb spot on his jaw warmed to pain, and with it, rage. It roared like a hundred thousand pounds of water smashing on the rocks below. He leapt on the guy, both fists wailing, completely lost in a wave of pure energy and purpose. Shouts, curses, and thumps filled the air along with the scent of mud and blood, followed by quick short blasts of police sirens. He was lost in the fray when someone caught one of his arms on a backswing.

"Whoa, whoa, buddy," Zeff said softly, in his ear. Logan's head pivoted, and it took a moment for him to register what he was seeing. Zeff's eyes were as big as a sad cartoon kitten's, swimming with so much concern and compassion that it instantly brought Logan back to himself. He allowed Zeff to pull him off the logger just as the police blasted commands through megaphones.

"We gotta get out of here," Zeff said as demonstrators flew in all directions.

The police clapped handcuffs onto Judi and Darryl as loggers picked themselves up and dusted themselves off.

Logan and Zeff ducked behind a van. "When I said you should get into the fight, I didn't mean like this," Zeff said, half laughing.

"That's the problem. I don't have an in-between."

As they ran from the crowd, Logan looked over his shoulder for Diana.

She was standing on the other side of the road, away from the melee, with a stricken look on her face.

Chapter 22

Diana

April 24 to May 13, 1990

That was the first of several fights and reunions over the next several weeks. The rage I saw in Logan, the swiftness with which he turned to violence was a total turn-off. He was no better than the loggers who acted like a bunch of meatheads. And that *gesture*. Pulling away from my touch. It kept playing through my head. It pissed me off to the point that I wanted to track him down and give him one of the tongue lashings that had won my debate team three trophies. That's when I realized I didn't know where he lived, much to my chagrin. I myself was staying at the Scotia Lodge, which was decent enough. No way was I going to stay at the Ingomar Club where my father was.

But Judi had been right, no one with a soul can walk in the redwoods and be unchanged. And Logan or no Logan, I was committed. So, I took refuge in the saner, more legalistic approach of EPIC. I went there the very next day, in fact.

"Hey," Jessica said when I walked in. She came toward me with her hand outstretched. I took hers in both of mine.

"I saw my first clearcut, and—" my eyes welled up, "I'm here to help."

"Welcome aboard," she said. "There's much you can do."

Much to my surprise, she took me back to her desk and gave me the first in a series of patient tutorials on everything she knew about existing environmental laws and practices.

The day after that, Logan showed up.

"Look what the cat dragged in," Jess said, hugging him, and glancing surreptitiously over her shoulder at me. I'd told her about what had happened at the rally.

My face grew hot when I saw him, but I was busy reading through the recent slate of timber harvest plans and cross-checking them with EPIC maps, and I angled my body so that he wasn't in my line of vision. Jessica took him over to a stack of papers, handed him canvassing maps and brochures, walked him through the main talking points, and pushed him out the door telling him not to come back until his hands were empty. She winked at me and went back to work.

The next day, Logan and I were both working in the office, trying to act like we didn't know each other, when Zeff flounced in. He was looking particularly smashing with eyeliner.

"Logan! Dude. I'm so proud of you, man," he said, giving him a full-body hug. "We miss you in the trees, but—this might just be the best place for you, considering your temper and all."

I snorted and went back to what I was doing.

"Dudette," Zeff pranced my way. "I can cut the sexual tension in here with a knife." He grabbed my wrist and pulled me toward Logan. "Now. I want you two lovebirds to kiss and make up."

"I've got nothing to apologize for," I said, stiffly, looking only at Zeff, but sneaking a peek at Logan.

"Now, now," Zeff said, pressing our hands together between his. "It takes two to tango," and he wiggled his hips. "Logan. You go first."

Logan looked at me. "I'm—sorry?"

"For what," I said, monotone.

"For—losing my cool. I'm not into violence. Really. I don't believe in it, I don't condone it, and I've literally never punched a guy in my life."

"It's true," Zeff said. "Between the two of us, he's the peaceful warrior. He doesn't even sabotage—" He caught himself.

"And I'm sorry for ditching you like that," Logan continued.

"Well, I'm pissed—"

Zeff cleared his throat exaggeratedly.

"I'm—sorry, too," I said, "for goading you." The minute I said it, I realized I meant it, and my anger at him vaporized.

It wasn't long before we were making out in the alley behind the office building.

Over the next few weeks, I took what I'd learned at EPIC to my father to plead the case for the trees. But the more I tried to reason with him, the more he condescended to me. He'd look at me over the glossy desktop from an office he'd commandeered at the Scotia head-quarters with that dead-on stare of his, his brows spread like the wings of an eagle diving for prey, and I began to see why it was so easy for the press to vilify him. The skin around his eyes was gray—probably from allergies, but it looked like a shadow from within was seeping to the surface. Maybe the way a person looks physically affects the way people perceive them, and then that partly shapes who they are. "You sound like a flake," he said after one of my more impassioned speeches. It caught me out cold.

And meanwhile, I kept catching glimpses of that guy, Detective Barnes, who worked for my father, spying on me. It galled me. I'd never fully faced how sexist my father was, how little regard he had for my intelligence and judgment. I began to think that all he had ever loved in me was his own DNA. My anger only served to embed me more deeply in Logan's world.

I had never hung out with people like this before. Everyone I grew up with had been groomed for professional success—which meant a few million in stocks, at least a quarter-million a year in salary, and a house no smaller than 3,000 square feet. In contrast, in Logan's world, wealth was an embarrassment, a vice, and success was good friends laughing around a homemade meal of Moroccan bean and barley salad and sourdough bread hot from a hand-made wood-fired oven.

I gave up my room at the hotel and stayed with Logan at his house, one room of which was an actual log cabin from the 1890s. It meant a lot because it was the first time he'd lived there since his father died. We visited Logan's tree whenever we could between political organizing, and he took me sailing a few times. We had a hard time keeping our hands off each other. Sexual chemistry is a thing that can't be denied.

My entry into Logan's world wasn't always easy. When some of the circle found out who I was, they made caustic remarks about how I was "slumming it" and would no doubt run back to my plastic bubble when my shoes got dirty. Some even told Logan they thought I was spying for my father. But Jessica never stopped believing in my sincerity, and who couldn't love Zeff—with his constant bubble of energy, spaciness, and expansive affection.

And the trees called. Huge, stately, a thrumming presence I could no longer ignore. Among the trees, I felt the contrast between myself as I was in Texas and myself now. I had spent my whole life spinning. I could talk a million miles an hour, spit any fact I'd read back at a person, dance all night, and crack jokes at dawn, but I had mistaken spinning for joy. In the forest, a different kind of joy took root, slow and still. Before, I had despised meditation. Sure, my friends did yoga, and I did too, on occasion, but hot yoga, or yoga taught by ex-gymnasts who were all about achieving the perfect body. I had always hated the part where we were asked to sit still and count breaths. It was agony. My mind refused to be stilled.

In the woods, though, as I walked, all the arguments on both sides, all thoughts about who I was or who anyone else was vanished. I was simply there, mind still, no difference between outside and inside. The trees marked three-dimensional space with such clarity and depth, it was as if, until now, my entire life had taken place on a two-dimensional plane. The older the grove, the quieter it got. At times, when I went alone, without Logan, I felt I could hear them, a decibel so low and slow. It wasn't perceptible to the human ear, but it laid out the map from tree to mind, and there was no difference.

The more I learned by attending rallies, meetings, and parties, the more I admired this complex web of teachers, activists, farmers, waiters, and artists—even loggers. Most were utterly original, walking the walk, as they liked to say, living off the grid, farming, and bartering. Judi Bari lived in a 500-square-foot shack, and Darryl Cherney lived in a tiny solar-powered geodesic dome. But the community wasn't in total accord. Paul Watson, famous for sinking whaling ships, urged violence, but at one meeting, Judi called him out on his sexism, much to everyone's amusement. And there were a lot of debates about the effectiveness of being arrested. And some activists were just annoying. There was this one white chick, excuse me, woman, who wore a lot of Navajo silver and herself Purewalker. She'd pounce on me if I said anything that could be even remotely construed as supporting the status quo. Jessica derided her as a wannabe Indian, and Logan said she was "politically correct," a term that meant insincere, a person who was more concerned with being perceived as morally superior but didn't really do much. Purewalker often argued loudly against any and all action in organizing meetings, accusing even Jessica of compromising her values because she wasn't trying to shut down all logging.

"Hurt people hurt people," Zeff explained, his large eyes melting with their particular mix of sorrow and glee.

Meanwhile, the more time I spent with Logan, the more in love I fell. Don't get me wrong, before him, I had had my share of sex. I had never been shy about that sort of thing. I'd always been in charge of everything I did, including my orgasms. And I could tell Logan had never been with a woman who was so sure of herself in bed. It surprised and delighted him. But sex was different for me with Logan. I was awash in him, awash in the sensations he provoked in me, and I loved that feeling. I knew I was more in love with him than he was with me. Once in a rare while, he'd get this half apologetic look in his eyes after we made love. But I didn't care. I was grateful that he elicited this torrent of feelings. We spent as many nights as we could up in his tree making love in her heights. I felt as if I was making love *to* the trees, and that the trees were making love to us, that our sexual interaction was inextricably entwined with their branches.

Chapter 23

The Party

May 15, 1990

Logan's feelings for Diana deepened one night at a large party at Rita's spread, a farm outside of Arcata.

"Lovely Rita, meter maid, where would we be without you?" Zeff sang to Rita in the flickering light of the fire behind her house. Rita's lawn meandered into a mowed field that sloped toward the ocean in one direction and back toward wooded hills in the other. More than a hundred people clustered in small groups around several fires, sparks drifting upward between. Guitar chords and flute notes floated up with woodsmoke and weed, as people drifted and danced between clusters.

"Di, this is Rita," said Zeff, "an organizer par excellence who has been fighting the corporate dragon for the last three decades."

Rita smiled and rolled her eyes. "Except lately." Her gray hair flowed like her clothes. "I've been out of town the last month, taking care of my mother."

"Pleased to meet you," Diana said, wondering if Rita would accept her.

"There's more food in the house, and if you need a place to crash for the night, find yourself a corner in the barn, and call it home," she said and nodded toward the rough-cut, post-and-beam barn to the right.

"Thank you," Diana gushed, aware that she was overdoing it.

The wind changed direction and wafted smoke right at Diana. Her eyes watered and she coughed.

"Smoke follows beauty," Logan observed. They laughed and moved to the other side of the fire, only to have the plume of smoke follow them. Diana's hair had a wave to it now that she didn't blow-dry it anymore. And though she still wore eyeliner and mascara, visually, she blended with the crowd.

"So, you're new to the area?" Rita asked.

"Yeah."

"People are coming from all over to join Redwood Summer," Rita said.

"She's not just anyone," Zeff said, large eyes crinkling with laughter. Logan and Diana shot him a warning look, which he blithely ignored. "This is Diana Jamison. As in, daughter of Darth Vader. We've won her over from the dark side."

Rita's eyes widened and she looked at Diana appraisingly.

"I'm a total convert," Diana said. "We don't have anything like this in Texas," she gestured to the trees. "I was just your average rich girl, growing up in oblivion until I got here and met these characters." She slipped her arm through Logan's and kicked Zeff affectionately. "Now, I'm doing what I can."

"I'd think you'd start with your father."

"Believe me, I'm trying. I'm not getting anywhere, but I won't give up."

"That-a-girl. Welcome." Rita hugged her. "Mi casa es su casa."

Diana was relieved by her quick acceptance.

They drifted down into the field and passed the next hour joining different circles, some in song and others in avid discussion, and still others just smoking weed and laughing with the odd dancer undulating between like seaweed underwater.

Firelight played across their faces, and from a distance, they were their own constellations on a black field mirroring the star-pierced sky.

Diana, Zeff, and Logan joined a circle where a passionate discussion was taking place. A man with a long beard was saying "They grew up in plastic houses. They're out of touch."

A woman across from him said, "How did our culture get to be so destructive?"

Logan said, "I think it comes from the Bible." They turned to him. "In Genesis, God says, you shall have dominion over the animals and all the earth."

"You know," the woman across from them said. "I just started learning Hebrew. Turns out, that's a mistranslation."

"How so?" Logan asked.

"The Hebrew word for dominion in the Torah—radah— actually means stewardship. So God was actually saying, you should take care of them all."

"That's not true," said the man with the long beard. "I can see why you want it to be true, but the word is used throughout the Bible again and again to mean military authority."

"Who cares what the Bible says, anyway?" said Zeff. "We need to stop being so anthropocentric."

"You don't even know what that word means," Logan said, thumping Zeff's bare chest where his beads and leather medicine bag hung between his shearling vest.

"Do too!" Zeff locked his arm around Logan's neck and gave him a noogie.

"Sweden's creation myth puts a tree at the center of the universe," said a woman with very light blonde hair, the fire flickering across her high cheekbones.

"Yggdrasil, yes!" said Logan, pushing Zeff off laughingly.

"It's no accident that we have a much better environmental track record than the United States," the woman rejoined.

The group theorized about the ethos at the center of Western culture, debating whether it was capitalism, Christianity, dualism, or some inherent flaw of white people's nature that caused them to be the colonizers, rapists, and slave-owners of the world. Some defensively pointed to Egypt's slave history, while others explained that whereas indigenous cultures in North America saw the world through the paradigm of a wheel with all beings connected like spokes at the center, European culture saw the world as a vertical hierarchy with God at the top and the land at the bottom. In the flickering light of the fire, they debated how to fix the problem, whether by meditation or violence. Zeff weighed in here. "Violence is never justified."

"What do you call it when we destroy their dozers, then?" Jim teased.

"Civil disobedience. Those are machines. Not people."

The group splintered into many sub-conversations, with some people nodding vigorously and adding examples while others argued. Zeff hooked up with Jim, and they disappeared into the darkness.

Diana tapped Logan's arm, "Can we wander?"

They strolled through the field to the next group.

"I still get a little uncomfortable with those conversations," said Diana

"I know you do. They're just talking."

"It gets so judgmental. It makes me feel like I'll never be good enough, never pure enough."

They wandered over to a food table with various bean and rice salads.

"What's this?" Diana said, pointing to what looked like chicken tenders.

"Try it," Logan said.

Diana bit into a nubbly brown strip and spit it out. "Ugh! What *is it*?"

Logan laughed: "Tempeh."

"What on earth is tempeh?"

"I don't know. Soybeans. Fermented something. Hippie food."

"Disgusting. You did that on purpose!" She punched his shoulder and he laughed.

"Try this," he said, holding up a spoonful of lumpy custard.

"No way! What is it?"

"Chia pudding," he said, taking a bite. "Delicious. Like tapioca."

"Like that chia pet thing?" Diana said, remembering the clay chia pet from the commercial from childhood that sprouted green fur.

"It grows on you," Logan said.

"I hope not!!!!" Diana laughed.

He strolled over to a table with three basins, one with soapy water, one, with clear water, and one empty, and did a quick rinse.

Diana both admired the earth-friendly set-up or felt exhausted by it.

"I mean—it's so cool how there's not a spec of plastic in sight, no paper napkins or paper plates. But where does it end? Are we supposed to make sure we never step on an ant?"

"Just do the best you can," Logan said with a shrug.

"But didn't everyone drive to get out here?"

"There you go with the hypocrisy argument. All it does is shut the whole argument down. If the only people who can credibly criticize have to be perfect, then no one can criticize."

"I hadn't thought of it that way," Diana mused.

"No one is saying we need to go back to caveman days."

"You sure about that? A few of your friends look like they live in a cave," Diana said with a smile.

"Beats looking like a Ken doll. Anyway, most people carpooled out here. The whole country has been laid out for the car, so you do what you can do."

"I know. I was just—I worry about the didacticism. Extremism. Violence."

"So far, most of the violence comes from the police, the FBI, and the logging companies. Loggers have been running activists off the road, things like that. And you heard Judi. She's all about bringing people together."

"But did you see that picture of Judi Bari posing with an Uzi? I mean, if that's not a clear message, what is?"

"That picture was a setup," Logan said.

"Looked real to me."

"Zeff told me that it was one of these infiltrators. The guy started hanging out with Darryl and Judi and then he showed them the Uzi in the trunk of his car. They were just goofing around, probably stoned. He totally set it up, and then he took a picture and sent it to the police."

"You really think the FBI would spend time on this group? Don't you think I'd know if my dad was being protected by the FBI?"

"It's not just your dad. The government is protecting corporate interests. Ever heard of COINTELPRO?"

"No."

"It was a J. Edgar Hoover program. Counter Intelligence Program. Their stated purpose was to disrupt and isolate 'radical' groups." Logan hunched and made air quotes, miming their attitude. "As if wanting to live in harmony with nature is a radical idea. The reality is, *they* are the extreme ones, ignoring basic life-affirming principles, racing us over a cliff for some weird shit called money."

Diana looked out over the field of people, their pink and brown faces glowing in the firelight, their laughter floating above them, bubbling like a brook. Their happiness and camaraderie emerged from human interaction rather than material goods, whereas her people bought and spent endlessly, looking for the happiness they could never find. And all that money only bred conformism.

"They did it to the Black Panthers," Logan continued. "They manufactured death threats among activists to foster infighting and to give the police an excuse to handle them with deadly force. Remember that talk at Beanheads about the bomb workshops?"

"No, I missed that."

"Yeah, the FBI was giving the *police* bomb-making workshops on Louisiana Pacific Lumber grounds."

"What?"

"I mean, supposedly to help them learn how to disarm bombs...but...."

"God. I had no idea." Diana felt a little sick inside. The world she'd come from was turning out to be a very different place than she had imagined it to be. The nail salons, the shopping malls, a thin veneer over...what? Human beings were such a mass of twisted confusion. How could it ever be untangled?

They wandered further down the field, passing Zeff doing hand-stand push-ups by a fire.

"How many is that?" asked Jim.

"I have no idea," Zeff said, not breaking his rhythm.

"You don't count?"

"It's not about counting, man," Zeff said

"Dig," said Jim.

"Show-off," said Logan, and pushed him off balance.

Zeff turned the fall into a somersault and popped back up, grinning, "Methinks thou doth *project* too much."

Logan grinned wolfishly over his shoulder, as he and Diana wandered over to another group around a different fire. A woman was talking, and people were leaning in close, following every word.

"So, the thing is, underground, all the trees are connected by the mycelium, which is a network of fungi that form a symbiotic relationship to trees," the woman explained.

Diana's interest was piqued, and she found a seat in the circle near the woman.

"The fungi—called mycorrhizae—need sugar but can't produce it. They attach to the roots of the trees and get sugar from the tree, and in turn, feed the tree with nitrogen and nutrients. Then the trees can actually communicate through this network, and they can help each other."

"Wow, that is so cool," someone said.

Diana was riveted. "What kinds of things do they communicate?" she asked.

The woman looked at her. "It's quite amazing. They can warn each other about drought or insect infestations. There's even some cross-species talk—like the birch and the fir. But other trees are separate, like the cedar. This network connects trees as much as a mile away."

"Do trees make a sound?" Diana asked.

"Funny you should ask. I haven't been able to ascertain that. But we know that grain makes a crackling noise at 200 hertz —and that seedlings turn toward that noise." Her audience nodded and smiled.

"We know for sure though that they speak through carbon, phosphorus, water, and even aerosols. Take the acacia tree," she went on. "If a giraffe takes a bite from it, it pulls bitter chemicals into its leaves to make them taste bad so the giraffes move on. Then it emits an aerosol that tells the other acacia trees to do the same—and it happens in minutes. But they talk fairly slowly. It might take a message three seconds to get an inch. So, if two trees were ten feet apart, and one was calling for more sun, it would take six hours for the nutrients of a tree in the sun to travel to a tree in the shade."

As the woman talked, Diana listened with every part of her body. It felt like she was finally getting fed food she had only just now realized she'd been starved for. As Logan watched her, his feelings for her magnified. This worried him. Their physical chemistry was exciting, but he didn't want to love again. It was too soon and too fast. However, her ability to completely absorb this—her easy connection to the trees—that fact she seemed to hear them as he did—the way she had changed so deeply yet naturally filled him with so much admiration and hope that he felt a sudden urge to pull her into one of the tents and make love to her.

Chapter 24

Skirmish

May 16, 1990

Like a watercolor brush drawn across wet paper, the blue dawn feathered the sky over Rita's sleeping revelers. Diana and Logan had been dozing by a fire, wrapped in a quilt when a commotion up at the house woke them.

A cluster of people ran down the path toward them shouting, Zeff among them. Blurred sounds distilled into, "They're cutting the Grove of the Ancients!"

Logan snapped to crystalline awareness, and Diana lifted her head groggily.

"What's going on?"

"There you are!" Zeff said, detaching from the group who ran on, stirring sleepers throughout the field. "Machines! Right now."

"But what about the stay—the study or whatever—" Diana said.

"I don't know. I think they're just doing it," Zeff said.

"Those motherfuckers," said Logan

"But that's illegal!" Diana exclaimed, now fully awake.

"You say that like legality matters to this bunch."

"They're cutting on a Sunday? Now?" Diana looked at her watch, "At four in the morning?"

"It's get up and go time," Zeff said.

"Is anyone out there?" Logan asked.

"Yeah, Kev and Moon are in the trees still, and more are headed that way, but we need more people," Zeff said, looking pointedly at Logan.

Logan went dead inside. "Yes, of course."

"We're meeting at North Fisher Road. We're forming a blockade there, and others are making circles around the trees."

"I'll drive," Diana said.

They all looked at her.

"Don't look so surprised."

"No—we know you're in... but maybe you should call your dad, or better yet, pull him out of bed," Zeff said.

As people ran up the path toward the house, Logan, Diana, and Zeff banked the fire. Diana was torn. She wanted to prove herself to this community and get involved in direct action. Up until now, she'd done most of her work from the EPIC office. "I'll come with you and identify myself. I'll get them to stop."

"They won't listen to you."

Diana debated internally before she said, "You're right. Okay—I'll find my father, and I'll meet you there. Be careful!" She gave Logan a kiss and Zeff a hug and ran off.

Zeff and Logan arrived at a scene already in chaos. Cars were parked every which way along the road leading to the Grove of the Ancients. Security guards were there with blinding searchlights and rifles. A crowd had linked arms around a few trees, but the dozers were going for the others. Trucks, skidders, and men with four-foot chainsaws were everywhere, revving engines and spewing exhaust.

Logan and Zeff jumped out of Zeff's van just as one of the smaller trees was felled with heartbreaking speed. The tree, by design, fell toward Zeff's tree, Arcadia, and people on the ground screamed as it glanced off the side of it. The impact jolted and jostled the platform, and Kev and Moon grabbed the tree trunk in terror. The falling log scraped bark off Arcadia all the way down.

"The bastards aren't even trying to save the wood, they're cutting as fast as they can, just to destroy habitat," Logan said, dizzy with rage. Zeff and Logan stood indecisively, swearing, trying to figure out what to do next. An organizer came by. "We're forming a ring around Arcadia. You pull together a circle around that dozer and lock arms."

Logan said, "It's fucking hopeless. We've lost."

"We'll save a few trees," Zeff said. "They might get away with this, but it will cost them. The press is coming."

Police cars arrived, sirens blaring, lights flashing, and they skidded to a halt with a flourish.

The crowd was shouting at the loggers. Security guards pointed guns at them and yelled, "Back up. Don't make me shoot."

Logan and Zeff pulled in another ten people and formed a circle around one of the dozers. In Logan's chest, conflicting urges to kill and to run away toppled over each other like two wrestlers, now one on top, now the other. But as Zeff locked arms with him on one side, and a woman on the other, and as the circle closed around the dozer, an unexpected joy radiated through his chest like hot whiskey. Zeff looked up at him and grinned, and Logan grinned back, then they stared into the headlights of the roaring metal monster and chanted, "Stop the slaughter, stop the slaughter, stop the slaughter." The driver backed, then switched gears, and roared toward them. A few people to Logan's left screamed and let go, but the ring closed around the gap, and the dozer paused.

The driver shoved his head out the window, "If you don't get out of the way, someone's gonna die. I don't want to kill you."

The police fanned out, going from group to group, "You're trespassing on private property. Disperse." When that didn't work, they shot pepper spray into the crowd. People coughed and doubled over. A few news vans pulled up, and reporters with cameras stepped out.

As more and more trees came down over the next few hours, people wept and screamed. Some ran into the woods, while others were handcuffed. The police arrested at least fifty people, Zeff and Logan among them, and shoved them into vans.

Chapter 25

Dad

May 16, 1990

Atlas awoke to furious pounding. He struggled to a sitting position.

"Dad! Dad! Open up!" The pounding was from the door.

"Diana?" Atlas jumped out of bed and stumbled to the door. "What's wrong?" He unlocked it.

Diana pushed the door back so violently she almost knocked him over. He steadied himself surreptitiously by grabbing ahold of the side table by the door. A dried flower arrangement trembled slightly. He switched on the lamp above it.

She strode into the center of the oriental rug and whipped around. "How could you? How dare you?"

"Whoa, Nellie. What's wrong? Are you alright?"

"I'm fine! But the trees! You're cutting the trees."

He held out his hands and tilted his head, as if to say, yes, as always.

"You don't know?"

His concern shifted to annoyance.

"Right now. Today. Sunday. The Grove of the Ancients. They're cutting!"

He turned his back to her, reached for his dressing gown and shrugged it on over his pajamas.

"They're not cutting the Gr—lot 2-86. It's an adjacent lot. We filed that THP last month and no one appealed it."

"That's not what I was told. And rushing in and cutting on a Sunday—they're destroying as much as they can out of spite— "

"Spite's got nothing to do with it." His words came out louder than he intended. He caught himself and continued with hushed intensity. "It's my right. No one can tell me what to do with *my property*."

"But, Dad, we need those trees to survive."

"My God," he said with disgust. "You've been drinking the Kool-aid."

"Dad," she stepped closer to him, suppressing the urge to grab him by the lapels. "It's not an either/or proposition. We don't have to choose. You can make a profit *and log* sustainably. I can show you the facts and figures. It might take a little longer, but what's the rush?"

"You wouldn't understand. I have loans, bills to be paid. It's all about the timing."

"Will you please just hold off? Just for a week or two. What's the difference?"

"The difference is that we embolden the rioters. Do you know how many timber harvest plans they've scuttled? Every time we turn around, someone's running to court, hanging from trees, or sabotaging equipment. We need to send a message. We will not tolerate terror-ists. They nearly killed one of the millworkers. Did you hear about that? Spiked a tree and the accident at the mill nearly decapitated him."

Diana was speechless for a moment. She'd heard about it, but they'd said it was another landowner. What if she was on the wrong side? Seeing her waver, he pressed his advantage with a softer tone.

"Trees grow back, honey. It's a renewable resource. And we're replanting."

"Replanting?! Even if you could get anything to live in the soil after you've finished bulldozing and spraying toxic herbicides, mono-crops are *not* the same thing as a habitat. The spotted owl, the marbled murrelet—"

"Spare me. You think these people really care about a damn bird?!"

"Yes! And they're putting their lives on the line to do it. And it's not just a damn bird. It's an ecosystem."

"Oh, for God's sake, Diana."

Diana gulped air, exhaled, and closed in on him, lowering her voice, "Dad. Remember what you told me about the Calder? It's like that. Taking one piece out sends the whole thing out of balance. If you ever loved me, if you ever thought I had a few good ideas, will you please just delay this one cut for me? Just for a few days. What's the harm?" She touched his face.

He looked at her face in the dim light. The trust, the tenderness. He didn't like being manipulated, but he was in a position of power. Sometimes a show of mercy made you more powerful.

"Let me make a few phone calls."

Her face lit up.

He dialed. Stanton wasn't answering his home phone. Stanton would be in his truck. He opened the CB radio case, fiddled with the dials, and pressed the transmission button. Eddie Cox answered.

"Where's Stanton?"

"It's chaos out here," Eddie said. "Rioters everywhere and cops." In the background shouts and shots could be heard.

"What about the press?"

"Yep. They're here, too."

"Call it off."

"Look, if it's overtime you're worried about—"

"I'm not. Just tell them to shut it down—"

"But—"

"Just for today. And call a meeting with all the field managers and board members first thing tomorrow morning."

"Yes sir."

After he'd talked Eddie down and made arrangements to please his daughter, and signed off, Diana threw her arms around him. "Thank you, Dad."

Half of him was irritated by her blatant pulling of heartstrings, and the other half was a tiny bit choked up.

"Thank you. Thank you so much. I can show you my calculations tomorrow. There's a better way."

"We'll see."

"I gotta go. Love you!" She hugged him and raced off.

As he closed the door behind her, he smiled slightly. She'd be okay. She hadn't been totally brainwashed by the crowd she was spending time with. She still had a business head. And she wasn't at all like her mother. Underneath the fine blonde hair, the only thing she'd inherited from Christine was a head as hard as his. He admired her warrior instinct, however misdirected it was at the moment. He would have to have another talk with her about consequences. He'd accommodate her this once, but if she came back again, he'd get her to see the bigger picture. And if that didn't work, he'd read her the riot act. She'd learn.

He nudged the dried flower arrangement on the side table with a knuckle. It reminded him of Christine, fragile, dry, decorative. She had never pursued her own business or career. She sat on boards and organized charities, but it was always someone else's agenda. They had never discussed it directly, but he had always felt that her participation in only charitable endeavors implied judgment of his own pursuits. It didn't matter. It worked as good PR for Titan, Inc. In a way, it was why he married her. Of all the women who threw themselves at him, obviously for his money, she had a stately, moral presence, and a social pedigree that lent him legitimacy in the upper echelons of society. But over their ten years of marriage, they'd grown apart. Then she got cancer. The ugliness of it. The smells, the pallor, the clumps of hair. The way it distorted everything before finally taking her life. There was nothing he could do. It was a relief when she finally died, now fifteen years ago. One isn't supposed to admit that to anyone, so he didn't. But it was an end to her suffering.

People thought he was heartless, no doubt, because outwardly, he didn't appear to mourn. He had thought he was heartless, too. It had taken him a few years to feel anything at all. Three years later, he met Linda. She was different from Christine. Linda owned a few businesses, and he was glad for it. She was indestructible. Diana seemed to get over her mother's death, too, and she had accepted her stepmother without rebellion. For a second, looking at the flower arrangement still quivering in reaction to his touch, a darker, bigger grief loomed. Before it could get anywhere, he swatted the flower arrangement off the table into the wastebasket. He hated that kind of decoration. All they did was collect dust.

He'd call Linda later and tell her he would be staying here longer than anticipated.

Chapter 26

Cox

May 16, 1990

Eddie was pissed. The Sunday Morning Surprise was his brainchild. The plan was to start the cut in the plot they'd gotten approved for, then, "Oops," catch enough trees in lot 2-86 that the whole habitat argument would be moot. By starting early on Sunday, the cutting would be done before anyone was the wiser. He was proud of the cunning, and he secretly expected that it would impress the boss. So, when he got the call from Atlas to shut it all down, amidst the revving engines, screaming chainsaws, and chanting hippies, he wanted to slam the CB radio mic into the dashboard of the company truck.

"It's bad for our image," Jamison said.

"Sir. A show of force is just what we need."

"I don't disagree with you, but for now, let's take a beat and consider a new angle."

Eddie snorted in exasperation. "We're still pressing charges, I assume."

"Of course," Jamison said. "Hold on."

Jamison seemed to be talking to someone in the room with him. Cops were now breaking up the ring of hippies that had surrounded their dozer, handcuffing them and shoving them into their van. The sun was up, piercing the cool forest air with multiple swords of light.

Jamison came back on. "We won't press charges."

"What?" Cox couldn't suppress his outrage.

"Let them cool their heels in jail for a few days."

"Sir. If we let them get away with this, they're gonna—"

"I know. But dropping charges will buy us a little public goodwill."

Cox slammed down the mic.

He waved Stanton over.

What's up?" Stanton hollered, opening the cab door, the roar filling the cab. He climbed in, wheezing heavily, and slammed the door, muting the chaos.

"Boss called. We've gotta wrap this thing up."

"No kidding."

"Yeah."

"Why?"

"I have no idea. He just said call it. Meet with the board tomorrow."

"God damn. Well, let's give it another quarter-hour. Time difference. You know?"

"Exactly."

"You know what this is gonna do? It's gonna fan the flames. It's gonna encourage them."

"I know," said Eddie, deep in thought. "The ring leaders are those two over there," he pointed to Judi and Darryl, part of a circle around a tree who had locked their arms together inside metal tubes. The cops were screaming at them to unlock themselves, and one of the loggers was revving a three-foot chainsaw behind them with glee, bringing the blade down close to the tubes as if to saw through. One cop was gesturing him back as if taking his threat seriously. The cops donned gas masks and released pepper spray.

"If we cut off the head, the whole thing dies."

"What do you have in mind?" Stanton asked.

"I'm thinking," Eddie said. "All this could be to our advantage. Bad press will drive PL stock prices down. Might be time to make the move."

"I'll leave all of that stuff to you." He was leery of the whole plot, but he didn't have much choice in the matter since that conversation about the gyppos on the take.

"I talked with Molton. He'll loan me the money. With your stock, we're almost there."

"Just tell me what you want me to do."

PuraaNam

Today Candra died. A return to Bhūr is usually cause for joy. But Candra, being one of the ancients, knew this was different, so she fought it. As the rootless ones laid their terrible teeth into her, Candra made her energy sharp and shot it outward to ward off the naked ones and warn all in her vicinity. The fire of her fight reached me. I was as if our mindroots had reconnected directly through Kulaaya, but it was by other means. I sent her all my air and sugar, but it was to no avail. Kulaaya has been stamped out between us.

Through her aerosols, I felt the clevertongue's thunderteeth tear into her. First one side, then the other, sending a vibration like a million cicadas, but with the frequency discordant. The water in her mindroot ran to the surface and spilled as they cut from one side to the other. Then finally, when they cut through, the vibrations of their instruments stopped. Candra continued to stand in shocked stillness. Then a trembling began in her trunk and spread upward through her branches. Her energy thinned out to trickle. Then her body began to fall. The waves of impact when her body hit the ground blasted through our trunks all around.

Her energy flowed meekly in the form of sap from her stump. But she was still alive. Yet none of us could reach her.

She has gone silent. She will live as they drag her away. She will live until they cut her into smaller pieces that will never be transformed into another kind of energy, which will instead stay still in the nests of the rootless ones, or she will be shredded and pressed flat. For *her, the circle has ended, unless fire consumes their nests and sends her back.*

We must pull ourselves away from the rootless ones. We must stop caring for them. We must let them end their own cycle so that Bhūr can maintain her balance.

Chapter 27

Sprung

May 17, 1990

The next day, at the Humboldt County jail, Diane sat in a plastic bucket chair, staring at the green walls, waiting for Zeff and Logan to be released. She couldn't wait to see the look of love and admiration in Logan's eyes as he hugged her, and Zeff's joyous high-five. She was a force for good and she glowed with it.

But when Logan came through the door, with Zeff behind him, he looked different. Like his skin had gone gray. His brows were drawn down at the center like the outspread wings of a hawk, and he not only didn't hug her, he avoided eye contact.

"What's wrong?" she asked.

"Why are we being released before the others?"

"I bailed you out."

"And that's supposed to make me happy?"

Diana took a step back like he'd splashed her with a bucket of ice water. "Yes?"

"What about all the others?"

"I don't know, I just—I did what I could. He called off the cut—for the time being—and I'm pretty sure the police are going to drop charges in another day or two—against everyone."

"Look, don't do me any favors."

"Wow. Okay," she said as she backed away, hands in the air. He was opaque to her.

"Hey, but thanks," Zeff said, his delicate features crumpled in sorrow. He reached out to her, but his warmth only accentuated the absence of it in Logan.

She pushed his hands away. "No, I get the picture. I'm the spoiled rich girl with no ethics. You're welcome." She turned on her heel and stormed out of the station.

"Harsh," said Zeff.

"Doesn't surprise me," said Logan.

"No. I meant you."

Logan could barely hear Zeff. Everything was dark, his surroundings barely there. The skirmish in the grove had torn a part of him open. All through the night in jail, rain pounded and mud surged in his head, swallowing trees, raking the land, and toppling his father's dozer. He had left. Yes, his father had ordered him to leave, but he should have climbed the dozer, knocked him off, and dragged him out of there. Instead, he'd obeyed orders and watched from a distance like a coward.

Zeff was still talking, but Logan couldn't hear him. "I gotta go," was all he could say. His blood swelled like the mudslide with too much volume for his veins and arteries, and rage tore at the roots of all his organs. It wouldn't be slaked until he tore Jamison's or Cox's heart out. They were the ones who put him here. As if through a mist, he could see the triple lines of worry across Zeff's brow, he could see Zeff's hand on his arm, but he couldn't feel it.

Chapter 28

Diana

May 17 to 23, 1990

I drifted listlessly around Arcata, Eureka, and Fortuna for days, furious at Logan for not appreciating me, and furious at myself for having fallen for him so hard. Each day, I waited for him to reach out and each day that he didn't, I couldn't believe what an asshole he was, to cut me off so completely. He had to know I'd gone back to the seedy motel in Arcata where I stayed before we met. I felt erased. He seemed to have zero regard for my feelings. I debated whether I should contact him, but I was clearly the injured party here. He had rejected me. It had to be his move to rectify things.

I stopped in at EPIC and helped where I could, but the volunteers' eyes rested on me a moment too long and my cheeriness struck a false note in their unreceptive silence.

"How's it going?" Jess came over, her eyes wide and watchful.

"Okay. Any word on the study PL is supposed to be conducting?" I said.

"We should know in a few days, but we feel good about the judge reviewing the case, and we have our own study."

"That's a relief."

"Thank you for getting your father to back off."

I didn't know what to say. I looked down. "It was the least I could do." Of all the people at EPIC, I felt the most comfortable with Jess.

A cloud hung over me the color of a tea stain. It had to do with the word "entitlement" and my spoiled, rich kid assumption that any problem could be solved by using my money to free my friends. Logan didn't want the preferential treatment. He wanted justice. But all I was trying to do was use my privilege for the cause. Isn't that what you were supposed to do with it? It wasn't supposed to be a mark of Cain. But it felt that way.

"Have you seen Logan?" Jess asked as if reading my mind.

"No. Have you?"

"No. But I ran into Zeff. He's worried. He said Logan is in a dark place. He isn't answering the door or the phone."

A twinge of nausea twisted my gut. "Do you think I should..." I broke off, deep in thought. That strange new feeling intensified, clouding my vision for a second. How could I have been so self-centered? I'd been walking around for days feeling like the injured party, imagining Logan and his friends scoffing at me, and all this time he'd been hurting. It should have been obvious to me.

"Activism takes a toll emotionally," Jess said. "I think this event kicked up grief over his father."

"Of course. I'm such an idiot," I said. "Excuse me."

I drove out of town to his house and pulled tentatively up the drive. When I saw his car, my heart contracted painfully. The look of hatred—worse—disgust on his face in the county jail came back to me. My mouth went dry.

I parked quietly and cut the engine. Nothing stirred but the tree in the wind. I scanned the wood-shingled house. No movement in the windows, shades drawn. I knocked on the door.

"Logan?" My heart thudded in my neck. Nothing. I went around the side of the house and to the back door and knocked and called again. "Logan, it's me." Still nothing. The feeling of stain deepened. How did I get here? What was this fucking feeling? As I turned the doorknob, my heartbeat intensified. Locked.

"Look, I just want to see if you're okay. I understand why you're mad at me, and I'm not asking you for anything. But I heard from Jess and Zeff." I paused. "They're worried about you!" I felt like an idiot, talking to a closed door. I wasn't used to this feeling. I was always the smartest one in the room, the one with the answers, the energy, the resources.

I could feel him in there. Lying in the dark, listening.

"I'm worried about you," I said more quietly. I looked around at the debris on the back porch, buckets, tools, work gloves, a crumpled hat, oil rags.

"Logan!" I grabbed the door handle and shook the door in its frame. "I don't care what happens to us. But your friends love you. We love you. Let us in!"

Silence inside. The wind blew. The trees undulated far above. The windows, eaves, and doors of the house gave nothing away. I looked up at the trees, and the lift and sway of their branches called to me. I followed.

In the cool of the forest, I opened like a sleeper's palm. The deeper I got into the forest, the cleaner and clearer I felt. Looking up at the trees, unshed tears ached in my throat. When I found our tree, I sat down at her base, leaned my back against her, and closed my eyes.

Uuma and Dina

The rootless one who visits with Laghu is here now.

She sits at our base. Her rhythms are disordered with this thing they call yearning. All the rootless ones yearn. We don't understand. Yearning seems to be an always-hunger for what is not. Even when Varsa doesn't visit enough with us and Mrid is dry, even when one of us is rooted too deeply in the shade, we do not yearn. We adjust to what is. In contrast, the clevertongues quiver at a faster rate for what they do not have, until they become a ball of not-being. Not-being is one of the many talents of the clevertongues. Their deafness and blindness is so loud. But it must also serve a purpose.

We like this one, this Dina, we call her, this blazing light. We like how she flits over our leaves like pieces of the Bright One. She has changed much over the recent brightsides, become more absorbent. Many pockets have opened between her fibers for Kulaaya to grow.

But in this moment, her open spaces are filled with brown liquid, and she quivers at a faster rate.

I shower her, I cloud her, I send a fine spray down upon her. She breathes. The more tiny bits of our being she breathes, the more her jagged edges smooth out into the round edges of petals.

The brown liquid evaporates, and she is open again. I hum to her. She hums back!

There, there, sweet one. You are one of us.

We bask.

PuraaNam forgets their beauty, these naked ones, particularly the beauty of their sounds, which alone can move more earth and water than a single one of us.

Chapter 29

Lost

May 17 to 23, 1990

Wound in dirty sheets, Logan lay in the dark, wedged into the crack where the sloped ceiling met the wall. He didn't know how he got from the jail to his house. His brain was muddled, and he had ended up here, exhausted.

A night passed, a morning, another night, perhaps, he wasn't sure, because all that rolled through his head were film clips on an endless loop: his father's body pitching over, a close-up of his neck, the pulse beating under a tent of pink skin. Logan thrashed onto his stomach to shake off the loop, but it never stopped playing, and the sheets only tangled tighter, his father's body pressed down into the mud. Logan torqued his body onto his back, trying to dislodge the image. Had his father been struck on the head and died instantly? Or did he fight, inhale mud, and choke on grit until his consciousness dimmed? Had his last minutes been panic? Hopelessness? Horror? Logan twisted away from the wall and curled into a ball, grasping his head as if to physically pull the thoughts from it.

But he couldn't have seen his father's neck from that distance, through the rain, in the cab, under his collar. Even through binoculars. Nevertheless, it was the brightest part of the memory, that dogged pulse pushing up that warm skin, insisting on life, again, and again, and again.

When he pulled himself out of bed, he wobbled dizzily down the dark hall to the bathroom.

The phone in the downstairs hall rang. The answering machine picked up. "Logan, it's your mother," a voice spoke tentatively. "I saw your name in the paper. When did you get back?"

Logan cursed and his stream of piss drowned out her voice. He went back to bed.

The funeral two years ago had been a blur. He knew he had been cruel to her. He heard himself saying something, he didn't remember what, but he'd physically pushed her away. The look of love on her face turned quickly to hurt, then to blankness. She walked away. That was what he wanted, but he couldn't forgive her for it.

And now Zeff was pounding on the door.

As painful as being shut in with all these thoughts was, having others bring him to the present only made it worse, so he didn't answer. Uncountable days later, Zeff was back. He broke into the house, the little bastard, and came up to his room, hauled him out of bed, and talked to him. Made him eat a few things. But Logan couldn't deal. He stared at Zeff, deaf and mute, and Zeff finally turned away sadly and walked out of the house.

A few other friends knocked. He didn't answer. He was lost in the past.

After the funeral, Logan was unable to cope with the house. The press of all the objects, so many tools and knick-knacks that had meaning when his father was alive, now just clutter. Like all that shit at a flea market.

Why had he returned, now? He hadn't wanted to get sucked back into the tangle of short-lived victories and relentless loss.

At first being home was okay. He had stayed cool. But next thing he knew, he was making love to a total stranger, literally sleeping with the enemy, feeling feelings again. Then, just a few demonstrations later, he was trying to strangle a logger. Then jail. The cool had given way to rage, which had given way to mud. Mud in his veins. Mud everywhere.

One morning, though, sunlight crept through the fog onto the ceiling, and he realized he had been in bed so long his backside hurt. He looked at the clock, it was seven a.m. He rose.

He pissed in the darkness of the bathroom, which stank of urine, and he wandered down the narrow staircase, through the cluttered kitchen, out the back door to the shed. He should sort some of the tools, sell them, give them away at least. Not let them rust to hell. He stood among the boxes and picked up a chainsaw. The chain was fused with rust. The moisture in the air was doing the same to him. He dropped the tool and sat down, his head heavy in his hands. He didn't know how long he sat there, but the fog burned off, and his armpits began to sweat.

When he heard the car pull up, he hurried into the kitchen, pulled the curtains, and locked the back door. The person knocked at the front door, and as she walked around the side of the house past the curtained kitchen window, he saw it was Diana.

"Logan?" She called and knocked on the back door. He crouched at the kitchen table, not breathing. Her calling and knocking went on for a long time. Her voice tore him in different directions. He had to physically plug his ears and hold his breath because each knock was like a fist to the chest.

Finally, silence. Blessed silence.

An alien feeling stirred in his stomach. What was it?

Hunger, possibly. Dulled.

He opened a can of beans and ate a forkful straight from the can. At first, it was just weird rubbery stuff on a dry tongue. But then—as if his body suddenly remembered what food was, saliva squirted into his mouth and his forkfuls picked up pace until the can was empty. He threw it into the sink, pushed his hair back from his brow, and straightened up. He felt a little better. His mind was blank. Another blessing. He might be able to go on.

A breeze found its way into the house through a crack, the woody-citrus scent of redwoods with a touch of earth.

Diana was gone, so he unlocked the kitchen door, stepped outside, and stood awhile in the sunlight, blinking. The trees undulated in the breeze, clouds of green, revolving, dancing, filling his brain, replacing the images and words with nothing but green beckoning. They had never hurt him. He followed.

As soon as he stepped into the woods, the temperature dropped ten degrees, and his energy smoothed. Fern, sorrel, fallen logs, squirrels, and soaring columns pulled his eyes from one thing to another as he walked, like a dance, mesmerizing him, cleaning him out. The morass of human feelings melted away as one foot followed the other over the springy ground, thudding softly like the pulse of his own heart. Unthinkingly, he found his way to his tree. Their tree.

The first thing he saw was Diana's face growing out of the trunk, eyes closed, hawkish nose, arms and legs melded with the roots as if she had been partially absorbed by Uuma. But when he stepped out from behind the fern, she was whole, sitting at the base of the tree, face upturned, spirit as smooth as her closed eyelids.

When she opened her eyes, there was no going back, no backing out, no question. He reached out to her, she jumped up wordlessly, and they hugged, melding from head to foot, warm and right as loam.

Chapter 30

Bomb

May 23, 1990

The landscape between Ukiah and Oakland was brown and scrubby, and more dominated by suburban sprawl than Arcata. The vineyards had just started to bud along the grapevine trunks, all neatly wired in rows that cascaded over the hills. Rocks, sheds, telephone poles, and the occasional yucca speckled the highway.

Judi had spent the night with Darryl in his cluttered geodesic dome, more hut than house, warmed by a tiny wood stove and down sleeping bags. In the morning, they huddled over coffee warmed on a propane camp stove. His hut was even smaller than her shack. Judi's girls, aged nine and five, were staying with their father in his much larger home.

After a short conference with organizers in Ukiah, they set out in her white Subaru for the combination rally-concert at the University of California at Santa Cruz, one of their many recruitment efforts for Redwood Summer. On their way, they stopped for a meeting with Seeds for Peace, headquartered in a gray bungalow on stilts in Berkeley. Then they headed to Oakland for dinner with more friends and fellow activists, Luke and Zoe.

Judi was cranky because of an argument with her ex-husband over who was going to take care of their daughters, the same argument that led to their divorce.

"I told him about these plans weeks ago. He wasn't listening, as usual."

"I know," Darryl said.

"You could have handled this event yourself," she added, checking the rearview mirror as she changed lanes.

"A promise is a promise," Darryl said with forced cheerfulness.

"Here we go again. It's just a better division of labor if you do the college visits and I do the meetings."

"You see me as a liability," he said matter of factly.

"I never said that—but those monkey-wrenching manuals you and Dave published don't help us any. Honestly, it's just about time management."

"You're not the leader, Judi."

"I know that. Don't you think I know that? I'm just the one who does most of the work."

"Oh, fuck you," Darryl said. "I work as hard as anybody."

"Look, we've been over this. I'm here, aren't I? Let's just do this and have a good time."

"Okay by me," Darryl said with a sigh, looking out the window.

The official stance of Earth First! was that there was no leader. They were individuals united by a cause. But Judi and Darryl did so much of the actual phone calling, flyer hanging, and meetings to coordinate Redwood Summer, that they were the de facto leaders. Judi's organizing skills had been honed when she became a labor organizer at the grocery store chain where she worked after she dropped out of college. Later she organized a wildcat strike at the US Postal Service in DC.

Zoe and Luke lived in a brown clapboard Cape Cod. It was modest, yet solidly middle class, and at least four times the size of both Judi's and Darryl's house, not that Judi and Darryl judged them. It made large gatherings possible. It took all kinds. The plan was to caravan with them and a few others the next day to the rally at UC Santa Cruz.

It was a festive potluck. Luke had made his famous wheat berry salad with humanely raised chicken, while other guests supplied grilled tofu and crusty bread. Judi brought goat milk cheese from her favorite organic farm in Ukiah, and Zoe made blueberry cobbler from frozen berries she'd handpicked last summer. Local wine flowed, cannabis billowed, and laughter bounced by turns softly and riotously around their tapestried living room, buffeting everyone with good vibes.

The next morning, after coffee (fair trade only) and breakfast, they all set out for UC Santa Cruz. Zoe and Luke drove ahead with the others, while Judi and Darryl followed. Judi's white Subaru was filled with musical instruments, flyers, speakers, and speaker wire. They crept along slowly, getting ready to merge onto the highway. Luke turned right onto the entrance ramp, and Judi turned the wheel to follow, but the car wouldn't obey.

"What the fuck?"

She tapped the breaks. Nothing. She stomped on the breaks. A blast rocked the car and ripped through Judi's pelvis. The shock wave of sound bashed through them as powerful as the explosive, and car parts whizzed in every direction. The pain was instant. Darryl hit the dashboard and bounced back, thinking, "Not again," because they'd been deliberately rear-ended only two weeks ago by a logging truck. But the high-pitched ringing that filled his ears and the blue-gray smoke that filled the car with sulfur and other chemicals was not normal.

With the cold logic that frequently accompanies trauma, Judi knew her back was broken, that she was paralyzed, and that she was dying. Pain thrashed her body, while waves of nausea pulsed like sewer gas. Peculiar animal moans came to her through the smoke, a muffled sound she didn't recognize. Then, she realized it was her, and the rhythm of the moans wasn't so much an expression of pain as they were the oars she was using to pull herself through the pain, from one second to the next, and the next, and the next. There was so much smoke she couldn't see anything, but she heard Darryl asking as if underwater, "What happened?" and she or someone else from the outside, cried, "It's a bomb."

Darryl said, "I love you, Judi. You're gonna live." The car rolled slowly down the street with them still in it. An oncoming truck swerved out of the way, and a woman screamed on a crosswalk before the Subaru scraped along the sides of a few parked cars and came to a halt at the curb in front of a school. Time passed disjointedly, like static between two radio stations. A pleasant numbness had begun to creep over her when police, FBI, and emergency workers showed up.

"What is your name?" she made out through the static.

"Judi," she muttered. She was unsure where her body ended and the car began. She felt like the Scarecrow in the Wizard of Oz after the monkey attack, all head and legs. No middle. That cracked her up and she started coughing.

"Okay, Judi, we're gonna get you out of the car and get you to a hospital, okay?"

Darryl got out of the car, blood gushing down over his left eye, yelling, "They tried to kill us," to the bystanders. When he saw the FBI, he said to onlookers, "My name is Darryl Cherney. Write it down. They're going to disappear us." Once the EMT workers patched up his eye, the police led him away in handcuffs.

Vaguely, Judi heard the hum of the motor of the "jaws of life" as it cut through the mangled door to extract her from the wreck.

Hands grasped her body and pulled, igniting the pain all over. She screamed. Something was strapped over her face. Dimly, she knew they were lifting her into the back of an ambulance. Then she lost consciousness.

She woke up in the hospital, staring groggily at two police officers, one male, and one female.

"Judi Bari," they said, "you're under arrest for illegally transporting explosives."

Chapter 31

Emergency

May 24, 1990

P re-dawn light curved around the horizon and cast the world in its image, soft-edged, ephemeral. High in their tree platform, Diana slept. Logan lay, propped on one elbow, studying her profile, a pale mountain range against the tree-tasseled horizon. He loved the bump in her nose. Feeling his gaze, she awoke and smiled, and something inside him broke and bloomed at the same time. They kissed.

Diana took in the fresh air, the lemon-earth scent, the dampness, the slight sway of being so high in the tree. "Have you named this tree?" she asked.

"Why do you ask?"

"I noticed a lot of people named the trees, and the groves all have names."

"Greg King decided we should name all the groves, to get people to connect with them, invest in them emotionally."

"So have you?"

Logan smiled, "Uuma."

"Uuma. That's beautiful. How did you come up with it?"

Logan looked up at the top of the tree. "I don't know. It just came to me after a while."

"What does it mean?"

"Well, that's the odd part. I looked it up. Turns out it means friend in Sanskrit."

"That made my spine tingle."

Logan smiled.

"Well, thank you, Uuma, for all that you have given us, but especially for bringing Logan and me together."

"Yes, thank you," he said looking up at Uuma's crown.

"I'm starved!" Diana said, suddenly. "Do you have any food at the house?"

"Nothing edible."

"Let's go into town for breakfast!" she said.

An hour later, they were sitting down at Beanheads with other Arcatans, luxuriating in hot coffee and bagel breakfast sandwiches, when Zeff burst through the door. "I've been looking all over for you! They're back in the grove, and they're cutting. Again!"

"Shit. It never stops. It just never fucking stops," Logan said.

"What about the survey?" said Diana.

"Apparently they filed it, and now they're cutting as fast as possible before anyone can appeal it."

"Pacific Lumber is fucking ruthless, and Atlas Jamison is a heartless prick—oh. I'm sorry," Zeff said, suddenly remembering who Diana was.

"I didn't want to believe it of him, but—" she said.

"And did you hear about the bomb?" Zeff said.

Diana's neck and back prickled like it was being stung by nettles. "Bomb?"

"Judi Bari. Early this morning. She's still in critical care. Someone put a pipe bomb under her seat."

"My God," Diana said.

"But Greg King and the others are leading the protest. Jessica has activated the phone tree, and people are already there, forming barricades across Fisher Road. We need all hands on deck. Especially tree climbers."

The nettle pricks along Diana's back turned to fire, and she jumped up. "I'll go find my goddamned father and meet you there."

"Deal. Fisher Road. You won't be able to miss us," Zeff flashed her a brilliant warrior's grin.

Logan left with Zeff.

Diana jumped into her jeep and raced for the Ingomar Club in Eureka, only ten minutes away, and on the way to the Grove.

Chapter 32

Over the Line

May 24, 1990

He wasn't at the Ingomar Club, but she compelled the startled front desk clerk to allow her to use the phone. He was at the Scotia headquarters. She drove like a banshee and burst through the double doors. "I'm Diana Jamison, and I'm here to see my father," she said, slapping her license down on the wood counter in front of the security guard on duty.

He looked at her skeptically, but when he read her name, he relaxed.

"I'll just call—"

"Don't bother." She bounded down the hall to her father's office.

"Dad! What the fuck?" she said, skidding to a stop in front of him. Her heart slammed against her breastbone painfully, as she panted to catch her breath.

His look of alarm was immediately replaced by lightly narrowed eyes. "Keep it down," he said, rising from his glossy desk to close the door behind her.

"How could you?!"

"Girl, if you want to get anywhere with me, you'll have to conduct yourself—"

"I don't give a flying fuck about what you—"

"I will not tolerate—" He drew himself up to his full height of six three.

"PL is going after the Grove of the Ancients. You promised to stop."

"Did you honestly think I was going to mothball all the logging shows?"

Diana quelled her breath and drew up all her power. "At least the old-growth!"

"This is none of your business."

"It's everyone's business! The Endangered Species Act is law!"

Atlas stepped close to her and spoke with quiet fury: "We filed the goddamned study. I'll be damned if I let the government, let alone a bunch of pot-smoking criminals tell me what to do. I especially don't intend to be lectured by my own daughter."

"That's all it is for you, ego. Money and ego. Mom expected more of you than—"

Atlas grabbed her arm. "That's enough!" He squeezed his nails into her arm, his voice like a serrated knife. "You will conduct yourself with respect, or I'll have you arrested just like the rest of them!"

The crown of Diana's head turned to ice. "Take your hand off me! Take your fucking hand off me!"

The security guard knocked and opened the office door without waiting for an answer. "Sir?"

"If you don't stop them, I fucking will!" Diana said as she yanked her arm from his grasp. She pushed past the guard and raced out of the building.

Atlas was used to being hated. People hated the rich, the successful. Of course, they were just jealous. But this was getting under his skin in a way he didn't understand. So much fuss about trees! And they wouldn't give up. Every time he turned around, he was slapped with another injunction. And the newspapers loved to go on and on about how he was a Wall Street outsider, a hedge fund operator, a raider, the perfect villain. They made much of how saintly Pacific Lumber had been before him, taking care of their workers, cutting sustainably. It was a lie. They were an international corporation and they'd done clearcuts aplenty. They'd just gotten old and out of shape.

But this, his own daughter coming at him like a filthy, screaming animal. He was bitterly disappointed. He thought she'd come to her senses. Instead, she was hanging around with that lowlife Logan Blackburn who was probably revenge-fucking his daughter. He winced. He wanted that mongrel to suffer.

Chapter 33

A Fight to the Death

May 24, 1990

As they drove to the site, Zeff filled Logan in on Judi and Darryl. The FBI had shown up to the accident within ten minutes.

"Must be some kind of record," Logan said.

"It was almost like they were waiting around the corner with their ears plugged."

"So, you think the FBI did it?" Logan asked.

"Or Pacific Lumber."

An electric current buzzed down Logan's spine. An ancient, dark, and relentless force rose in response. As they bumped along the winding roads into the woods, he leaned his head out the window and looked up at the trees, their lemon-earth scent filling his lungs. "Whatever the cost," echoed in his head, and he gave himself over to the thought utterly. It didn't matter if he lived or died.

They arrived to chaos. Protesters parked their cars every which way across the road at the entrance of the Grove of the Ancients. A handful of overweight security guards in wrap-around shades paraded with rifles, fighting back a crowd of sixty protesters chanting "Earth first! Profits Last!" and "Hey, hey, ho, ho, Pacific Lumber has got to go!" Signs on sticks reading "Save our Trees" and "Stop Sacrificing Virgins" bobbed over the crowd.

Meanwhile, a couple of D-10 Cats roared along, scoring new paths between the trees under the direction of Harry Stanton and Eddie Cox, who communicated by walkie-talkies, and creating a barrier between the tree fellers and the protesters. Diesel fumes and burnt oil clouded the forest air and hot spikes of sun tore through the forest cool where two trees had already been felled. Two loading-trucks idled on the road and a third was being loaded. One dozer was ramming Zeff's tree, with Kev and Moon in it. They had roped themselves to the trunk determined to go down with the tree if necessary, but they screamed in spite of themselves.

Zeff and Logan joined the crowd and took up the chant, the crowd developing a single mind.

"I don't see Jessica," Logan said, looking around.

"She went straight to the judge's house to see if he would issue a stay order. Should be here soon."

The dozer rammed the tree again and Kev and Moon locked hands as Arcadia trembled with the shock. Protesters from the ground screamed, "You're gonna kill them."

Logan scanned the grounds and spied another dozer. Zeff followed his gaze.

"You thinking what I'm thinking?" Zeff said. Logan nodded and they took off. They scaled the beast from behind, and while Zeff distracted the driver, Logan yanked him out and tossed him clear of the treads. Then he slipped into the seat, grabbed the controls and fired it up. Zeff rode outside the cab hanging on with one hand, raising his other fist high, and howling like a wolf. Logan steered the dozer to intercept the one ramming the tree. Others looked on and cheered.

Chapter 34

Fall

May 24, 1990

D iana came tearing up the road and screeched to a halt. She jumped out of the car and scanned the scene. Locating Harry Stanton next to the equipment shed, she raced toward him.

A thunderous collision distracted her. One dozer had smashed sideways into another. Smoke billowed, shouting escalated, and Logan stood atop his dozer, fists raised to congratulatory cheers.

"Goddamn it," Stanton yelled. He motioned to a security guard standing next to him. "Get that bastard, now!"

Eddie, out from the redwood-sided office trailer, put down the CB radio mic.

Logan, sensing Diana's presence from afar, looked across the crowd at Stanton, and found her effortlessly. Even at that distance, their eyes locked. Diana raised a fist to him and grinned wildly. He grinned back. He looked beyond her, and his expression changed instantly to alarm.

"Call your men off," she told Stanton as commandingly as she could muster. A security guard, face impassive, eyes obscured by sunglasses, stepped between them. "You're trespassing. Back off."

"I'm Diana Jamison and you work for me. Get out of my way."

The guard glanced back at Stanton, and she pushed past him.

Behind Stanton, the crane arm of a loader dropped a grappling hook over a 1,000-year-old felled tree the girth of a trailer. Two men on either side secured the hooks and chains in place.

Sirens screamed in the background, reaching a fevered pitch as two police cars careened to a stop behind the chanting crowd, lights flashing.

"Stop this! I order you to stop," Diana yelled over the roar.

"Get out of my face, little girl," Stanton said.

"Who do you think you're talking to?! This is my company, too. I'm ordering you to stop all the cutting, *now!*"

"Your orders don't mean a tinker's damn," he yelled.

The grappler hook rose, slowly pulling the huge tree trunk into the air fifteen feet behind Diana.

Logan jumped off the D-10 and ran toward Diana shouting. But she couldn't hear him in all the noise. A security guard stepped in Logan's way.

Diana shoved Stanton in the chest with both hands. He fell back only a few inches, and in a moment of rage, grabbed her under the armpits and tossed her back like a small log. Diana hit the ground and rolled while Logan rammed the guard to the ground. Diana sprang up like a panther ready to re-engage. As she reached the zenith of her jump, she looked left. The cross-cut of the oncoming log, its rings beaded with sap, filled up her vision. She knew instantly it was inescapable. Time slowed. This was the end. In the silence of the log's approach, in that very long instant, she split, and one part of her was amazed that she had no fear. The other part felt sad for Logan and, a nanosecond later, her father. She turned her head to find Logan, her fine hair slicing the air like stalks of wheat, and she caught his eyes as he lunged toward her. When their eyes met, she whispered, "I'm sorry."

Real-time commenced abruptly. The sounds of the present jarred back to life.

"Diana!" Logan screamed.

The log hit her in the head and knocked her body out of the way as it rose in the air. Onlookers screamed and ran toward her fallen figure. Logan reached her, turned her over, and hugged her limp body to his chest. All anyone could see was her silky hair escaping between his grasping fingers, covering the real damage.

Eddie grabbed Stanton by the elbow. "Come with me." They both moved away from the scene toward the road to intercept the oncoming policemen.

Zeff, still on the dozer, saw it all. Over Logan's head, he could see the police talking to Cox and Stanton. Cox was pointing back and forth between Logan, the dozer, and the air-borne log.

"The crowd was getting out of control," said Cox, "and that guy came at Diana Jamison and pushed her. Isn't that right, Harry?" Cox said.

"That's right. She's the daughter of the boss, and I guess he thought she was in charge, and he just pushed her into the path of the oncoming log."

Zeff pushed his way through the crowd as fast as he could. The police nodded, radioed for backup, unclipped their guns, and headed for Logan, whose face was buried in Diana's hair. Zeff dashed to Logan and grabbed him by the shoulders. "Come on, man, we've gotta go."

"Leave me alone. Just leave me alone," Logan shouted.

"Come *on*, man. It'll be their word against yours. We've gotta *go*, and we've gotta go *now*," he yanked at Logan.

"Everyone stand back," said one of the officers. "Give us some room." The crowd made way for the police, "You there," he said coming up behind Logan. "Stay where you are and put your hands up."

Zeff yanked Logan up by the collar and wrenched him into the crowd who instinctively opened for them and then closed behind them, blocking the officers' path.

"Clear the way!" the officers yelled, to no effect.

Logan stumbled along beside Zeff like a three-legged dog, barely able to find his feet, pushing himself up with his hands when he fell, and Zeff, hand still on his collar, steered him toward six-foot ferns at the edge of a ravine, and they tumbled and slid down it, out of sight.

Chapter 35

On the Run

May 24, 1990

A few minutes later, in the thick of the woods, out of the earshot of the rally, Logan paced and panted. "This can't be happening. This can't be happening."

"I know, I know, I can't believe it, was she really—?" Zeff said, his large eyes, now larger, and shining with tears.

"I don't know. I don't *know*. There was so much blood, I couldn't see her face, but—when I held her—when I held—it was—she was so —still, so—empty."

"Maybe she'll be okay—"

Logan grabbed his head in both hands "I never should have—"

"It wasn't your fault, man. Pacific Lumber, man. That guy *pushed* her!"

"But if I had—"

"Logan, Logan. Don't do this to yourself. They're fucking *murderers*. First Judi, now *this?*"

As a new wave of reality staggered Logan, he nearly fell. Instead, he grabbed a branch and beat the tree with it, putting his entire body into each swing. Zeff moved to stop him. "Logan, don't. They'll hear us."

Logan grabbed Zeff with both hands and slammed him up against the tree, staring into the face of Atlas Jamison.

"*Dude... It's me.*"

Logan released him with an apologetic hand gesture and began pacing and mumbling to himself. The sound of two men crashing through the woods reached them. Zeff gestured to be quiet and they both listened, then dropped soundlessly into a cavity under a fallen redwood log.

"This is Robert Blackburn's kid, right?" said one of the policemen.

"Yeah. And the likelihood of finding him out here is about as good as finding one of those marbled murrelets," said the other.

The first policeman stumbled and cursed. "His old man was a real nut-case. Getting himself killed over a few trees."

Hearing that, Logan jerked as if to leap out, but Zeff clapped his hand down on his shoulder and gestured silence.

"So, it was vengeance?" asked the second.

"No doubt. They get all upset about the life of a tree, but fuck humans," said the first.

"You think she's dead?"

"I don't see how she could have survived a blow like that."

"Did they take her to Fortuna or Eureka?"

"Fortuna."

They walked out of earshot. Zeff continued to hold Logan until he was sure they were gone, then he let Logan go. Logan's face hardened to a metal mask, and he sprang from the hole.

"I've got to see her."

"What. *Now?*"

"Yes, now. What if she's alive?"

"You're crazy. You can't go anywhere near her. They'll spot you in a heartbeat."

"No, they won't." Logan pulled a buck knife out of his belt, leaned over, and began hacking his hair off. It fell to the forest floor in hanks.

Chapter 36

Reckoning

May 24, 1990

Sitting in the back of his Range Rover, Atlas Jamison checked the car's mobile phone again. No reception. He tapped the heavy receiver to see if it was broken. He'd gotten a call that the protest at the cutting site was getting out of hand, but the damn road was so twisty it was taking forever to get there. Now, as they neared the site, there was a slowdown. The police had orange cones out and were directing traffic to the left. The already narrow road was down to one lane, and they had stopped moving. Atlas tapped on the glass

"What's the hold-up?" he asked the driver.

"Not sure, sir."

Atlas glanced impatiently through the front windshield, seeing the bumper stickers on the battered car in front of him, "EPIC" and "InterTribal Sinkyone Wilderness Council." He vaguely recognized the car of the woman who'd served him the first stay order. The police waved them further to the side of the road. Atlas's driver eased them onto the slanted shoulder to make way for an ambulance heading back toward town. That wasn't a good sign. Atlas sighed. The whole Pacific Lumber takeover was turning out to be a big mistake. He'd never encountered this much resistance before. Such a mess. But the only way out was through.

Jessica, Atlas, and his driver all looked over their shoulders as it passed. After it passed, an officer approached Jessica's car. She rolled down the window, and Atlas saw the police lean in, talk to her, and then gesture that she should turn around. Atlas looked at his watch impatiently as she made the three-point turn and headed back toward town. The officer approached and Atlas lowered his window.

"Sir, you'll have to turn around—" As soon as he recognized Atlas, he paled.

"What seems to be the problem, officer?" Atlas asked.

"There's been an accident, sir. I'll radio you ahead." He pulled out a walkie-talkie and spoke into it, then waved Atlas past the other cars that had been pulled over.

By the time Atlas's driver pulled onto the site and parked, the scene was eerily silent. All the machinery had been cut dead, and the protesters, cordoned off by the police with caution tape, sat and knelt on the ground, oddly subdued while the police questioned them a few at a time.

Next to a log on the ground under a crane, Eddie and Stanton bent their heads together.

As Atlas approached, he overheard Eddie. "All you have to do is stick to the statement you gave the police."

Stanton rubbed his eyes, his shoulders slumping. "Okay. Right."

"This may work out very well for us. The law will be all over the protesters. With the right publicity—"

"Cox! Stanton! What the hell is going on?" Atlas cut in.

"Mr. Jamison, sir. Uh. There's been an accident."

"I see that. What happened?"

Stanton spoke slowly as if feeling his way forward through the dark, avoiding eye contact with Atlas. "The crowd got out of control. One of the protesters pushed her into the path of the loader. She was hit."

"Pushed who?" Atlas asked, ice talons gripping the back of his neck.

"Your," Stanton hesitated, "daughter, sir."

"My daughter," Atlas' voice hushed.

"It was that kid, Logan Blackburn," Eddie spoke quickly.

"Is she alright? Where is she?"

"On the way to the hospital, in an ambulance."

Atlas swiveled and yelled at the driver. "Turn the car around! Cox, you're coming with me. Stanton, button up this operation. Nothing else happens here until we talk. Understood?"

"Yes, sir."

Minutes later, as they raced down the dirt road toward the hospital in Fortuna, Jamison said, "Tell me exactly what happened."

"Well, like we said," Cox's normally pale eyes burned oddly bright, "the crowd was getting out of control, and your daughter was trying to talk to them."

"To the protesters?" Atlas' eyes narrowed. "Or the loggers?"

"The protesters. She was trying to back them off."

Atlas's eyes went dead. "Go on."

"And this kid, Logan Blackburn, broke out of the crowd and shoved her right into the path of the loader."

"He did this on purpose?"

"Definitely."

"How badly was she hurt?"

"I don't know, sir," Eddie said, looking at the carpeted floor of the car.

"Well, who the hell told you to go ahead with the cut, anyway?"

"We finished the study, and the judge okayed it."

"I never gave you or Harry the go-ahead."

"He and I have been handling things out here for a while without you. What's changed?"

"What's changed is that I'm here now, and my daughter is involved."

"Sir. I'm sure she'll be all right."

Atlas fell silent. His dark reflection in the tinted window looked back at him, distorted.

"Look, sir. This is the situation. It's not good, but it's what's happened. So maybe we should see if there's a way to turn it to our advantage."

Reflexively, Atlas backhanded Eddie in the face, then grabbed him by the collar.

"My daughter is on the way to the hospital, and you think this could work to our advantage?"

Eddie spluttered, fingering his lip with one hand, looking for blood, pulling on Atlas's hand at his collar with the other. "I just meant—"

"Stop the car," Atlas yelled to the driver over his shoulder, then back at Eddie: "Pack your bags."

The car stopped, and Atlas reached across Eddie, opened the door, and shoved him out. "You're done here!"

Eddie stumbled in the loose dirt on the shoulder of the road, straightening his jacket in the wake of the car's exhaust as it sped off. Shock turned to rage turned to cold satisfaction. He'd get his revenge. He had already found another company to buy up another few percentages of PL stock and hold it for him. He was a little less than a half a percent away, and he had been talking to another board member who was about ready to come along. Like Jamison had done, he was keeping his ownership under the five percent that would trigger a Federal Trade Commission intervention to halt all sales until antitrust investigations could be conducted. Diana's injury would be bad press for PL, which would drive the stocks down. He'd call that board member the second he got home. With Jamison distracted, now would be the perfect time to make his move. Maybe even tomorrow, bright and early.

Chapter 37

Crazy Shit

May 24, 1990

Zeff and Logan had to wait for everyone to leave before they could backtrack to Zeff's '69 Dodge van, and from there it was a solid hour and a half to get to the hospital in Fortuna. Exhaustion overcame them both, and they drove in silence, muffled by the roar of the van's engine, which was situated in the front.

Zeff pulled up to the loading dock at the rear of the hospital and parked behind a dumpster.

"I gotta tell you, man, I think this is crazy. There's bound to be cops all over the place, and they think you did this."

"I'll get in."

"Yeah, but can you get out?"

"Just wait for me, here."

Logan climbed out of the van and entered the hospital via the loading dock. At the end of a long, linoleum-tiled hallway, he ducked into a utility room stashed with scrubs for custodians. He put one on and pushed a cleaning cart in front of him heading for the emergency room waiting area. Atlas Jamison sat forward on the edge of one of the blue chairs, elbows on knees, head in hands, staring at the floor. Logan emptied the trash and pushed the cart through the doors into the emergency area, keeping his head down. He pulled out a spray bottle and cloth and began cleaning the door lights slowly, his back to Jamison.

A tired doctor came down the hall toward Logan and walked

through the doors to Jamison. Jamison looked up, and from where
Logan stood, he could see the doctor shaking his head, and Jamison's
chest collapsing inward for a second before he caught himself. Logan
exhaled, his breath smelling like ammonia. His head spun and he
grabbed the edge of the door to steady himself. He couldn't
remember the last time he'd eaten or had water. Time had gone into a
slow backward eddy like a sharp turn in a river.

Jamison stood up and followed the doctor back through the doors.
Logan ducked to replace the window cleaner in the cart and then
followed at a discreet distance.

"I'm very sorry," he overheard the doctor say. "There was nothing
we could do. She never regained consciousness. Rest assured that she
suffered no pain."

They paused outside a private room.

"Can I see her?"

"Of course," the doctor said, opening the doors to the room.

"I'd like some time alone with her."

"Take all the time you need. If you have any more questions,
here's my private number," said the doctor, handing him a card.

"Thank you."

Logan waited until the doctor was out of sight, grabbed a huge
laundry bin, and pushed it up to the door of the room Jamison disappeared into. Glancing through the windows, he saw Jamison leaning
over a covered figure, his own body obscuring the face. Jamison held
her hand up to his lips, head bowed. Logan's mind went cold,
mechanical, hyper-logical. He grabbed a towel from the laundry bin,
bunched a sheet under his arm, and pushed through the door.

Without turning around, Jamison snapped, "I told you. I want to
be alone."

"Oh, you're gonna be alone, alright," Logan said slowly. "Very
alone."

Jamison, hearing the hostility in the speaker's tone, turned to
see a custodian, but in a nano-second recognized Logan. The
instant Logan saw recognition in his eyes, he closed the distance

between them, body-slammed him against the wall, forearm pressed against his throat, and shoved the towel into his mouth. Jamison struggled, but couldn't break Logan's maniacally strong grip, and within minutes, deprived of oxygen, lost consciousness. Logan threw the sheet over Jamison and dropped him into the laundry bin, careful to keep his eyes averted from the bed. Panting and shaking, he covered Jamison with a sheet, wiped the sweat from his face, and wheeled the cart down the hallway to the loading dock.

Zeff, meanwhile, had bitten his hangnails until they bled, keeping an eye out for Logan and making sure no one else saw them. He jumped when Logan burst through the doors pushing an overloaded laundry bin down the ramp. Zeff hurriedly exited the van.

"Open the door," Logan said.

"Holy shit, man," Zeff whispered-screamed, as he opened the doors. "Is that Diana?"

Logan didn't answer. The whites of his eyes showed around his pupils. He shoved the laundry bin up to the van doors and tipped it. Only half of Jamison's body tipped onto the van floor. Logan scrambled into the van over him and yanked him the rest of the way in.

"What did you do? What *the fuck* did you do?" Zeff said, recognizing Jamison, and scanning the parking lot for witnesses.

"Shut the fuck up and bring that bin back to the dock."

Zeff did as he was told as Logan climbed back out through the front seat and slammed the van doors closed.

"Let's go," Logan said.

Zeff ran to the driver's seat and Logan hopped into the front passenger seat.

"Where are we going?" Zeff asked as he backed the van around the dumpster and steered toward the parking lot exit.

"I don't know. Just drive north."

"Is he dead?"

"I don't know."

"You *don't know???*"

"Just give me a minute." Logan panted and rubbed his eyes with the palms of his hands.

"Oh, you crazy motherfucker. You crazy, crazy motherfucker."

"Take me to my Uncle Chester's place," Logan said, looking up through the windshield.

"What are you going to do?"

"I don't know. I just wanna give him a taste of his own medicine."

"Jesus, Logan. This is some *crazy* shit. We should bring him back to the hospital, leave him on the loading dock and call them. If they catch you, you're going away for life."

"What life? What fucking life?" Logan said, hitting the dashboard.

Zeff shut his mouth and kept his eyes on the road.

"Did you see her?"

Logan didn't answer, looking straight ahead. "I gotta secure him before he wakes up. You got rope or something?"

"My climbing gear, yeah. In the back."

Logan climbed into the back of the van, carefully bracing himself as Zeff rounded corners. He cut the rope into lengths with his knife and tied Jamison's hands and feet. He found a rag and gagged him.

"You got any drugs back here?"

"Yeah, man, back cabinet, weed, Benzos, and valium."

Logan found a thermos and shook it. "What's in this?" He opened and sniffed it.

"Just water, I think," Zeff said, looking at Logan in the rearview mirror.

Logan crushed three valiums, added them to the thermos, and gave it another shake. Jamison was on the floor in front of the bench seats. Logan propped him against the wall of the van so his head and shoulders were upright.

Jamison stirred and barely opened his eyes, then his eyes widened and he sat up and yelled, but his gag muffled the sound. He jerked at his ropes. Logan shoved him back against the wall of the van.

"Shut the fuck up. No one can hear you."

"I think I'm having a *heart* attack," Zeff said, clutching his chest.

Jamison collected himself and glared at Logan.

"Thirsty?"

Jamison nodded warily.

"If you promise not to scream, I'll take the gag out and give you a drink."

Jamison nodded again, and Logan untied the gag. He poured some water into the thermos cup and held it for Jamison, who drank.

"I don't know what you're planning to do," said Jamison, "but you can't get away with this. There will be a manhunt. If you let me go now—"

"Yeah, I've heard enough of you," Logan said and gagged him again.

It wasn't long before the drug took effect and Jamison started to nod out.

It was dark by the time Zeff pulled up to Logan's uncle's place, a grassy drive leading off into the woods past a donkey pasture. "Turn in here," Logan said as they approached a donkey stall.

Logan hopped out and reappeared with a harnessed donkey. Zeff joined Logan at the side door of the van, glancing around nervously. There was no traffic on this backroad and Logan's uncle's house was not in view.

"What are you going to do, man?" Zeff asked, searching Logan's face in the dark and getting no read.

"I don't know, but the less you know the better," Logan said, pulling Jamison out of the van and, with Zeff's automatic help, flipping him over the donkey's back. The donkey brayed in protest.

"Hey, no offense," Zeff said, "but I just can't have any more to do with this,"

"No offense taken, but as soon as they get wind that he's missing, the police will put out an APB on both of us."

"Yeah. Might be a good time for me to visit my aunt in L.A."

"Good plan. And if they do catch up to you, just say we got separated at the event and you haven't seen me since."

"What if someone saw my van at the hospital?"

"Say you were checking on—" Logan stopped, unable to say Diana's name. "Say you were looking for me."

"Logan, man. I feel like I should knock you to the ground, tie you up, stop you from *doing* this," Zeff's eyes turned down at the corners as he looked up at Logan.

Logan smiled cynically. "You couldn't if you tried. Just turn around and don't look back."

"But this is some serious shit. You can't kill the guy—I mean—he might deserve it but..."

"I won't kill him. But I don't give a shit about what happens to me or him. I have no future. The human race has no future. Nothing we do makes a damn bit of difference, so I might as well do what I want— and right now that's—"

"What?"

"I don't know. But you and me? We're done here," and he gave Zeff a gentle but dismissive push in the chest. He shouldered his backpack, hit the donkey's rump, and walked off into the darkness.

Chapter 38

Pacific Plots

May 24, 1990

S tanton had just gotten home and grabbed two beers when his phone rang.

"Hello, Mr. Stanton. This is Mr. Jamison's driver. I'm at the hospital."

"Yes?"

"Mr. Jamison went in about two hours ago. I inquired at the front desk, and no one knows where he went. I wasn't sure who to reach out to, because things went badly with Cox."

"What's the status of his daughter?"

"They're not saying, sir."

"I see," Stanton said, his voice dropping.

"I'm just not sure if I should wait for him or if I should go to the police."

"Hold on," Stanton said, thinking. "I'll call you back."

Stanton hung up and dialed Eddie Cox and filled him in on the situation.

"Really," Eddie said. "How interesting. Tell him to go home and that we'll look into it. If anyone asks, we'll say we heard he wanted to be alone for a few days. That may buy us the time we need to put the last pieces into place tomorrow. I've got to talk to my silent partner and we can make our move. By the time Jamison shows up, he won't be in charge of Pacific Lumber anymore."

"Sounds like a plan," Stanton said uneasily. He hung up and called the driver back.

"He probably just needs to be alone for a while. Go on home. I'll follow up. We'll call you if we need you."

"Very good, sir," said the driver and rang off.

Chapter 39

Ecology 101

May 25, 1990

A tlas awoke to a thick stream of urine spurting into the sky. The ground over his head was moving. When the hot urine vapor hit his nostrils, it woke him fully and brought with it the understanding that he was bundled face down across an animal's back. He groaned and tried to look around. The donkey stopped and someone flipped his feet over his back. He landed with a jolt face-up, staring up at the redwood forest canopy. Logan's jaggedly cropped head came into view, his face in shadow, and sunlight blazing around his head.

"Bahtrd," Atlas said through his gag. "Un hy ma."

"Having a little trouble with your diction, asshole?" said Logan.

"Mu-her fu-her."

"I'm gonna take this gag out of your mouth. If you scream, nobody's gonna hear, but it's really gonna piss me off."

Logan yanked the gag down around Atlas's neck.

"Help!" Atlas yelled.

Logan kicked him in his side. Atlas coughed and shut up. Logan turned the donkey around, took off the harness, and slapped its butt. It trotted back the way they had come.

Logan put his face close to Atlas's, and Atlas noticed how bloodshot his eyes were, the blue of them almost neon against the red, his lips chapped and flaking, his skin gray under the tan. His breath smelled like rotting meat. "We walk from here. Every time you hesi-

tate, I'm gonna hurt you. If you hesitate more, I'll hurt you more."
Atlas blinked reluctant assent. Logan yanked him to a sitting position,
tied a rope around his neck, and cut the ropes off his ankles. It was
dark and misty among the close trees.

Atlas's legs were stiff, so it took him more than one try to get to his
feet. No sooner had he achieved the standing position when Logan
yanked the rope around his neck and pulled him into the middle of a
wide, shallow stream. Atlas stumbled and fell to his knees, getting
doused. Logan turned and kicked him in the chest, knocking the
wind out of him. "Get up."

They splashed upstream in the shallow water. The stones were
slippery, and with his arms tied behind his back, Atlas couldn't maintain his balance. His city shoes were slick-soled, so he fell several
times, his face and arms taking the brunt of each fall. Logan would
stop and command him to get up each time, but in a robotic way. His
fire seemed to have cooled. Thirst filled Atlas's mind, made his mouth
dry, his lips sore. It was almost a relief to fall into the water, but he
wouldn't even consider drinking from it. Who knew what kind of dirt
was in it and what it would do to him? It was icy cold, and between
his wet clothes and chilled air, he had lost his vital warmth. The chill
crept into his core.

"I need water," he finally said. "And dry clothes."

His captor stopped and looked back at him for a long time as if
doing long division in his head, his face haggard.

Logan looked up at the trees, the land. He could care less if this
man died, but he didn't want him to die yet. He sloshed back to Atlas,
unzipped his backpack, pulled out a bottle of water, uncapped it, and
held it to Atlas's mouth. Atlas eyed him for a second and then took
the bottle in his mouth. Logan tipped it up. After he drank, Logan
helped him onto the bank, led him away from the stream, and tied
him to a tree. He retraced their steps, then walked backward, eyeing
the ground carefully, brushing twigs and branches back into place to
cover their tracks.

Logan said nothing, but from there on out, he kept Atlas on a shorter leash. They walked a long time in silence, bushwhacking off-trail, and then Logan began to talk, his words punctuated by silences as he searched the ground for the next root or log to step over, the next hole to avoid.

"For years, I've been trying to figure out what makes a guy like you tick. Is it phenomenal greed? Or are you too stupid to know the consequences of your actions?"

Atlas's foot punched through the crust of humus, and he fell to his knees. Thereafter, he tried to put his feet where Logan's had been.

"You've seen these forests. You can't be totally impervious to their presence. I mean, you can feel that, can't you?" Logan turned around and gestured to the giants towering over them, the weight of the silence all around them. "You've seen the clearcuts. So, it can only be that you're a greedy, motherfucking pig, right? *Right?*"

Atlas just glared at him. "I called my wife, you know. I told her I was waiting to see the doctors about Diana's condition. She'll wonder why I'm not following up." He was lying though. News had traveled fast that the boss's daughter was injured. She'd reached him by the mobile phone in the Rover. He'd told her to leave him alone for a few days. She was used to that, so she didn't fight it.

Logan turned around and kept walking.

"I mean, how much money does it take to fill a guy like you up? Do you have to cut down every single tree?"

They came to a huge fallen log, and Logan pushed Atlas onto it, then grabbed his legs and heaved. Atlas tumbled over the other side. Logan scrambled over and pulled Atlas to his feet, then took the lead again.

"What I just don't get is, after the first twenty or thirty million, what do you DO with all that money? I mean, doesn't the second and third yacht get boring? Is that what it is? Boredom? Or are you a junkie? Always looking for the next hit, and each time it's gotta be bigger?" Logan stopped and turned around. "Is that it? Huh? I'm asking you a question!" he shook Atlas.

Atlas swayed. He looked up at the trees blearily. Was this really happening? Was his daughter really dead? Was he really here in the woods with a madman? He shook his head to clear it. "You're not looking for answers. You've got them all."

"No, I really wanna know!"

Atlas searched himself. It all seemed so far away now. What was it? "I provide jobs. I stimulate the economy," he said, but even as he was speaking, he knew how hollow the words rang.

"Economy! In five years, this'll all be gone, and loggers'll be piping gas for a living. You'll be long gone too. Try again."

Altas searched Logan's face. With his hair cut jagged and the gray hue, he looked like a prisoner of war.

"Go on!" Logan said.

On any given day, he'd know the answer to that question, but today, after what happened, he had no idea.

"It's all about power, isn't it?" Logan said.

"I'm not going to explain myself to a—" as he paused to search for the word, two separate thoughts—that his daughter was dead, and that this man had killed her—collided, "a fucking murderer—you killed my—"

"No, motherfucker—" Logan grabbed him by his lapels, their faces inches apart. "*You* killed your daughter." Up close, Logan's contorted face and foam-flecked mouth didn't look human. "Was it worth it?"

Logan flipped Atlas around, pushing his face up against the rough bark of a redwood. "How many of these trees, how much life had to be destroyed to add eight zeroes to your bank account?"

"GET OFF ME!" Atlas yelled. Logan let go.

Atlas turned back toward Logan and slid to the ground. "You want to kill me. Fine. Kill me now. I'm not playing this game. This is as far as I go."

Logan pulled out his buck knife, and said with no emotion, "Glad to oblige."

Atlas's eyes fastened on the knife. Logan knocked him sideways to the ground, straddled him, smashed his right cheek into the ground and buried the knife into the earth inches from Atlas's eyes.

The knife filled his vision.

Logan carved out a circle of humus and popped it out of the ground.

"Ecology 101. It takes hundreds of years for this much topsoil to develop."

He broke apart a layer of soil revealing silvery-white threads.

"See these strands? Mycorrhizal fungi. It interfaces with the roots of the redwoods. A symbiotic relationship that is broken when D-8 Grapplers and D-10 Cats grind up the roots and compress the soil. It breaks the chain. No more redwoods. Got it?"

Atlas's eyes leapt to Logan's, letting him know he was listening.

"Now, Anatomy 101."

He grabbed a twig the diameter of a finger and snapped it. Then he grabbed Atlas's pinky and bent it backward. Jagged pain shot up Atlas's arm, leaving a sickening path of heat.

"This finger is going to break the same way that stick did. You start moving, or I demonstrate my point. And there are nine other points I can make."

Atlas nodded. Logan got off him and stood up. Atlas rolled over and struggled to his feet.

Uuma

More True Ones have fallen near PuraaNam. Dina has left her bark. Laghu! Kulaaya shudders with his energy. It buzzes like the thunderteeth the naked ones use. PuraaNam also buzzes. I do not contain their thought. Death is only a change of form. Dina has joined Atman. But Laghu swings out of balance, in a state of Vikriti. We hum to him. He does not answer.

Chapter 40

Shift

May 25, 1990

When Atlas stood up, his mind shut down. He stumbled after Logan like an automaton. But after what was either hours or interminable minutes, the trees grew brighter, in tiny increments, their silence louder, the space between them more palpable. Altas had never noticed how three-dimensional the trees were, how they occupied space front and back. He'd only ever seen them as a picture. Now, as he walked between them, he felt them differently. Under it all, he thought he heard a low thrumming, like an engine, or the echo of a highway, or waves, he wasn't sure. He was dizzy, and when a dark blue bird with a black crest flew in front of him, it left a trail of blue in the air behind it. He shook his head. He must be in shock. The jay landed on a branch above his head and squawked at him, a high piercing sound, like ungreased metal on metal. Other jays joined in, their harsh cries grating on his eardrums.

Further up the path, a chipmunk darted up the trunk of a tree, stopped, and eyed him. The blackness of the chipmunk's eyes pierced him.

They hiked steadily uphill in silence and Atlas's thirst grew unbearable. His head ached, his mouth was gummy, and his lips stuck to his teeth. His legs felt like inanimate stumps he had to drag forward. They crossed a creek, and the cool, sweet clarity of water sang to him like a siren. He dropped to his knees and leaned down to quench his thirst, awed by this liquid light. But just as his lips touched the water, a boot crashed down next to his head, stirring up mud, and Logan yanked him back by the rope.

"Nope. Not for you. Ichthyology 101. Salmon spawn here. They swim out to sea, but they always return to their place of birth. They fight their way upstream, lay their eggs in the sand, and die. Their death fertilizes the soil and starts the next generation. Raise the temperature of this water just one degree and you kill the whole cycle. That's exactly what happens when you cut close to the river. That's why you don't get any."

The sound of the water filled Atlas's ears as Logan yanked him away from it, and his hatred for Logan gave him a different kind of fuel.

When they came to a tree larger than all the rest, Logan stopped and put his hand on it. "The first time Diana and I hiked, I brought her here. At first, she was giving me all that crap you gave me about jobs, but when she saw this, she just knew. She changed. I didn't know a person could change like that. Most can't."

The sounds of the forest amplified in Atlas's mind, the creak of the trees swaying, the click and chatter of insects and animals. The ground was undulating and he was having a harder and harder time figuring out how to navigate. He paused and looked up to the top of the slope they'd been ascending. It was brighter up there. A figure was standing between two trees, the sun streaming around it. With a whip-like spin of flying hair, she was gone. "Diana?" he whispered.

"What did you say—what did you say?" Logan said quickly, urgently. He followed Atlas's gaze and searched the haze of sunlight at the top of the hill.

"Nothing," Atlas mumbled. Now the forest was bombarding him with sounds, chittering, tapping, humming, all pierced occasionally by the Steller's jay, and under that, a rushing, a shushing.

Logan turned away from him and continued their climb. Atlas waited until the rope went taut and stumbled onward.

"I hated showing Diana this. But I'm gonna love showing you."

They cleared the top of the ridge and the sun blazed as they walked out into the desolation of the clearcut. It was like stepping from a refrigerator into an oven. Stumps spread every which way threaded by tractor tread marks that crisscrossed like insanity itself.

"Welcome to hell," Logan said. "Diana wept when she saw this." He paused letting Atlas take it all in. "Did you make enough money off this cut? Is it worth never seeing your daughter again? Because this is what killed her."

Logan's words hit Atlas so hard that he couldn't breathe. With a guttural scream, he body-slammed Logan, knocking them both off their feet. They tumbled down the bank, rolling over each other and tangling in the rope, coming to rest at the foot of a stump with Atlas on top.

Atlas straddled Logan, but before he could balance himself, Logan jackknifed and head-butted him in the nose, knocking him unconscious.

Logan fell back to the ground, panting.

Chapter 41

Cox and Stanton

May 25, 1990. Earlier the Same Day

W hile Atlas was draped over the back of a donkey like a bag of
sand, Eddie was calling an emergency meeting with the PL
Board. Right before the meeting, scratching a mosquito bite on his
wrist until it bled, Eddie was firming things up on the phone with
Matthew Molten.

"Matthew, there has been a turn of events out here that requires
immediate action."

"How immediate?"

"Tomorrow morning."

"Will do. I'll transfer the shares as soon as the market opens
tomorrow."

"It's a pleasure doing business with you."

Jamison still hadn't turned up, and that was just fine with Cox.
The longer he was out of the picture, the better. When the news
leaked out that Diana was dead, it made national news, and Linda
Jamison had called. Cox assured her that Atlas needed to be left
alone, and she confessed that was his usual mode of operation when
things got bad. It had never been this bad, though, she said, and
should they report him as missing? No, no, Cox assured her. Atlas
just needed to lay low for a while. He promised her he'd find him and
give her a status update when he did.

Now he stood in the redwood paneled boardroom, a row of men

seated before him on each side of the conference table, his reflection shining in the table's glossy surface.

"Gentleman, no one has heard from Atlas Jamison for nearly 24 hours. Given the crisis, with the death of his daughter, the bad press, and the plummeting stock, as your vice president, I make a motion to take over as acting CEO until Mr. Jamison returns."

"I second the motion," Stanton said. "Any discussion?"

Silence.

"Has anyone heard from Mr. Jamison?" asked one board member.

More silence and some shaking of heads.

"Should we be worried?"

"Point of order," said another board member. "The motion on the table is whether to vote Mr. Cox in as acting CEO."

"He is the next in line, after all. And the constitution speaks to this," said one of the lawyers.

"I call the question," said Stanton. "Any objections?"

Silence and shaking of heads.

"All in favor?"

"Aye," the group said in unison.

Cox's heart hammered out his victory. "Next item on the agenda," he said.

"PL stock has plummeted from $50 a share to $45 since yesterday. I'm prepared to buy out anyone who wants to sell for $50 a share."

There was a general stir in the boardroom, and a few men murmured to their neighbors.

"This is not a hostile takeover. I think you can all agree that my management style is more in line with traditional Pacific Lumber values. There has been a lot of unrest among the workers and local activists since Jamison took over. He has brought the company nothing but bad press. He has sold off some of our diverse interests and has cashed out our worker's pension funds. Your vote to sell stocks to me and my silent partner will restore PL's reputation and value. I'll restore the pension fund, and that will calm the workers down."

There was a general murmur of approval.

"I move that we investigate this offer," said Stanton.

The board assented. By law, they had twenty days to decide.

As they left the building, Cox called Stanton aside. "Well done."

"You've got the funds lined up?" Stanton said.

"Do you seriously think I would have made that motion if I didn't? In the meantime, I want you to return to the job at lot 2-86 first thing tomorrow morning. Word is that EPIC is challenging our study and got a court in Sacramento to hear the case. So, get as many trees down as you can. Get ten crews up there. Just cut. Don't even bother to load them. Let's make a million dollars before lunch."

As they turned toward their cars, from behind the bushes, Zeff lowered his shot-gun mic and smiled grimly at Brian and Jim. "Get the word out. Pinko Commy Freaks to the rescue."

Chapter 42

Stake-Out

May 25, 1990

L ogan crouched by the creek and washed the blood off his hands and face. He was surprised at how easy it was to hurt another person. The person he had been most of his life had been turned off. He was a house of many rooms, and right now, he was living in the burnt-out wing no one used. In this place, he didn't have a problem with anything he'd done. Could it be this easy? The forest also seemed dead, the colors flat, the sounds random. It was the same as the corpse on the table at the hospital. Just a shell. He could never go back.

Atlas awoke to find himself lying on his back, spread-eagle, roasting in the blazing sun. His throat burned with thirst, and his whole body felt like it was going into organ failure leaving him awash in toxins. A turkey vulture the size of a German shepherd paced back and forth ten feet away from him. He stared at it bleary-eyed. He'd never seen anything so ugly in his life. He had no idea they were so large. The way its red wrinkled head hunched into a collar of black feathers like a boa was obscene. Its hooked beak had a boney point perfect for tearing flesh, and below its yellow eyes, enormous nostrils flared like ear coils except there was a hole clean through to the other side of the beak. Truly monstrous.

He tried to sit up, but his outstretched arms were bound to a redwood limb, like a crucifixion. Only then did he feel the lump of it digging into his back. The buzzard unfurled its black wings when he moved. Its wings spanned six feet, as wide as he was tall.

"Get away from me!" Atlas said, but his throat was so dry it came out as a croak. The vulture wasn't the least bit perturbed.

After some awkward maneuvering, he managed to get to a sitting position. The branch his arms were tied to extended a foot past his hands on either end. The vulture watched him with increased interest, opening and closing its wings slowly as if undecided about flight.

"Filthy piece of shit. I'm not dead yet!" He pivoted the branch toward the vulture, and his back wrenched in pain.

The vulture winged lazily up into the trees at the edge of the clearcut.

Through a series of contortions, Atlas managed to get to his feet and walk toward the shade, but he was pulled short by a rope. He turned around, tangling the rope around his legs, and saw he was tied to a stump. He looked around for Logan. Nowhere. The bastard had left him to die. He bent double, twisting sideways to try to grab the rope with his hand, but the branch bumped into the ground before he could reach it. He cursed and walked back to the stump where the rope came off the ground. With some satisfaction, he was able to grasp it. He pulled but couldn't get a purchase on it. He rubbed the knot against the stump hoping to jar it loose, but quickly realized the futility of this task.

"Help," he screamed but the action set his throat on fire, and he began to cough. The screaming only fueled his fear. Desperate for water, and noticing a little puddle behind the stump, he dropped to his knees and, because there was no other way to do it, flopped forward onto his chest. An iridescent sheen of diesel fuel floated across the top. Disgusting, but it was better than dying. He nosed the oil aside and drank, but the fuel smell overtook his senses. There were only a few sips of water, anyway. He submitted to his exhaustion and lay with his cheek in the mud, gazing down at the clearcut as it sloped away from him.

The vulture returned, alighting eight feet away, and began to pace. Atlas lifted his head and lay on his other cheek, looking back toward the abundant life of the forest above him. Something white flickered there, and his heart rose in hope. A breeze blew, cooling his brow. The whiteness twirled like a dancing woman. The hairs along his arms and the back of his neck rose. "Diana?" He shook his head and stared, but he couldn't focus. He knew it wasn't possible, yet he both hoped and feared it was. The wind died down and the white shape dropped. It was just a piece of plastic sheeting. Her bright eyes, her sharp wit, her laughter, all gone. He ran his mind over this impossible fact. Behind it, around it, palpable darkness rose and surrounded him. Regret. Guilt, and another emotion he recognized when his wife died. A dustier, more obdurate feeling from another lifetime, a lifetime to which the door was permanently closed.

"I'm so sorry," he said. Darkness diffused in his mind like ink dropped into water until he lost consciousness.

When he awoke, he wasn't sure how much time had passed, but the sun had changed position and beat on him less directly. He turned his face toward the vulture, who regarded him with yellow eyes. The black pinpricks at the centers of the vulture's eyes held no emotion.

"You're no eagle," he croaked with a whisper of a laugh. "An eagle. Now that's my kind of bird. Dives right in for the kill. But you...well, you're a rather polite fellow, aren't you? At least you'll wait for me to die."

The bird cocked its head and paced a few steps in one direction, then turned around and paced back. Its wrinkled head looked small in comparison with its huge, feathered body. It settled, now six feet away from Atlas, and pulled its neck back into its feathered caul. It looked almost like a king with an ermine collar, Atlas thought. The line of its mouth curved down like it was frowning, and its eyes looked more contemplative now, almost sad as they regarded him.

This close, he could see that its head was fuzzy, like an old man. This thought stabbed Atlas in the heart briefly before he let it go.

In sudden alarm, the vulture flapped its wings and took off, opening up a terrible emptiness that was filled, in the next moment, by Logan's muddy hiking boots.

"Oh, thank God," Atlas croaked, almost laughing with relief, then coughing because his throat was so dry. "I thought you'd left me here to die."

"So did I," Logan said. He pulled Atlas to a seated position, untied him from the branch but kept his hands bound in front of him. The relief of lowering his arms was unspeakable. Logan tossed him a bottle of water. Atlas fumbled with it frantically, but his hands didn't work, so Logan had to twist the cap off and help him drink. Water never tasted so good. How had he never noticed? He emptied the bottle.

"Time to go," Logan said.

Stop

Logan, stop. I'm still here. I see it now.

Chapter 43

Climb

May 25, 1990, Sunset

As he stumbled after Logan through the forest, Atlas entered a fugue state, his mind and body one entity, the pain and fatigue a new normal. His shoes were worse than useless, full of water, causing him to slip and slide, but his feet were too city-slicker-soft to go bare. As he picked his way over the springy earth so different than unforgiving asphalt, his glance bounced from fern, to sorrel, to ruffled redwood bark, in a rhythm that was soothing, a kind of song, a forest orchestration. The sweet-spicy scents, the burbling creeks, the shift of feathered shadow, and the darting of animals replaced all thought. He felt an order, a whole, a consciousness as if the forest itself was a mind. It contained a splash of the random, so that things repeated, but never in the same way. His former life of straight lines and right angles now seemed insanely rigid and redundant. Indoors, there was no place for vision to expand, to think beyond itself. Indoors, humans were the biggest and most active entity. It was all an illusion. They were horses with blinders on. He looked up at the trees, at the patches of green and yellow, and a distant memory stirred then vanished.

When Logan brought him to the base of a tree and strapped him into a harness, he looked at the young man from the vantage point of a bird soaring in the sky, as if he'd never seen him before. At this distance, he felt an unfamiliar curiosity. This young man was in terrible pain. He couldn't remember why. The young man was talking as he tugged at his ropes, but the words didn't register.

Then Atlas was rising slowly, surely, up into the canopy as if he truly were a bird. Someone grabbed him under his armpits and hauled him onto a platform, propping him up, untying his hands and feet. They were just feet and hands, after all, not wings, not talons. Someone was holding water to his lips, putting something in his hands.

He looked down at it. A bar of something. Food? He held it to his lips. His mouth was dry. The first few chews felt like cardboard. Then saliva filled his mouth and the sugar shot directly to his head. He swallowed. Hunger filled him. He gobbled down the rest of it with a rush of energy and joy. He finished the bar and drained the water from the canteen next to him. Every molecule of his body rang. He looked around with fresh eyes. They were on a platform hundreds of feet off the ground, swaying gently in the crotch where the tree divided into two massive trunks. It was like another level of Earth up here, with the hanging gardens of Babylon growing in the tree branches. A breeze blew, and floral, humid, earthy leaf scents swirled around him, each with a distinctively different message. The sun was setting, shining orange through the canopies. The air itself had substance. Breathing felt like reading a vast, mysterious book with his lungs. He hadn't known his lungs could read.

The young man sat six feet away from him, his knees drawn up, elbows on knees, head in hands. This was the man who was said to have killed his daughter, a man he had hated only—how long ago was it? A day that seemed like years. To his surprise, he pitied this young man...and there was something wrong with the story. The pieces didn't match.

For his part, Logan was lost. The elation of shock and emergency was gone. Everything was grayscale. Last night, kidnapping and killing Atlas had seemed to be the only thing to do. Even this morning, he felt he was rebalancing the world by punishing evil—forcing evil to see what it had done. He was certain, driven. But now, with exhaustion, came a small measure of sanity. He knew he'd passed a societal point of no return—what he was doing was a crime. He would never be forgiven. Going back to civilization meant prison. No matter how evil this man was, he was a living being, and Logan had a sacred obligation to safeguard all life.

On the other hand, he couldn't imagine going back to a world where men like this won, where Diana had been killed, where these ancient beings were destroyed and turned into suburban lawn furniture, and where the people trying to save them were sent to jail. It was unacceptable.

The last of the water in his canteen and the weeks-old granola bar at the bottom of his knapsack looked alien to him as if his body had permanently gone off food and drink, so he gave them to his nemesis. He wasn't sure why. Maybe to buy himself time before he decided what to do next.

Chapter 44

EPIC Night

May 25, 1990

I t had been a long day at the EPIC office. Their one paid assistant and all their volunteers had gone home, and Jessica was staying late to go over a few legal filings. She sighed, and her knee hit the leg of the folding table that was her desk, jostling everything. She steadied the table, keeping the stacks of paper neat.

Usually, she took her work home and went over things in bed, but the last two days had been so hard that it felt better to keep a wall between work and home. Besides, she didn't want to wake her grandmother.

She filed the appeal on the bogus environmental study PL submitted. They'd just stuck it in the mail and started cutting before anyone even saw it. None of the local courts would take it, but she'd gotten the court of appeals in Sacramento to hear the case, but it was looking like another ancient grove would be cut.

The news headlines screamed, "Eco-terrorist Killed Daughter of Pacific Lumber CEO," and "Anarchists Descend into Chaos." The acting CEO of Pacific Lumber, Eddie Cox, had issued a statement that Atlas Jamison was in deep mourning, not to be disturbed, and would not be making any public appearances for a few days. The tragedy would sway the public against their cause, and they depended on the public's goodwill for success.

She hadn't had time to absorb the fact that Diana was dead. She had fielded two press conferences emphasizing EPIC's peaceful and legislative approach, but their alliance with Earth First! was questioned. Judi was still in the hospital, and Darryl was out of the hospital, but both were under arrest, and much was being made of the police report that they had been injured by their own bomb concealed in a guitar case in the back seat. When money was raised to post their bond, the judge ordered a higher bond.

A friend of hers pointed out that the image of the blasted remains of the white Suburu clearly indicated the bomb was under the driver's seat, not in the back seat, and another friend of hers on the police force said the report had been changed.

It was tempting to think things had never been this bad, but ancestral memory told her otherwise. Their only shot at saving the Headwaters now was more delay tactics via more demonstrations.

She put down her pen, stood, stretching her back, and wandered to the storefront window. The office was just down the street from the Minor Theater, a blue stucco building built in 1914 that still had the trap door Harry Houdini used to disappear from the stage. It was late, and the last movie had already ended. No trap door was going to make these bad guys disappear. She tried not to think of it as a battle between the bad guys and the good guys because that only made her more bitter. But today it was hard not to see it that way.

Watching things die was a constant part of this job, and to the people fighting to save the ancient redwoods, each loss carried with it the same grief as one carries for a human. Nonetheless, she had to admit, she ached over Diana's death differently. Diana had been a quicksilver flash of light: funny, confident, passionate. She strode into their lives full of privilege and arrogance, but once she understood, gave heart and soul to the cause. The love she and Logan developed was a beautiful thing to see. Diana's existence held out the hope that the gap of understanding between the two sides could be closed. Now that hope was dead and the gap yawned. Closing her fist around her medicine bag, she said a prayer for Diana, for Logan, for the town of Arcata, and for the trees.

There was no telling how Diana's death would affect Logan after the loss of his father. That was another thing that had frazzled her day. She'd done her best to track down witnesses and take statements to help clear him. Everyone knew he didn't do it, but the White man's money machine ground inexorably forward, shredding everything in its path, even its own people.

She sighed again, feeling tired and defeated. Across the street from The Minor was The Koop, an electronics recycling shop. It was founded by Charlie McDaniels, a venerated black businessman. It was stacked floor to ceiling with cast-off computers and televisions. It never failed to fill her with dread. But Charlie's wide warm smile as he explained how they could be pulled apart and how silver and gold could be extracted from them, gave her a measure of strength. So many people in Arcata were trying to do the right thing.

She knew from years of this work to take feelings of defeat with a grain of salt. "Don't water that," her grandmother always said. She thanked the great spirit for her grandmother. There was no way to be in this fight without occasionally crashing emotionally. She'd get some rest, and she'd feel better tomorrow. She always did. She fingered her medicine bag again. It contained bits of the shell of a pond turtle, her spirit animal. She'd spent most of her childhood in her grandmother's backyard playing with them. It was her grand-mother who told her they were her spirit animal. They were, of course, endangered now because of habitat fragmentation.

When her people's culture got popularized, a lot of white people picked powerful predators as their spirit animals, finding wolves and eagles more romantic, she supposed. They didn't wait for the animal to select *them,* as was the way of things. Her spirit animal was quiet, slow, and simple. Pond turtles didn't pick fights with others. She'd learned from them that if you were in a fight for the long haul, you had to pace yourself, carry a hard shell, and pull your head in when things got dangerous.

Down the street, Zeff materialized, his long curly hair showing blondish when he stepped under the streetlamp. He looked more waifish than usual, Jessica thought. He was such a pretty boy. His delicate features always looked a bit tragic when he wasn't smiling, but tonight he looked truly haunted.

"What's up?" she asked, unlocking the door.

"I've been dodging the cops all day, but I overheard that Coxsucker ordering Stanton to go back to the Grove of the Ancients first thing tomorrow morning."

"Diana's body is barely cold."

"I know, Brian and Jim are rounding people up."

"I'll activate my phone tree again."

"Yeah." Zeff's voice drifted off with a note of hopelessness.

"How's Logan holding up?"

Zeff's face went tight and he avoided her eyes. "Not good. Not good at all."

"Well, I've got notarized witness statements from three protesters and one mill worker saying that Logan was nowhere near Diana when she fell. In fact, people are saying it was Harry Stanton."

"That's great," Zeff said, without much enthusiasm.

"What's wrong?"

Zeff looked at her for a long moment in silence. "I gave my word."

"Is he in trouble?"

"He's in deep shit. He's *over the edge*. I don't know what to do."

"You better tell me."

Zeff's brow wrinkled like a T-shirt in rubber bands. "I don't want to make you an accessory."

"If I'm your lawyer, everything you tell me is privileged."

Images from last night assailed him: the crazed look in Logan's eyes, the jagged hair, Atlas's head flopping near the ground as the donkey trotted after Logan into the darkness.

"Okay, but you gotta swear this stays between us."

"I can only swear that I'll do whatever I can to help."

"Deal."

Chapter 45

Over the Edge

May 25, 1990, Sunset

"So," Atlas said after he finished the granola bar. "What are we doing here?"

Logan didn't look up.

"We've come a long way. There must be some point," he tried again.

A Steller's jay zipped onto the platform, cocked its head at them two or three times, and zipped off.

"I have no idea," Logan muttered.

"Are you going to kill me?"

Logan lifted his head slowly. "I was going to, I think, I don't know. I wasn't thinking. Maybe we're just a couple of salmon at the end of our run."

Atlas remembered what Logan had taught him at the creek.

"So... now we just sit here and ...die?"

Logan shrugged and looked at the orange sky beyond the trees, then leaned his head back against the tree, looking up.

"Why didn't you just leave me at the clearcut, then?"

"I guess...because I wanted to teach you a thing or two before this is over. So, take a fucking look around."

Atlas looked out at the ocean of trees, the orange light of the setting sun that seemed to light the branches from within. The horn blast of dinosaurs reached his ears. It was the sound of trees groaning as they swayed, he realized.

"Does *any* of this get in?" Logan cut into his thoughts.

Still lost in the trees, Atlas stared back at him blankly.

"That's what I thought. You'll never get it," Logan said.

"No, I think I get it. I—I see it now, the consequences of my actions."

"Oh, you get it, do you?" Logan said, slowly, softly. He leaned forward and his intensity built, "You see it now...the—quote," he made air quotes, "—consequences— of your actions."

Logan leapt to his feet and grabbed Atlas by the collar and shoved him out over the branch he and Diana had straddled only a few weeks ago. It faced east overlooking the plucked landscape of the mudslide that killed his father. "Do you understand the consequences of *that action?*"

Atlas looked out, surprised, at the still-scarred landscape. Then he remembered what Barnes had told him about Logan's father, and he felt like he was going to vomit with hatred.

"I thought I understood," he said, "I thought you were trying to teach me a lesson, to save the forest, but now I see it's just plain old vengeance," he paused as his rage billowed. "You fucked my daughter for vengeance, and you fucking killed her. Goddamn it."

Logan was shocked. "What?" He dragged Atlas back onto the platform, spinning him back around. "Have you got shit for brains? I *loved* your daughter. She was ashamed to be the daughter of an arrogant piece of shit that wasn't even a monkey when these trees seeded the earth, a puny hairless monkey that thinks he can own this immensity. These trees are so much greater than you in so many ways, but you wouldn't understand that. She did, though." He was shaking Atlas by the collar with each word, his spit speckling Atlas's face.

"Right. You loved her so much you threw her in front of the loader." Atlas thumped him in the chest with both hands.

"You fucking idiot. I wasn't anywhere near her. It was your goddamned foreman. And your precious VP did nothing to stop it. She jumped in his face and ordered him to stop cutting, and he pitched her aside like she was a ball of trash. She fell back but jumped back up, and...." A cannonball of grief blew through Logan's chest, and he gulped in air and choked, still holding onto Atlas. "If she had just stayed down...."

Atlas's eyes burned as images flicked like a spliced filmstrip through his mind. "If you won't stop them, I fucking will," she had said before she flew out of the office. Then Eddie talking to Stanton as he came up behind them, "Stick to your statement." The instant Eddie had told Atlas she was trying to stop the protesters, he'd known he was lying. As much as he hated this maniac, what he said made sense.

Logan saw the look of recognition on Atlas's face. "So, how does it feel to know your own men killed your daughter?"

"You rotten, fucking bastard," Atlas screamed, pushing Logan back. "This is all your fault. None of this would have happened if you hadn't brought her out here and brainwashed her with your hippie crap."

"And people think trees are stupid. I knew her for only a few weeks and it was clear to me there was no telling her anything, much less brainwashing her," Logan said as they grappled with each other. "Did you really not know her at all?"

"What do you know about anything," Atlas shot back, shame fueling his rage. "You're a worthless bum living in the trees making trouble. It's easy to sit on the sidelines and criticize. What have you ever *done* besides tear people down, and now you want to lecture me, you Communist dog?"

"Christ was a Communist, not that you'd care," Logan said, stepping back from Atlas.

Atlas laughed crazily. "Oh, so that's what it is? You're some kind of Tarzan Tree Messiah? Well, guess again."

As Atlas babbled on, the fight went out of Logan. His face went slack. Moving like a sleepwalker, he grabbed a branch above his head, pulled himself up, and with exhausted finality, said, "Enough," as he kicked Atlas off the platform

Atlas sailed out into the air. His eyes opened wide around the shocking realization that he was now going to die. A scream escaped his lungs as he plummeted for an eternal second, hands grasping and coming up with nothing.

Then a hard jerk to his groin flipped him around, and he slammed into the tree trunk. He was swinging back for another slam, but, scrambling furiously, he fended it off with his feet and managed to grab the rope above him to steady himself. Breathing hard, he twisted erratically in mid-air like a dropped ball of twine, and just as insignificant, but thankful to be alive.

On top of the platform, Logan sat against the tree trunk, pulled his knees up to his chest, and dropped his head onto them. The tears finally came as the forest darkened.

Slippage

It felt so good, Logan, to throw all my power at that man. His name is already escaping me.

I had one purpose. I was purpose. In flying at him, I flew also at my father. When he tossed me back, I sprang up stronger, my body-my power. My anger-my joy.

Something huge collided with me. An earthquake to the skull. Then nothing.

I lay on the ground. I tried to get up, but my arms and hands didn't obey. When I pushed harder, I slipped out of myself, like I was playing tug of war and the other side let go. I flew. I couldn't stop myself. I could see, but not through eyes. Like a radio tuner spinning between stations, I slid up and down the frequencies, sound is light, light is Atman, the all-spirit.

I now see from all angles.

Without a body to filter it, I was overwhelmed. It was all static and shafts of bent light. Terrifying. But the forcefield of True Ones bounced me back toward the ground.

A flickering, my old container, crumpled like a discarded robe. When I grasped it, all I wanted was to be back in that body. Home! It had carried me, fed me, breathed me. It was the steadiest best friend I had never acknowledged. It knew how to filter all these lights and sounds. I craved its familiar corridors.

You came running toward my body. I tried to squeeze myself back into it so that I could hug you as you pulled—what was me—to your chest.

Maybe, just maybe, I felt your arms around me. I reached for you but found only webs. The corridors of my body closed and squeezed me back out, too small, too cramped, too solid.

I grew large, full of space. I could never squeeze myself down into such a narrow place again. So, I surrounded you, became warp and weft through you. I could see myself, through your eyes. It was a shock to see how my face had been smashed in. That face that had been me, now a jack-o-lantern left on the porch too long, caved in.

I could feel how Vikriti you were inside your own body. Chaos. You couldn't feel me. But I was there, all the same. Your sadness was unbearable. I tried to inhale, but instead, I began to rise and spread out. Everything, Atman, was me, soil, water, True Ones! They filled me with joy and that joy made me even larger. And then I was pulled away, out and upward. I drifted toward the sky so curious to see what was next. Language was falling away. I was forgetting it all, and glad to forget.

But something made me look back. Your face came to me across all the frequencies, turned up to me, creased with sorrow, painted with blood. Two eyes, a nose, and a mouth, the first thing we ever see, a pattern inscribed beyond sight beyond time.

I turned back.

I knew, without knowing why, that I could stay if I inhabited something again. Something large enough to contain me. Uuma.

Chapter 46

Web

Darkness descended, and cool air came wreathing around them. Time went on hiatus. Atlas, dangling in a seated position in his harness, found a way to wrap the rope so he could rest against it and find a semblance of sleep. Logan pulled stiffly to his feet and rummaged in the tin chest at the corner of the platform. He attached one musty sleeping bag to a carabiner, clipped it to the rope holding Atlas, and sent it down. When it gently hit him, Atlas accepted it without comment and wrapped it around himself. Logan crawled into his own bag and turned on his side.

Sleep took them at different times, unawares, like a switch that had been flicked, conscious one moment—then not. Logan slept fitfully, awakening to a super moon, peculiarly bright, casting a web of black shadows and white space like snow. Each time he awoke, the shadows had shifted. His pulse pounded in his ears. His mouth was sealed shut with dryness. If his mouth never opened again, it would be okay. He couldn't tell the difference between sleeping and waking.

Atlas was awakened by the strangest screech he'd ever heard, like a woman screaming, but she had screamed so loud she barely had any voice left. She seemed to be hissing at the same time, as if carrying a message from the other side. It scraped through his chest and scoured his heart. Each and every hair on his body stood at full attention as the spirit screeched through the darkness, heading right at him, white arms open wide, round white face pierced by two black eyes. It swooped over him, its wings soundless as it passed, sucking the air out of him.

The moon was inconceivably bright. It had always been a distant thing in the sky, but now it was a god bearing down on him. It painted bold white strokes across everything. Branches slashed the white with black shadows that crisscrossed everything all around him like the *She Wolf* painting coming to life. He twisted slowly and looked up, mesmerized by the design. He had always thought the point of the Romulus and Remus myth was that civilization suckled at the teat of savagery. Now he understood it differently. Nature nurtured civilization. People weren't civilized unless they were in right relation to nature. He hung awake, turning slowly back and forth, like a spider at the end of a thread, until he couldn't tell whether he was awake or asleep.

Uuma-Dina

I went back to Uuma. I flowed into Uuma. Now we are Uuma, we are Uuma-Dina, and we Uooooma -Diiiiina you.

Laghu.

The nimble one.

But you are not Laghu just now. You are Vikriti, imbalance, as is this other clevertongue with you. Who is he? A rootless one I once called father. But all is becoming mist. I almost remember the drop of liquid I was that swam from him. His energy is as Vikriti as yours. You fight. You will kill each other. This is not the way. This thing you do. Called hate. We do not know this thing.

I claw my way back, trying to remember what it is to be a clevertongue. I surround you both. I make myself like Kulaaya and infiltrate you.

What is this? Your face is raining. Sadness. Like Samudra, the coming together of waters. Desire. Longing for what is not. Desire is how you befriend the void. Only the clevertongues feel this, not even the furred ones who befriended you feel this thing. It is Kulaaya, a strangely beautiful weave, part Kutastha, all-spirit. A way to balance light and dark.

Words, already dispersed, just fluctuations of air on vocal cords, just stops and clicks of the tongue, that bit of flesh no longer mine. It barely comes back to me. I will speak to you through pictures.

I will speak of love.

Chapter 47

Night Visions

May 26, 1990

When the owl screeched again, Atlas was lying face down on the ground. A deep rumbling filled his ears, like enduring thunder. He lifted his head. Leaves and needles stuck to his face. Two white feet stepped into his line of sight, slender, elegant.

"Diana?"

He leapt to his feet, but she flitted into the forest and disappeared behind a tree. He hobbled after her, but when he got to that tree, she was a flicker beyond the next, and the next, drawing him forward, ever deeper, to a place he might never find his way back from.

"Diana! Wait," he called, and she threw him a backward glance, her fine hair fanning out in slow motion. But she whipped her head away and disappeared behind another tree. Then another.

That low vibration, like thunder in the bones, resolved into the rumble of a truck jostling him. He was sitting on the tailgate, a young boy. He fell off and stood up crying, "Wait for me!" But the old truck rumbled off, the driver hidden, unaware, leaving him alone, forever lost.

Two hundred feet above, on the platform, Logan felt the itch of a web across his face. He brushed it away, and the back of his hand touched another's hand. He sat up, instantly awake, someone's breath still warm in his ear.

"Diana?" he whispered.

All he saw was a web of shadows across his legs. The moon had climbed higher in the sky, surreally bright, so close to the Earth, and yet so far away.

"Please, if you're here, come back," Logan whispered.

A barn owl screeched, and something at the edge of the platform flitted.

"Why won't you speak to me?" he said. He lay back down, shifting to his other side, and wondered how he'd ever sleep again. His wakefulness became shallow sleep, and he was climbing up something difficult, having to choose handholds and footholds carefully, strategically. It was a tree with many sharp branches that scraped and poked him, so unlike the redwoods. His hand searched for a handhold, but the bark came away from the tree. He reached up, and his hand fell on another hand, a woman's hand, coming out of the knothole as if she was inside the tree.

"Diana?" he called. The hand pulled away. When he got level with the knothole, it was empty, and the hole was too dark, too rotten to put his hand down inside.

Then he was on his boat, swaying gently, logs thumping against the side incessantly. He looked over the edge into the water. They weren't logs, but dead bodies, floating face down. Before the horror hit him, the scene switched.

Sunlight stippled his vision. He was talking on the phone, and the receiver's coil spiraled away from him endlessly. Diana was at the other end babbling happily, telling him she was reading a vast book in a new language that she couldn't wait for him to read. But a feathery itch of spider's legs crossed his cheek and woke him. The web of black and white shifted as if spelling an indecipherable message. He was Odin trying to learn how to read the twigs at the base of Yggdrasil.

Then she stepped out of Uuma's trunk. The shock of her sudden presence sparked tears. "You came back," he said.

"Love," she said as she knelt and wrapped her arms around him, her face soft and sharp in light and shadow. She climbed into his sleeping bag, and he knew it was real because the cold air rushed in with her. He ran his hands over her face, their bodies meshed like the trunks of two trees growing together. She was warm and solid, bone and flesh, and smelled of lemon-cedar. "Don't ever leave me," he said.

"Remember," she said.

"How could I ever forget?"

"No," she said. "Re-member."

Logan didn't know what she meant, but he melted into her body's warmth, and her body melted into his, and they revolved around each other like the spiral arms of a galaxy, he in her and she in him until they both fell into a deeply restful sleep.

Atlas, meanwhile, continued to wander lost in the woods, that subsonic rumble vibrating his sternum, making him queasy. Diana disappeared around the edge of a tree just ahead of him. When he got to it, he saw her hand, emerging from a knothole. He reached for it, but it pulled into the tree. "Diana!" he called, digging into the rotted wood to find what was left of her.

The low vibration intensified, rose in pitch, and resolved into the rumble of that truck again, coming toward him. He waved it down, but the driver, a shadow behind the windshield, seemed not to see him and came ever closer as if to run him down, forcing him off the path. He tumbled into a ditch and rose cursing, waving his arms. The truck pressed on, the driver oblivious or malicious.

Then Diana was at his side, smiling. He gasped and hugged her, and she hugged him back. "Is that your father?" she asked, pointing to the truck rumbling off into the distance. Even in the dream, he knew that was wrong, but he nodded.

"Do you want me to help you catch up?" she asked.

"I don't see how."

"It's easy," she said. "Just pick up your feet."

She took his hand, and he lifted one foot off the ground, then the other so that he was standing in the air. It turned out to be that easy. Why had he never known this? The two of them skimmed over the ground without friction, like light itself. She steered him through the night, through the trees themselves until they caught up to the truck, which stopped. As they neared the driver's window, it rolled down, and he saw, not his father, but his grandfather, his thin face a mass of tanned wrinkles that wreathed into a smile. "Re-member," Diana said and faded.

"I've been looking all over for you," his grandfather said, which surprised Atlas.

But the scene changed, and he was staring as if through the wrong end of a telescope at two tiny figures, a child at the back of a truck with his grandfather leaning over him. The next instant, he *was* the child, and his grandfather picked him up and set him on the truck bed.

"Trees don't talk," Atlas said, with childish scorn.

"How do you know?" his grandfather said, squeezing Atlas's knee. "Maybe they talk real slow and you don't stick around long enough to hear." He watched his grandfather limp around to the driver's side. Love and pride swelled his small chest. The engine roared, the gasoline fumes engulfed him with their comforting odor. As he jostled along the wooded road, his gaze soared into the sunlit canopy, patches of amber and green light. The subsonic rumble filled his body again, but this time, the vibrations felt organized, like they were separating into words, a message he was just starting to under-stand when the hoot of an owl woke him.

Above him on the platform, Logan woke up alone.

"Diana. Where did you go?" Logan looked up. A spotted owl perched on a branch above him. Its head swiveled slowly toward him, eyes like enormous searchlights drilling into him.

"Wait," Logan said as he launched himself toward the owl, but it took flight, and he awoke, belly down, head flopping over the edge of the platform looking at Atlas dangling ten feet below, like Odin hanging in the branches of Yggdrasil.

Diana's words reverberated in his head. Re-member. Put the pieces back together. He pulled up the rope. Atlas reached up for him, and Logan reached back. They clasped each other's wrists, and Logan hauled him up to standing.

They stood on the platform in awkward silence.

Searching through a sea of possible responses, Atlas finally settled on a quiet "Thank you."

Logan said nothing.

He turned away and climbed back into his sleeping bag.

Atlas did the same.

They both lay in silence, listening to the trees creak, the wind swish, and the occasional screech of owls. When Logan's breath became deep and regular, Atlas rolled over to look at him, a puff of down scented air escaping as he turned. Logan appeared to be curled in his sleeping bag around another form. It was easy for him to imagine Diana was there, asleep in his arms. A fatherly surge of love crushed his heart.

Chapter 48

Booby Trap

May 26, 1990

A caravan of logging trucks roared down the dirt road in the pre-dawn redwood forest toward the Grove of the Ancients. A half-mile ahead, pine branches camouflaged in dirt lay across the road. The empty loading truck in the lead roared toward the spot. The driver detected what looked like a hump of dirt but assessed it would be no problem and didn't check his speed. No sooner did he hit it, but the truck crashed into the three-foot ditch with a bang that reverberated through the forest. The front axle broke and the driver slammed against his seatbelt so hard it scored his chest.

"Goddamn!" the driver shouted as steam and acrid smoke filled the cab.

The truck behind him slammed on the breaks and its rear end swung around and slammed into the first truck in a cloud of burnt rubber.

"Fucking hell!"

In quick succession, another hauler and two pickups screeched and swerved every which way, some hitting, some landing in ditches to the side. All the PL employees, Cox and Stanton among them, hopped out of their cabs swearing and rubbing their necks and chests.

Well-hidden in their tree platform, Zeff, Jim, and Brian slapped silent high fives.

"That's one," Zeff whispered.

Stanton yelled, "Get those dozers off the truck and fill this patch immediately."

"Those cock-suckers aren't going to stop us," Cox yelled. "Those trees are coming down, today!"

An hour later, Cox and Stanton, faces red with fury, stared through a hole cut through their storage container at the field site. Three security guards were bound and gagged inside. Cables, chainsaws, and all the other tools were gone. Above the hole, spray painted in neon pink was: "Eco-Commie-Welcome Hole."

"You've got to be fucking kidding me," Cox said.

"That's two," Zeff said, high-fiving Brian and Jim. Cheers and whistles rose from two other tree-sitter platforms.

"You're not going to be cheering when we cut your asses out of those trees," Cox yelled.

Stanton turned and shouted to the workers, "Do we have any other saws up here?"

A couple of loggers reached into the toolboxes in the back of their trucks and pulled out two small chainsaws that looked like toys next to the trees. Stanton shook his head in disgust.

"I'll radio back to town to load up more trucks," he told Cox. "You two, unload those dozers and prep the cutting site for those two trees," he said, pointing at the two with tree-sitters in them.

The loggers ran to their machines. Three engines roared to life in quick succession, then one by one, they spluttered and quit. Stanton took off his hat and threw it at the ground, swearing.

From the platform, Zeff, Brian, and Jeff cheered, "Three strikes, they're out!" Zeff said and pulled down his pants and mooned the people below. The protesters cheered his bare butt.

"Supermoon!" someone called.

"Goddamn it!" yelled Cox, his voice high. "I'll see you in prison if I don't see you in hell first."

Chapter 49

Begin Again

May 26, 1990. Earlier that same morning.

Logan stirred in the early morning hours when all was blue, and the first birds were waking. Caught between consciousness and sleep, he still felt the weight of Diana's head on his arm, her leg across his belly, the humidity of her breath on his cheek. He knew it wasn't possible, but he held onto the illusion as long as he could. He dreaded finding the empty space beside him, but when he finally opened his eyes and sat up, he was oddly okay. His mind felt clear and calm.

Atlas was sitting against the tree, looking up into the canopy. "You're awake," Atlas said, simply. He had been thinking about grief. That it was a wily thing that disappeared like an underground spring, emerging unexpectedly, and often disguised as obsessions. Was it possible that his whole life, his obsession with art, with takeovers, with amassing wealth was all just grief? For his parents? His grandfather? His wife? It hadn't protected him. Now he was pierced by a sorrow for which there was only one salve. A complete about-face.

Logan said nothing and leaned back against the opposing half of the tree.

"I am not a superstitious man," Atlas began slowly, "but I dreamt about Diana last night." Logan couldn't help but search his face. He was different. The brackets between mouth and nose were smoother, his eyes rounder, his hair messy. He looked younger.

"I feel like she's still here," Atlas said.

A chill went down Logan's spine as he thought about the warm body beside him moments ago.

"In the night, she led me through the woods, and it's like she's inside this tree."

Logan and Atlas locked eyes.

"You saw it too," Atlas said.

Logan frowned and looked down, shaking his head slightly, not wanting to give Atlas any satisfaction or comfort.

"After you went to sleep, I could swear she was lying beside you, under the covers."

Shivers renewed and amplified down Logan's spine, and he couldn't help making eye contact with Atlas again.

"I can't believe I'm saying this, but you did something for me... bringing me out here. You put me through this ordeal. I never would have seen what I've seen if—" he paused, searching for the words. "It has changed me."

"People don't change," Logan said, bitterly.

"Maybe so. I guess it's not really a change. It's more like a reclamation."

Atlas waited for him to ask for more, but when Logan didn't, he pushed forward.

"I was born in the '30s, right at the end of the Great Depression. My parents abandoned me when I was only a few years old."

"Spare me your sob story."

"Hear me out. I'm trying to prove to you that I can change."

Logan looked away.

"My grandfather took me in. He was a handyman, a jack of all trades. We spent a lot of time together, and a lot of it in the woods, collecting firewood in his old truck of his. He was a good man. He used to tell me the trees could talk. And I loved that idea. I loved him.

"But he died, one day, when I was only about eight. I found him at the bottom of the steps to the back porch early one morning. I ran down the street in my holey pajamas, knocking on doors, trying to get someone to help.

"I ended up at an orphanage and was put out to work at the age of thirteen. Those were dark years, and I banished them from my mind. I found work was an elixir. I could outwit just about anyone. I was good at whatever I did. I rose in the ranks quickly and discovered stock trading early. It was an addiction. I made money. Then a *lot of money.*"

"Big surprise there. It was always about money."

"But you see," Atlas rushed ahead, as if he was discovering what he said as he said it. "It wasn't really about the money. It was about winning. It was about never looking back. It was about making a wall so thick I'd never see or feel that...," he paused, searching for the word, "helplessness...again. The sun couldn't make me hot and the rain couldn't make me wet. I was invincible, my only tool was my brain. I didn't need anyone, you see, to survive. I could bring down giants all on my own."

"And so you have."

Atlas stopped like he'd just come to the edge of a cliff.

He restarted in a quieter tone. "That's what Diana showed me last night. She brought me back to my grandfather. She reminded me.... And she made a request.... Now I have a debt to pay. And I'm going to need your help to pay it."

"My help?" Logan exclaimed. "What the fuck? Why do you think I would *ever* help you?"

"Because you loved Diana. Because this is what she wants."

"What?"

"I know I'm to blame. But I can't let her go. All that is left of her is this forest...and...you."

Logan stared at him, unbelieving.

"She wants me to stop the cutting. I can. And I will."

In the distance, the sounds of rumbling trucks reached their ears. They both turned toward the sound and listened.

"You'd say anything to get out of this tree," Logan said.

"Yes, I would, but not for the reasons you think. Look, that's them, coming after the—what do you call it?—the Grove of the

Ancients. Let me down now and come with me. I won't press charges. What happened here stays between us. I'll give you my word."

"Your word," Logan snorted. "I could never trust you. Or forgive you."

"I'm not sure I can forgive myself. But that's what she was telling me last night. Re-member. Put the pieces back together."

The rumbling of trucks grew.

"She told me that, too," Logan blurted, a note of wonder in his voice.

"I loved her, too, you know," Atlas said. "I loved her fire." A raucous screech and crash buffeted the air and startled birds to flight, followed by three sets of shrieking brakes and two more explosions of metal. They could feel the faint tremor even up in the tree. "Please, you've got to trust me! Time is running out."

"Alright," Logan said, rising to his feet. "She did speak to me...and she said the same thing you said you heard. Re-member."

The confirmation of the truth of it shot down Atlas's spine like an arrow.

Logan picked up a climbing harness. He paused and looked out over the tessellating trees. "We're going back."

He rummaged in the metal locker. "You're gonna need these," he said, tossing Atlas a pair of hiking boots. "And these," he tossed him a few energy bars.

"You had these all the time?"

"I forgot. Now get those boots on. And remember, I've got nothing to lose. If you don't follow through, I'll—"

"I know, I know," Atlas said, sitting down to switch out his shoes as quickly as possible.

Logan threaded a rope through Atlas's harness and checked the carabiners and pulleys with a few jerks. Atlas stood at the edge of the platform, back to the fall, facing Logan. He tried to catch Logan's eye. "Son?" He held out his hand for a shake.

"I'm not your son," Logan said.

"Okay then. Let's just do this. For Diana."

Logan paused, then clasped Atlas's hand. "For Diana." He paused awkwardly again. "Now take a flying leap. I'll belay you to the ground and then come down myself."

Atlas took the measure of him. Logan could let him drop and say it was an accident. But the flash of Diana reminded him that Logan was no killer. He knelt and eased his body off the platform until he was hanging by his hands from the edge, two hundred feet off the ground.

Then, he let go.

Chapter 50

The Last Stand

May 26, 1990

A dozer roared onto the cutting site and a band of thirty protesters linked arms to block its way. The driver paused, then raised the blade, revved his engine, and advanced slowly toward them. The protesters backed up ten feet then dug in their heels. The driver halted and jerked forward in increments, the tank-like tread mashing the ground. Jessica Wild arrived, and instantly assessing the situation, drove between the protesters and the tank, squealing to a halt.

She jumped out of the car waving papers, "One step further and we'll charge you with assault," she yelled.

Cox yanked a rifle away from one of the security guards and strode up to her aiming the rifle at her.

"One more step and I'll shoot your ass. Get off my land. Now!"

The protesters, who had been murmuring amongst themselves, turned and ran for the trees.

"Shit," a logger yelled, "don't let them get into the trees."

A few loggers stepped in their paths and fistfights broke out. Some ran to trees not already inhabited by tree-sitters, others formed human chains around trees, and a few others began scaling the tree Zeff, Jim, and Brian were in.

Cox turned around and screamed at the D-10 drivers, "Knock those goddamned trees *down*."

The drivers of two D-10s looked at him like he was out of his mind.

"Do it!" he screamed again, his voice gratingly high. "Now!"

The drivers revved their engines and started moving toward the tree Zeff was in.

"You'll kill them," Jessica yelled.

"Tell them to get the fuck out of my trees!"

"Now hold on, Eddie," Stanton said, putting his hand on Cox's shoulder, but Cox shrugged him off. "I'm in charge here. I call the shots. And it's sir, to you, from now on."

Stanton's face reddened, and he turned his back on Cox. That's why he was the first to see Logan and Atlas run onto the site just as the D-10 rammed into the redwood where Zeff stood high on a platform. The crash shredded ears. The impact jarred the tree so severely that Zeff lost his balance and tumbled over the edge of the platform, grabbing onto the edge just in time. The first D-10 backed up just as another D-10 rammed the tree with another crack. The tree shook and groaned, and a long crack appeared in its side, and Zeff lost one handgrip. The protesters screamed from all angles as diesel fumes filled the air. Brian and Jim lay down on the platform and grabbed Zeff's wrists.

Logan paused just long enough to see what was going on, then raced to the first D-10 now closing in on the tree as the second one backed up. He scaled the drawbar between the tracks, opened the cab door, and yanked the nonplussed driver out by the collar. He seized the controls and stopped the machine's advance just before it hit.

Zeff, still hanging by one hand, laughed hysterically and shouted down, "Nice timing, Rambo!"

Logan leaned out of the cab and grinned back up at him. Meanwhile, waving both arms, Atlas ran toward the other D-10 still advancing on the tree, shouting, "Shut that down! Now!"

The driver's eyes bulged, recognizing Atlas despite his natty hair and rumpled, stained clothes. He cut the engine.

Silence poured over the site like an icy river as everyone became aware of Atlas's presence. They stared at him as if holding their breath, taking in the blood and bruises across his arms and face. The silence deepened as Logan descended the D-10 and stood by Atlas's side. From above, Zeff's eyes widened. "I'll be damned," he whispered, as he and Jessica exchanged looks across the distance from tree to ground. Police sirens reached everyone's ears.

Atlas spotted Cox, Stanton, and Jessica standing in a triangle. The whites of Cox's eyes showed around his pupils as he stared at Atlas. Atlas strode over to him.

"Sir, are...are you alright? Where have you been? We've been looking all over—"

"I've been...," Altas spoke slowly and paused, searching for an answer, "taking inventory...."

Stanton and Cox exchanged glances.

Atlas faced Stanton. "...and reassessing the cause of my daughter's death."

"What do you mean, sir?" Stanton stuttered.

"I'll spell it out," Atlas said. He grabbed the front of Stanton's shirt just as police skidded onto the scene and sprang from their cruisers.

"Officers," Cox yelled, pointing at Logan, "I'm the CEO. Arrest this man. This is Logan Blackburn."

The officers un-holstered their guns and advanced on Logan, guns raised.

"Just a minute, officers," Atlas said, shoving Stanton toward them. "Mr. Stanton wants to revise his statement."

Stanton pushed Atlas off, "I told you, it was him!" He pointed at Logan.

The officers stopped, confused, looking from Cox, to Atlas, to Stanton to Logan.

Jessica Wild stepped forward. "Officers, I'm here with Sheriff Saunders. I have several affidavits proving that Logan is innocent and that the man who pushed Diana into the path of a loader was that man, Harry Stanon."

The cops looked nonplussed. They all knew Harry Stanton.

"I have also filed for an emergency stay with the Court of Appeals in Sacramento," Jessica continued, "charging that the environmental study filed by Pacific Lumber was designed to fail, and that they suppressed more than seventy sightings of marbled murrelets and spotted owls."

The officers lowered their guns, and two took the papers from Jessica while the other two stepped toward Stanton, who looked back and forth angrily between them and Cox, hands spread wide in disbelief.

"You're not gonna believe this crap, are you?" Cox said. "We filed the study."

"But you started cutting before it even left the mailbox," Jessica said. "This THP has not been officially sanctioned."

"I'm sorry, sir," the one examining the papers said to Stanton, as if embarrassed. "You'll have to come with us."

"This is bullshit," Stanton said.

"And you," said the first officer, looking at Logan. "You're Logan Blackburn?"

"Yes."

"You're wanted for questioning."

Atlas stepped in. "Officer, I can give you my word. He will come later."

The officer hesitated, then turned away.

Atlas turned to Cox. "Shut this all down. Now."

"Sir," Cox said, thrusting his chin up and his chest out a fraction, "that's not your call to make anymore."

"Oh, really?" Atlas said, stepping closer to him, his voice sinisterly casual. "And how have you come by this assessment?"

"No one has heard from you for over thirty-six hours," Cox said, tone dripping with disdain and then careening into bravado. "We called an emergency board meeting, and I was named acting CEO."

Atlas's laugh came out like a bark. "Well, I'm back."

"Also, while you were off on your little field trip, PL stock crashed, and I put together a deal and made a lucrative tender offer. I expect a call any minute confirming the board's acceptance."

"Hm," Atlas said, hand to chin in mock contemplation. "Apparently you haven't read the most recent bylaws," Atlas said without missing a beat. "Such a vote requires a supermajority and a five-year waiting period."

"What do you mean?" Cox said, turning bright red and shaking visibly.

"What I mean is, do you really think I'd let anyone do to me what I did to them? Ask our lawyer."

Sweating, Cox headed to the office trailer to operate the radio.

Atlas turned to Jessica. "And now, Ms. Wild, I have a proposition for you."

"Oh?" Jessica looked at him skeptically.

The two of them walked away, talking. In the background, Cox's voice could be heard rising an octave before he threw the mic and cursed.

Zeff belayed down the tree in record speed, ran at Logan and nearly knocked him over with bear hug.

"Man, am I glad to see you. You had me *seriously* worried, dude."

"Me? You're the one who was hanging by a thumbnail."

"Yeah, I was about to surf that baby to the great beyond!" Zeff said, his face melting into an earnest expression as he lowered his voice. "What happened?? Last thing I knew you were gonna kill the bastard and there was nothing I could do to talk you out of it. Next thing I know, you come charging in together like Batman and Robin."

"I'm not sure I know what happened," Logan said, looking down at the ground and then up at the trees. "Something got to us...both. We changed."

PuraaNam

Thunderteeth and groundquakers sent the whole grove into chaos. Akasha, only three trees away bore the brunt like lightning strikes. We fed her and pulled lightning from her, but Kulaaya too was a chaos of messaging. Many clevertongues like our feathered friends fluttered over us, crying out, striving with their own. After much striving, all went quiet.

When finally the last clevertongues went away, our furred and feathered relations returned. Kulaaya evened out, and we let down our branches and rode the curve of Bhūr into the dark. Uuma was right. The clevertongues can be reached.

Chapter 51

Reunion

April, 1991

Nearly a year later, there came a hesitant knock on Logan's door. He jumped up from the battered kitchen table and answered. His hair now reached his shoulders.

On the doorstep stood a woman who resembled Logan, with a sculpted nose, generous lips, and striking brows. She looked up at him, nervously.

"Mom," he said, pushing his hair back. An iota of silence stretched to the point of discomfort. "Come in."

She held out her arms, and after a fraction of a second, he wrapped his arms around her and squeezed.

"So, where do we start?" he said, stepping back.

She absorbed every detail of his face like she was studying a work of art.

"How about we start with breakfast," she said, and they turned toward the kitchen.

Epilogue

May 24, 1991

The One-Year Anniversary of Diana's Death

A man stood next to his RV reading a small wooden plaque that read, "Headwaters Preserve, Dedicated in Loving and Living Memory of Diana Jamison."

He got back into the driver's seat next to his wife who was chewing a piece of gum and checking her makeup in the mirror.

"I can't believe it. There's no more road. There's not even a trail."

"You mean we dragged our rig over this gravel to look at a plaque?" said his wife.

"Seems so," said the man.

"What's the point of preserving it if we're not allowed to use it?"

"No wonder Pacific Lumber booted their CEO," he said, picking up the *Humboldt Chronicle*, the headline of which read, "Molten in, Jamison Out." The opening of the article read, "Charging that Jamison's new policies had failed to maximize Pacific Lumber's profits,

Matthew Molten, citing the 'shareholder of particular interest exemption clause,' staged a hostile takeover. Stockholders agree. Jamison has five years to transition out. He leaves with a golden parachute."

The man crumpled the newspaper and threw it out the window and hit the power button. "Let's drive back to town and get a beer," he said.

Someone rapped on his window. Startled, he turned back to it. There stood a slender Sasquatch.

Fear rippled across the man's face.

On closer inspection, the Sasquatch had a long, curly mane of hair, a goatee, and a nose ring. Zeff motioned for him to roll down his window.

The tourist did as he was told.

"Thanks for the TP, man," Zeff said, holding up the crumpled newspaper. "Mind if I take a crap in the back of your ride?" Aghast, the man punched at the power button and missed three times before the window rolled up. He revved the engine, backed up, and turned around. Zeff thumped the side of the RV as they drove off. He turned and grinned at Logan and Jessica, who stood in the distance.

"Coming?" Logan said. Zeff caught up to them as they hiked into the main grove of the Headwaters Preserve.

"I gotta admit, Logan," said Jessica, "after Diana died, I thought you'd leave again. Think you're here for good?"

Logan looked up at the trees. "These trees can't walk away. How can I?"

"Word," Zeff said.

"Do you think she's still here?" asked Jessica, following his gaze into the canopy.

"If she is, she has let go of her human form and become one of them," Logan said.

"The grief never really goes away, does it?" Jessica answered.

"No," Logan admitted, "it just becomes another part of you...but it has its own kind of fertility."

"Dude, as part of the trees she'll live forever."

"As will we all," said Logan. "It's just a matter of how much suffering happens along the way."

"One Love," Zeff said, bobbing his head to the Bob Marley tune playing in his veins.

They walked in silence.

"Do you believe we will ever stop them?" Logan asked, contemplatively.

"Yes," Jessica said emphatically.

"Why?"

"Because we have to."

They all accepted this for a beat.

"And if we don't," Zeff added, "we've at least got this little piece of heaven on earth." He swung his arms wide and twirled as he spoke. "And this one," he said, motioning a circle between the three of them. They all smiled, and their love for each other combined with their mutual sense of purpose and lifted them like pollen into sunlight, particles of untold messages able to travel miles on a simple breeze and fertilize untold others.

They continued to hike in silence, concentrating on navigating over roots and between ferns so as not to crush a single living thing or leave a single mark. But they also knew it was not possible, that death was part of the equation.

"So, have you talked to Jamison since he was ousted?" asked Logan.

"Yes, in fact, he called me right after to let me know that his commitment is as strong as ever. He's never wavered since the day he came out of the forest. I don't know what you said to him."

"I don't think it was what *I* said," Logan answered.

The trees reverberated in silence. The wind blew and tree aerosols filtered down around them.

"It helped that he got a major payout from the government for this preserve," Zeff added with an eye roll.

"I know," Jessica said, "And it's only a fraction of what we asked for, but it's something."

"Sure is," Logan said.

Around them the giants soared, earth's green-headed arbiters covered in bark as wrinkled and storied as elephants' skin, sentinels of the air, partitioners of the sky, translators of sun and soil, teaching by example how to live as a diverse, yet symbiotic, whole. It was nature's definition of love. No matter what the rest of humanity did or whether they achieved their goals, today, these three friends were pierced by joy.

Uuma-Dina and PuraaNam

Listen, loved ones, we are all speaking to you. Loving you is hard. We breathe into your mouths as when you breathe into your drowned ones, as the feathered ones tuck life into their nested young. Quiet your bodies. See us. Feel our bark, stippled, shiny, furrowed, white, black, red. We are the True Ones. We speak by being. We have stood for eons before you, alone on Bhūr, the sustainer. We will be here long after. Hear us now.

THE END

Postscript

🌳 The old-growth forests of the Pacific Coast once stretched for 2,000 miles from the redwoods of Big Sur California to the Sitka Spruce of Alaska. Only four percent remain (figures vary).

🌳 Old-growth redwoods capture three to ten times more carbon than most forests on earth (*Save the Redwoods*).

🌳 Eighty percent of land animals depend on forests to live (*National Geographic*).

🌳 "Stopping deforestation and restoring damaged forests could provide up to thirty percent of the climate solution" (IPCC, *Yale Environment 360*).

🌳 In the last hundred years, we lost as much forest as was lost over the last 9,000 years (Ritchie).

🌳 Primary rainforest destruction increased by twelve percent from 2019 to 2020, equivalent to a soccer field every six seconds. The primary causes are logging, forest fires, land conversion for infrastructure, urban sprawl, and commercial agriculture (*Global Forest Watch*).

🌳 Virtually all of the world's protected forests have come under protection thanks to the efforts of "environmental activists," ordinary people from all over the planet and all walks of life who made something extraordinary happen by giving their time, hearts, minds, and bodies for a greater cause.

Tree Glossary

(Why Trees Sometimes Speak Sanskrit)

Friends of mine who are yoga masters told me that the reason yogis chant in Sanskrit is that the vibrations of Sanskrit words are said to manifest the things they name. The universe is a great evolving vibration of energy (the "big bang") and the yogis hear the vibrations relating to the individual things. While I couldn't find scientific verification of this, I loved the idea. Because all human language descended from Indo-European roots, and because Sanskrit is one of the oldest languages, it seemed like a good fit for the trees. Other compound words came to me as I considered the trees' point of view.

Atman soul, universal self

Akaasha ether, air, sky, Zeff's tree, he calls her Arcadia

Avani earth, dirt

Bhūr Earth, the planet

Bright-One sun

Brightside day

Candra moon, name of a tree

Circle around the Bright-One year

Clevertongues humans

Darkside night

Dina blazing light, what Uuma calls Diana

Earthquakers bulldozers, trucks, skidders, loaders

Kulaaya web, what they call mycorrhizal fungi.

Lightpath energy pathway in the human brain, a place where trees can track, enter

Laghu nimble one, what Uuma calls Logan

Mrid earth, dirt

Naked Ones humans

PuraaNam The Ancient One, the name of a tree

Rootless Ones humans, and other animals

Samudra from sam-together, udra-water, the coming
together of waters, ocean

Shunya void

Thunderteeth chainsaw

True Ones Trees

Udra rain, water

Uuma friend, Logan's tree

Varsa rain

Vikriti out of balance

Windbear strong wind

Bibliography

Bari, Judi. "The Secret History of Tree Spiking." *International Workers of the World Archives*. Anderson Valley Advertiser, February 17, 1993, and the Earth First! Journal, December 21, 1994; reprinted in Timber Wars, © 1994 Common Courage Press.

Bari, Judi. *Timber Wars: Footloose Wobs Urgently Needed* Industrial Worker, October 1989; Reprinted in Timber Wars, © 1994 Common Courage Press.

Dunning, Joan. *From the Redwood Forests*. With Photographs by Doug Thron. Chelsea Green Publishing Company. 1998. Global Forest Watch. GlobalForestWatch.org.

Harris, David. *The Last Stand*. Sierra Club Books. 1996.

Jacobelli, Sara. "Who is Alicia Littletree?" *Anderson Valley Advertiser*. 25 June 1997.

"Judi Bari Revisited: New Film Exposes FBI Coverup of 1990 Car Bombing (Part 1 of 2)" *Democracy Now*. 2012.

Lanman, Cecilia. Interview. *Living on Earth*. 1996.

Montaigne, Fen. "Why Keeping Mature Forests Intact Is Key to the Climate Fight." *Yale Environment 360*. Yale School of the Environment. October 2019.

Nunez, Christina. "Climate 101: Deforestation." *National Geographic*. 2022.

Pearce, Fred. "Conflicting Data: How Fast Is the World Losing its

Forests?" *Yale Environment* 360. Yale School of the Environment. October 2018.

Thompson, Mary Liz and Darryl Cherney. *Who Bombed Judi Bari?* Whobombedjudibari.com.

United States Department of Forestry. "U.S. Forest Resource Facts and Historical Trends." 2014.

Ritchie, Hanna and Max Roser. "Deforestation and Forest Loss" *Our World in Data,* 2021.

Speece, Darren Frederick. *Defending Giants: The Redwood Wars and the Transformation of American Environmental Politics.* Weyerhaeuser Environmental Books. 2016.

Wohlleben, Peter. *The Hidden Life of Trees.* Greystone Books. 2016.

Zinn Education Project "May 24, 1990: Judi Bari's Car Bombed." *This Day in History, Zinn Education Project Teaching People's History.*

Against the Grain
Book Club Discussion Questions

1. Why did you pick up this book? What drew you to it?
2. Did it meet your expectations or surprise or disappoint you in any way? Was this a result of what happened in the story, or the quality of the writing?
3. What passages stuck with you the most?
4. How would you characterize Diana's relationship to her father?
5. What similarities do you see between Atlas and Logan?
6. How are the trees different from each other and from humans?
7. Were you willing to suspend your disbelief for the tree sections? Why or why not?
8. What is Logan's central dilemma and how does he overcome it?
9. Was Diana's change believable? Why or why not?
10. Does Atlas change truly and permanently? What had the greatest impact? Violence, love or loss? Was this change believable?
11. What role does activism play in the book? In what ways is it positive or negative? What issues does this raise for you as you witness various marches and movements occurring in the world today?
12. What themes in the book resonated most with your life?
13. Has the novel moved you to do or think about anything differently?

Author's Note

Lâle Davidson grew up splitting time between a college town in Oneonta, NY, where her mother taught literature, and her father's farm outside of Pittsburgh. This land had been farmed, timbered and strip-mined, before her father bought it from his father. Over her lifetime, he fostered  it into a rich wild forestland. She spent many summer days sloshing after him through the woods carrying buckets of water or walnuts, trimming and wiring saplings to protect them from deer. Ancient apple trees provided warty comfort during a lonely childhood. When she and her husband visited the redwoods in California in the late 1990s, and stumbled across the story of Redwood summer and the saving of the Headwaters, she dreamt of the Sierras as if seeing them from above. While the camera's eye roved over trees and mountains, a voice-over said, "These are worth saving. No matter the cost." She gave that voice to Logan's father.

Her stories have appeared in *The North American Review, Big Lucks,* and *The Collagist,* among others. Her story "The Opal Maker" made the *Wigleaf* Top 50 (Very) Short Fictions of 2015. Her short story collection *Strange Appetites* won the Adirondack Center for Writing's People's Choice Award. Her novel *Blue Woman Burning* was published by Emperor Books in 2021. She is the recipient of the SUNY Chancellor's Award for Scholarship and Creative Activities.

She teaches creative writing at SUNY Adirondack and does her best to fight climate change. Visit laledavidson.com for contact for readings, book club visits, and workshops.

(Author photo Deborah Neary)

CPSIA information can be obtained
at www.ICGtesting.com
Printed in the USA
BVHW042356270922
648047BV00002B/89